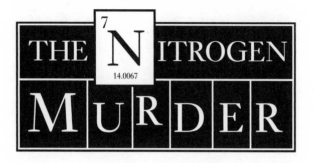

GLORIA LAMERINO MYSTERIES BY
CAMILLE MINICHINO

THE NITROGEN MURDER

A PERIODIC TABLE MYSTERY

CAMILLE MINICHINO

NEW YORK

THOMAS DUNNE BOOKS

ST. MARTIN'S MINOTAUR

1/06 LAD 1/06 16(0)
3/09 Qad 4/06 18(0)

THOMAS DUNNE BOOKS.
An imprint of St. Martin's Press.

www.minotaurbooks.com

ISBN 0-312-33383-8
EAN 978-0312-33383-6

First Edition: May 2005

10   9   8   7   6   5   4   3   2   1

For my husband, Dick Rufer

ACKNOWLEDGMENTS

My special thanks to my niece, Mary Ellen Schnur, for her inspiration and advice; and to Inspector Christopher Lux of the Alameda County, California, District Attorney's Office for his interest and willingness to answer my questions, often the same ones more than once.

As usual, I drew enormous amounts of information and inspiration from Robert Durkin, my cousin and expert in all things mortuary; and from my cousin Jean Stokowski, who was constantly available and supportive.

Thanks also to the many writers, family members, and friends who reviewed the manuscript or offered generous research assistance, in particular: Judy Barnett, Barry Black, Verna Cefalu, Erin Chan, Darla Granzow, Margaret Hamilton, Dr. Eileen Hotte, Jonnie Jacobs, Anna Lipjhart, Peggy Lucke, Philip "Buddy" Marcus, Robert Olson, Ann Parker, Lisa Shapiro, Susan Shapiro, Sue Stephenson, Karen Streich, and Jennifer York.

I'm most grateful to my loving husband, Dick Rufer, the best there is. I can't imagine working without his 24/7 tech support.

Any misinterpretation of such excellent resources is purely my fault.

Special thanks to Marcia Markland, my wonderful editor, who has been with me in one way or another from my first book and continues to be my guide; and to my patient, extraordinary agent, Elaine Koster.

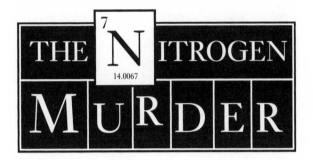

CHAPTER ONE

Summer is the wrong time for me to visit California.

First, I've always hated desert heat, claiming membership in the tiny club—a *nano*club, in scientific terms—of people who prefer humidity. Second, there's only a meager Fourth of July in California. You might see modest fireworks displays, but nothing like the shows on Revere Beach, in Massachusetts, back in the old days. Magnificent sprays of color and thunderous bursts of stars and stripes came from giant barges out on the Atlantic Ocean, the finale perhaps a replica of the flag-raising at Iwo Jima or an image of the presidential faces of Mount Rushmore.

Elaine Cody, whose wedding was the reason I was dragging my own fiancé from Revere to Berkeley in mid-June, reminded me that I spent too much time dwelling on how things used to be.

"I'm going to find you a Fourth of July celebration you won't forget," she said. "We had a terrific fireworks show at the marina last year. Great new designs, with interlocking circles and geometric figures. You'd have loved them."

I rolled my eyes. "Did I ever tell you about Aida?" I asked.

Elaine sighed and maneuvered her army green Saab into her Northside garage. We'd just made a harrowing trip from the San Francisco airport, across the Bay Bridge at rush hour on a Friday. "The amazing Aida, the horse that dives into a bucket of water."

"*Dove*. Past tense. I'm sure she's dead by now," Matt offered from the backseat. His gray head rested on one of my oversized carry-ons. I'd used Elaine's wedding—her third—as an excuse to bring an extra forty pounds of luggage.

"It was a large tank, not a bucket," I said, letting decades-old memories of Aida crowd out maid-of-honor images. A graceful pony and flowered-bathing-capped rider falling through space with style and flair, versus me, in a plus-size floor-length dress.

No contest.

In my mind I heard a drum roll and a cymbal crash, as I followed Aida's leap off a fifty-foot tower. A larger horse whose name I'd forgotten would twist in the air and land on his side, making it more difficult for his rider to land safely. But Aida tucked up her willowy legs as if she were going over a jump and plunged into the water. I felt wet from the enormous splash, then realized the doors of the Saab were open and I was dripping perspiration. We'd arrived in Elaine's sweltering garage.

I'd lived and worked in Berkeley for thirty years before returning home to Revere, so I knew the heat wave would be short-lived, and unbearable only during the daytime. The fog would roll in, and breezes from the San Francisco Bay would take over after a magnificent sunset, compliments of the Bay Area's particular spectrum of air pollution.

". . . so I chose navy blue for you, Gloria," I heard Elaine say. "I thought it would be better for you than a pastel."

No kidding.

Elaine had redone the interior of her two-tone brown Tudor. Her built-in dark oak bookshelves were still in place, but new living room furniture in various shades of brown and burgundy leather had replaced the floral set that was there on my last visit. During our long friendship, I'd often teased her that she changed furniture and men with equal frequency.

Her Hummel collection was now distributed around the room on various small tables instead of lined up on her mantel.

She owned at least two dozen of the figurines, mostly children or angels, at play, napping, petting small animals, or fingering tiny musical instruments. Her newest figure, a special edition Hummel-ized policeman, claimed the center of her glass-topped coffee table. Behind his back the cherub-cop held a scroll with an imprint of an NYPD badge.

"I have the fireman on back order," Elaine said when she saw me pick up the *Salute to American Heroes,* as the script on the base of the statuette proclaimed.

Hummels were Elaine's only "cute" habit. At five-nine, with shoulder-length gray-blond hair, Elaine still dressed like the Radcliffe graduate she was. Tailored clothing of fine fabric, nicely matched. No polyester, no shoes with ties, no jeans or pants with an elastic waist unless she was in the act of jogging. Her long neck could sport a scarf two inches wide without wrinkling. Mine was best suited to the silver chain that had held my lab ID badge for three decades.

Elaine's two-story home was at the top of a hill in an older, tree-lined neighborhood a few streets north of the University of California Berkeley campus and the laboratory where I'd cleaned my first laser windows. She was still a technical editor at that lab, Berkeley University Laboratory—BUL. I was glad labs didn't choose mascots.

"I can't wait for you to meet Phil and his daughter," Elaine said as the three of us toted bags up the stairs to her guest room.

Matt grumbled at being forced, by a vote of two to one, to carry only the lightest suitcase. His recovery from prostate cancer treatment was going well, and I wanted to keep it that way. I hoped this wedding trip would be a vacation for him, away from the homicide desk of the Revere Police Department. *Service, courage, and commitment,* the RPD motto, had me tired just thinking about it.

"And I can't wait to wear my new tie that matches Gloria's little navy dress," Matt teased. Unburdened as he was by heavy luggage,

Matt ran his fingers up my back, where the zipper of my dress would lie in two weeks. That neither of us had ever had the physique to wear "little" clothes didn't seem worth mentioning.

I'd had transcontinental briefings from Elaine since her first date with Philip Chambers, a retired BUL chemist now working as a consultant. "I know I said 'never again,' Gloria," she'd told me, "but he's a scientist like you. How can I go wrong?"

I had a feeling she'd mistaken my silence to mean I understood her logic. The courtship with Phil had been even shorter than her usual prenuptial process, but I reminded myself that my role in Elaine's love life was to be her support, not her critic. What was so awful about Elaine's record of four engagements and two ex-husbands, anyway? At least she tried. I'd cut and run when my first engagement ended decades ago. My only fiancé had died—which was why I put my hand on Matt's chest at night unless I could hear him breathe. I was most reassured when his snoring filled the room of our Revere home, the hazards of sleep apnea notwithstanding.

Matt and I took a few moments with Elaine to catch the view of Berkeley from our guest room windows, which were elaborately treated with yards of rich fabric. I felt sure the design had a technical name. Framed by the draperies, the UC campanile stood out, more impressive in the soft evening light than BUL's sister lab, Lawrence Berkeley National Laboratory, and the giant concrete building that held its cyclotron.

Elaine pointed out a flat-topped, rectangular white building in the distance, with an array of satellite antennae on its roof. "Phil works in that facility. Dorman Industries, kind of a midsize consulting firm." She turned to Matt. "This is one of the few days you can make it out; it's usually too foggy."

Elaine was right, but even Alcatraz was visible today, in the middle of San Francisco Bay. I remembered touring "the Rock" many times with East Coast guests when I lived here. I was glad

Matt wasn't the tourist type. I'd passed the point where riding the cable cars up and down the streets of San Francisco, angled at nearly ninety degrees, was fun.

Elaine hadn't stopped talking about her fiancé. "Most of what Phil's doing is classified, as I've told Gloria. It's a kind of extension of what he was doing at BUL."

"He's retired and now consults in his field? What a novel concept," Matt said. He nudged me in my ticklish zone, which, I supposed, was meant to say he was glad I'd veered off course to police work.

Not that I'd deliberately chosen a career as a Revere Police Department consultant—I drifted into it when they needed technical help with the murder investigation of a hydrogen researcher, shortly after I returned to Revere. I met Detective Matt Gennaro at that time, and one contract had led to another.

Elaine had stocked the guest room with pear-scented soap and lotions, which she knew I liked, and a vase of white and orange flowers. On the bedside table she'd placed a Hummel—a little boy in an old-fashioned (of course) wooden cart, with an American flag pinned to the back. If it were a music box, it would be playing a John Philip Sousa march.

"In honor of your favorite holiday," she said.

"Sweet," I said, and meant it.

After impressive hors d'oeuvres, prepared by Phil, we were told, and Elaine's famous chicken Kiev, Matt went up to bed. One side effect of his anticancer medication was that he needed more sleep. Elaine and I began our usual program of "remember whens." The monthly dinner club we'd belonged to (Berkeley was a hub for ethnic restaurants); the time I'd tried to keep up with her on a bike trip through the steep, winding paths of Grizzly Peak (what had I been thinking?); her ten least favorite BUL authors to edit (not me). We laughed at engineers' infatuation with putting capital letters in the middle of words: MicroCell assembly, LasAmp module, ForBal spindle, BioAssayFlow device. It was Elaine's job to talk them out of such language gimmicks.

"It demeans your amazingly creative engineering breakthrough to have its name look like some popular commercial product," I said in a deep, mock-serious voice. "How's that for an imitation of your tech-editor bedside manner?"

"What I want to say is 'You idiot, you're not working for Disneyland.'"

We had another laugh at BUL engineers' expense as Elaine refilled our espresso cups.

"It's so wonderful to have you here, Gloria. I know Phil's sorry he couldn't come to dinner tonight."

"It was nice of him to make the hors d'oeuvres."

"Poor guy slashed his hand in the process." Elaine pointed to the tiny, delicious shrimp wraps that had been the culprits in a kitchen accident. "He was working here and isn't used to my new knives. He had to go to the ER in the middle of the project, but still he came back to finish the tray." Elaine smiled, a proud fiancée. "And then back to work until late tonight."

"I'll be sure to thank him profusely. But maybe it's just as well that he couldn't make it this evening. Matt's probably better off early to bed."

Elaine looked at her watch. "Early by Pacific time, anyway. Phil's set to meet us at Bette's for breakfast in the morning. And Dana—well, who knows. Being an EMT, she has a crazy schedule. I love her, though, and we get along really well. She's the one responsible for all the flowers around here tonight. She insisted they be right off the truck at the farmers' market and took care of it while I was at work."

I skipped over mention of the fresh California blooms and zeroed in on Dana's career. This was a new fascination of mine—high-risk vocations—traceable to my first dates with a cop. "Phil's daughter's an emergency medical technician? That sounds exciting. I don't remember your telling me that."

Since my return to my Massachusetts roots, Elaine and I had stayed in close touch, with daily e-mails and at least weekly telephone conversations. She'd met her latest fiancé less than a year ago at their health club Christmas party. Still, about all I knew was that he was handsome, that his job was extremely important and highly confidential, and that Elaine and he were "very much in love."

"Not really that exciting," Elaine said. It took a moment to realize she was referring to Dana's EMT job, not Phil himself, or their relationship. "Dana works for an ambulance transport company. They're not the ones who answer 911 calls; they just take patients from one hospital to another. Or from a convalescent home to an ER, and so on. Seems more like taxi service."

"A taxi with a gurney, I'm sure," I said.

Elaine's phone rang. She placed her cup next to a ceramic angel playing an accordion and went to the hallway to answer.

I settled back on one of the paisley pillows I'd sent her at Christmas. I was glad to see they fit nicely with the new color scheme. Sent by me, but not chosen by me. I'd left that job to my Revere friend Rose, whose elegant taste was a match for Elaine's; mine ran more to what the high-diving pony Aida's stall décor might have been.

I riffled through a large illustrated book on Elaine's coffee table, *Our Wedding*. The title alone gave me a headache. I'd successfully deferred all Gloria Lamerino/Matt Gennaro wedding talk until after our California trip, though Rose was chafing at the bit.

My coffee table books displayed the wonders of science and technology. I'd just acquired a large album of Harold Edgerton's pioneering high-speed, stop-motion photography: now-famous photos such as the milk drop coronet, a .30-caliber bullet passing through an apple, and the swinging arcs of golfers and tennis players. Elaine's photography books used to have exotic flower arrangements or black-and-white classics of New York City in the rain. Now she was displaying close-ups of wedding para-phernalia. I flipped past a lacy garter, a cake cutter decorated like a ballerina, glittery white slippers filled with candy. *Tsk-tsk,* I said mentally.

I looked at my bare ring finger. I hadn't wanted an engage-ment ring. "I'll wear one if you will," I'd told Matt.

Elaine also had chosen not to have an engagement ring, lead-ing me to believe her wedding would be for mature audiences. Surely she wasn't about to offer stale almonds wrapped in net-ting to her wedding guests?

"How awful," I heard her say. Had she overheard my mutter-ings about pink tulle? "She's . . . she's *dead?*"

Uh-oh. I hoped I'd heard incorrectly, but I sensed a cloud forming over Elaine's wedding, not to say someone's life, some-one's family and friends.

Elaine came back to the living room, a look of consternation on her face.

"That was Dana, Phil's daughter. Her partner's been shot. Dead." Elaine's speech was slow, as if she were weighing each word for credibility. Her voice was high-pitched, as usual when she was upset. She rubbed her bare arms as if a sudden chill had overtaken the warm room.

"Her partner?" I tried to recall what Elaine had told me about Phil Chambers's daughter. Twenty-four, living with a couple of roommates in a house in Oakland, working to earn money for med school. Dating preference? Male or female, I couldn't remember.

"Her ambulance partner," Elaine clarified. "A beautiful young black woman. Tanisha Hall. I've met her."

I moved closer and rubbed Elaine's shoulders. "I'm so sorry, Elaine."

"I just can't believe it. She was studying to take the fire-fighter's exam. She has a little daughter."

Had a daughter hadn't registered yet, I noted.

I continued my amateur massaging, though I wasn't sure Elaine was aware of my touch. "You said she was shot?" I asked.

Elaine took a deep breath; her voice told me she was close to tears. "Dana says Tanisha was walking from the ambulance to the trauma center entrance. They'd just delivered the patient on a gurney, and Tanisha was taking his property in after him." Elaine threw up her hands, as if newly surprised. Her voice became a whisper. "Someone ran up and shot Tanisha and stole the briefcase that belonged to the patient. And she died. While just doing her job."

In the line of duty. So much for the taxi driver theory.

CHAPTER TWO

Granted, I wasn't meeting Dr. Philip Chambers under the best of circumstances. He'd been interrupted during an important meeting the night before to talk to his traumatized daughter. She'd seen her friend and partner shot down in front of her. Phil may even have known Tanisha Hall and been grieving for her. On top of all that, he'd cut his hand making special hors d'oeuvres for Matt and me.

Still, I wished I liked him better. I'd always relied on my first impressions as holding true. I ran a checklist through my mind. Did his expensive-looking clothing intimidate me? Not likely—I wasn't put off by Elaine's cashmere sweater sets, nor by the dapper wardrobes of my friend Rose and her husband, Frank Galigani, the well-put-together mortician.

Was it his physical appearance? Phil Chambers was tall and thin; he had thick brown (I wondered about this) hair and wore strong cologne. Citrus, I guessed. Matt was short and stocky and odor-free, and his hair color matched my own more-salt-than-pepper locks. But I couldn't imagine that was what turned me off about Elaine's fiancé.

I hoped it wasn't solely his opening remark when Elaine introduced us.

We'd all met for breakfast on Saturday morning at Bette's Oceanview Diner, an award-winning Berkeley restaurant. Old-timers remembered when Bette's stood out on Fourth Street, one of the few operating businesses for blocks, surrounded by abandoned factories and warehouses and gravel lots that were empty except for debris. Now the diner was physically dwarfed by gentrification. In the early eighties, we referred to the whole neighborhood, close to the Berkeley marina, as *"Bette's"*; now it was "the Fourth Street Shopping Center." I'd even heard "the Crate and Barrel Mall." Still, Bette's managed to attract both locals and tourists on its own merits, and in great numbers, as evidenced by the long sign-up sheet for seating.

Bette's itself hadn't changed much since its opening: black-and-white harlequin floor; long, shiny counter with swivel stools; authentic 1950s jukebox that crowded the minimal waiting area; and chrome trim wherever possible. Bette's was always densely populated with the eclectic mix we expected in Berkeley. Elaine and I used to play at naming the customers. The long-haired family in the booth next to ours today, for instance—we would have imagined the children's names to be Sunflower (a girl), Redwood (a boy), and Mulberry (too young to tell). A twenty-something couple waiting by the jukebox, on the other hand, dressed nearly identically in khaki shorts and white tops, had to be Ashley and Josh.

Phil had been seated in a red Naugahyde booth when Elaine, Matt, and I arrived. He stood and shook Matt's hand, protecting his bandaged left hand with his right underarm, then turned to greet me. His eyes narrowed as he half said, half asked, "Elaine tells me you have a doctorate in physics?" As if he hadn't believed his fiancée and, now that he'd seen me, he was sure she'd been mistaken.

I called up a questioning look of my own. "And you have one in chemistry? Amazing!" I said.

Elaine and Matt laughed, both better prepared than Phil for the nastier, sarcastic side of me. Most people don't expect much from a short, gray-haired female.

"We need a diner like this in Revere," Matt said, redirecting our attention to what no one could be acerbic about. He slid in next to me and unobtrusively patted my knee. *Relax.* "I've been craving homemade pancakes, and I see that's a specialty here."

"Made with locally milled flour and all natural ingredients," Elaine said. "After all, this is Berkeley."

I took a deep breath, deciding I might order according to smell. Bacon or fruit? Buttery pancakes or hash browns? Even the salad that swished by us in the hands of a waitress had a fresh, handpicked aroma.

I resisted a reminder to Matt to choose an item with a heart icon: low-fat, low-cholesterol choices. I didn't remember noticing his diet before his prostate cancer; I know I never kept surreptitious track of his fat and calorie intake every day. But since his diagnosis I'd been on guard, as if everything he ate, every choice of movement or activity, was related to his illness, which had to be kept at bay.

To his credit, Phil rushed to clarify his comment to me. "I didn't mean to sound surprised, Gloria. I work with a lot of women these days."

"You're not helping yourself, Phil," Elaine said, containing a laugh. And then to me, "He's old-school, as you can see."

It wasn't the first time I'd met sexism as a woman in science, but I didn't often meet it among scientists themselves. And I wondered about the "old-school" designation. Did that mean he and Elaine never went out without a chaperone? *Too snide,* I told myself, and held that remark back.

I thought of Elaine's two ex-husbands and her "extra" fiancé. Where were they now? I wondered. Not in our lives. Elaine had lost track of Greg, a lab engineer; Skyler, a San Francisco street artist; and Rene, a Parisian chemist, whom she'd been engaged to but never married. In between, there had been Bruce, Mel, José . . .

Looking at Phil, I missed them all.

We spoke only briefly of Tanisha Hall's death, but the fact of it was there, hovering over the heavy white mugs of strong coffee and the wide-bottomed glasses of orange juice. Every time we laughed, someone cut the moment short, as if it were improper to be frivolous so soon after hearing of the young woman's murder.

"How's Dana holding up?" I asked Phil, once our pancake and French toast specials had arrived. I knew he'd had a lengthy conversation with his daughter last night, though he hadn't left his meeting to visit her.

I saw a pained look cross Phil's face, but it passed quickly. He shrugged his shoulders, then swung his syrupy fork in the air, its tines pointing upward, carving out a small circle a few inches from his face. "You know Dana," he said, turning to Elaine. "She takes everything so seriously."

"Murder is pretty serious, don't you think?" Matt asked. A simple question from one who'd made a career out of bringing killers to justice. His voice was calm, his eating uninterrupted, and he saved me from making another remark I might later regret.

"Sure, sure," Phil said. "It must be hard seeing someone you know get shot. And over a duffel bag." He shook his head: *the futility of it all*. "But Dana's strong. She'll be okay."

I caught the error in Phil's comment. According to Elaine, the shooter had taken a briefcase, not a duffel bag. I almost corrected Phil, but I thought I'd caused enough friction already.

I did my best to be pleasant for the rest of the meal, though anyone who knew me would have been able to tell I was in a polite-but-cold mood. Then I saw the look on Elaine's face. She *did* know me well, and she was distressed.

I felt guilt settle in my stomach, making Bette's double-egg-dipped sourdough French toast seem feather-light by comparison. Elaine had chosen Phil; it was my shortcoming that I couldn't find his redeeming qualities. And what about Phil having to sit through breakfast with his fiancée's flighty friend, going from one coast to another every twenty or thirty years?

I gave myself a mental slap. I needed to get with the program and behave like a normal maid of honor. I'd come to help with bridal tasks. I'd been Elaine's attendant twice before, and I knew there were endless errands to run and phone calls to make concerning the food, the champagne, the minister, the flowers, the rings, the photographer, the decorations, the music, the outfits. I was out of breath thinking about it.

"So, when are we going shopping for our shoes?" I asked Elaine. "I'm favoring some navy patent leather flats with a little Mary Jane T-strap."

Poor Elaine choked on a piece of Bette's famous lemon scone.

Phil was a connected guy. Not connected like my long-deceased Uncle Pasquale, a small-time Revere bookie, but connected to his cell phone and pager and state-of-the-art PDA, each of which he fingered at one time or another during our breakfast. Taking a call, entering a date, answering a page, making a note with a sleek black stylus. Elaine didn't seem to mind this, so I tried not to. Not surprisingly, Phil had to leave our company earlier than he'd hoped, to attend an important meeting. I congratulated myself on resisting the temptation to ask why he couldn't clear a whole Saturday morning for his fiancée and her maid of honor.

Outside Bette's, Phil kissed Elaine, shook Matt's hand and mine, and crossed the street. He got into a snazzy BMW driven by a white-haired man, about the same age as all of us.

Elaine waved at the BMW driver. "Howard Christopher, Phil's boss," she told us. "Nice guy, but always on Phil's back to do more, work more hours. You know the drill. I keep telling him, 'You're not marrying Christopher.' "

I'd caught the parting I-love-yous between Elaine and Phil.

That had made me happy, but by the time Phil left, I'd given myself enough mental slaps to keep me alert for two weeks.

Elaine wanted to check out the wedding site—the magnificent Berkeley Rose Garden. True to her name, my best East Coast friend, Rose Galigani, loved roses and insisted on visiting the garden every trip she made to visit me when I lived in California.

"There are three thousand bushes and two hundred fifty varieties," I'd told her the first time, reading from the guidebook, pleased with myself for finding such a treasure for her.

"They're not all blooming at once, Gloria. Different varieties peak at different times."

"You mean pink one month, red another?"

Rose shook her head and rolled her eyes at the idea that a woman whose bedtime reading was the latest news on the Big Bang wouldn't know the life cycles of roses.

What I liked best about the Rose Garden was the surprise of it. Even with the newly installed viewing area, walking or driving along Euclid Avenue in northeast Berkeley, you might miss it. Bushes and trees partly hid the entrance. Once you turned down the path, however, an enormous amphitheater of six terraces opened up below you. Berkeley's own Hanging Gardens of Babylon. Roses everywhere.

In the bright sun, I enjoyed sharing the pleasure with Matt.

"Whoa," he said. The expression he reserved for special occasions.

Today's roses were a breathtaking pink and white, their scent swirling around like clouds of charge around a heavy nucleus. Steep, wide stone steps, as beautiful as they could be treacherous to any but the sure-footed, led down, down, down, to a small clearing—a few square feet that were as lovely as any sanctuary.

Straight ahead, looking across to the horizon from the street level, were San Francisco Bay and the hills of Marin County. A postcard scene in Elaine's backyard, and mine at one time.

A wedding ceremony was coming to a close as we arrived. In the Rose Garden, no invitations were needed. It was normal for families and passersby enjoying the park's tennis courts, paths, and picnic areas to pause and "attend" a wedding in progress, settling on the stone steps or leaning on bikes and scooters. We watched as the bride and groom and their attendants—all youngsters, compared to Elaine's and my wedding parties—climbed up to the street level and rode off in a Model A Ford appropriately decked out in streamers. Cameras clicked and rolled as the driver, in a vintage 1930s cap, cranked up the car.

For no good reason, I wondered whether Hollywood producers had ever used the Rose Garden for an action-movie car-chase scene, sending motorcycles and police cars up and down the narrow walkways. For all I knew it had been done.

Elaine had made arrangements for us to hold a rehearsal here in two weeks, before the Saturday afternoon Cody/Chambers wedding. Saturday was the third of July, so everyone would be celebrating all night, Elaine had told me.

"You'll walk in from this direction, Gloria," Elaine said, indicating a set of steps that began at the Euclid Avenue entrance. Her arm swept to the aisle sixty degrees away. "Dana will come in from there. Phil and I are going to come in together from the other side." She turned to me and said in a soft voice, "Too late for me to be given away, don't you think?"

I smiled. "No comment."

Elaine felt it would be a good idea for us to stop in to see Dana. She called ahead and reported that Dana sounded very grateful we'd thought of it. We stopped at Fourth Street again and picked up pastry from Bette's takeout annex, coffee beans from Peet's, and a small purple plant (Elaine called it by name) at one of the many home and garden shops. If Dana was at all ready to be cheered, these items would do it.

I could hardly wait to meet Dana Chambers. Like father, like daughter? I hoped not.

"Open mind," Matt whispered as he held the car door for me. I always marveled at how well he knew me.

CHAPTER Three

D ana's neighborhood in the flats, where the cities of Berkeley and Oakland overlapped, was densely packed with single homes and duplexes, mostly run-down, their unkempt front yards dotted with rusty toys and car parts. Battered old autos and trucks were parked bumper to bumper on both sides of the street. We'd been lucky to find a parking spot around the corner from Dana's. I doubted the *chirp chirp* of Elaine's car alarm meant a lot, but it did give some comfort.

The sun beat down on us. I'd remembered to wear long sleeves for protection against the intense California rays, but Matt had on a polo shirt and complained mildly about his skin burning up. "Summer wimps," Elaine called us both. Her sleeveless linen dress, a pale yellow, showed no sign she'd even sat in it.

As we picked our way along the broken sidewalk, skirting candy wrappers and cigarette butts, Matt assumed his assessing-the-environment attitude, scanning the area. The posture seemed incongruous with the pretty flowers he carried.

"Dana just moved in a couple of weeks ago. I've never been here," Elaine said. From her tone, she may have wanted to assure us that she had nothing to do with choosing the shabby neighborhood.

Except for several rowdy dogs, mercifully behind chain-link fences, there was no sign of life on the street until we arrived at the house Dana shared with two roommates. Her door was propped open by a large, bulging backpack. The purse of choice for recent generations.

Dana's house was old, built long before safety codes. The stairs were steep and narrow, with no railing, almost as precarious as the Rose Garden's terrace steps, but not at all as attractive. Neither were the few roses in the small front yard. They hung limply from their stems, as if they were sad, having just heard the news of Tanisha Hall's death.

I worried about Matt, who insisted on carrying everything up the steps. I strained to listen to his breathing, inexpertly evaluating his respiration. He'd awakened to news of a murder that affected someone close to Elaine, if not to us, and probably was concerned about my juvenile reaction to Phil Chambers. So far, not a fun vacation. I'd wondered about the wisdom of his making the trip in the first place, but his doctors enthusiastically had given permission.

"I was on the lookout for you," Dana said, appearing at her door. "It's hard to see the number here with all this greenery."

She'd swept aside a hanging plant, her gentle voice and sad eyes belying the obvious strength of her body. Fitting my stereotype of what an EMT should look like, Dana was tall and broad-shouldered; her long arms and legs, not very covered by short shorts and a tank top, were tanned and muscular.

Elaine embraced Dana, reaching up as high as when she'd embraced Phil a while earlier. "I'm so sorry, Dana," Elaine said. "This must be just . . . incredibly hard for you." The two women stayed together a moment or two. Elaine sobbed quietly; Dana stared over Elaine's shoulder, her eyes ringed with red. She patted Elaine's back, as if Elaine were the one needing comfort. My heart went out to Dana; I liked her immediately and pointlessly wished I'd been nicer to her father.

"We brought some sustenance from Fourth Street," Elaine said when she broke away.

Matt produced the food and the plant and a warm smile,

and we crossed the threshold into Dana's living room.

"Elaine's told me all about both of you, and I've been dying to meet you," Dana said, addressing Matt and me. "I'm sorry I'm not in better shape, but I'm so glad you came. My roommates both had things to do, and I told them I didn't need them to stay around, but I really don't want to be alone."

I had the feeling this visit would be free of hidden, or not so hidden, hostility and resolved to give Dana's father another chance.

We settled ourselves on a variety of mismatched chairs in Dana's living room. I took a wooden rocker with a multicolored braided pad; Dana and Elaine sat on the floral patterned couch, which I recognized from Elaine's old living room set; Matt dragged in a straight-backed chair from the dining room. I imagined three sets of parents, plus assorted stepparents, all contributing to furnishing the house for the three young women. I wondered what, if anything, Dana's mother had passed along. Elaine knew little about Phil's first wife, she'd told me, other than she now lived in Florida with a new family.

In spite of her cushy seat on the couch, Dana sat stiff as the bed board I'd used when I hurt my back lifting an oscilloscope. Her conversation was equally taut.

"How was your flight?" she asked. She swung her head from me to Matt, her eyes not quite focused on either of us.

"No incidents," I replied, regretting my word choice as soon as I said it. Dana showed no special reaction.

"Don't you hate airplane food?" Dana asked. She glanced at the buttery scones, the moist muffins, and the double-thick brownies we'd brought from Bette's as if they, too, had been served ice cold, wrapped in plastic on a tray of questionable cleanliness.

"We stopped at the Rose Garden," Elaine said, with no elaboration.

Elaine's tongue is stuck, too, I thought.

"Have you had your incident debriefing?" Matt asked Dana. I gasped, inaudibly, I hoped. He'd run in, guns blazing, so to speak, and addressed what was on all our minds.

Dana shook her head. Her long, straight hair was wet, as if from a swim or a shower, with no attempt at styling. "Not yet." A weak voice, but on the way to opening up.

"You know, I've been there, as you can imagine." Matt's face was as serious as I'd ever seen it, as if he'd just been through a life-changing experience. He reached back into his pants pocket. "I made some notes. Might be useful to you."

Dana looked at him, focused now. "Yeah?"

Matt patted his pockets. Front, back. Nothing. He clicked his tongue. "I guess I left them in the car. Want to walk out with me to get them?"

Dana pushed herself off the couch. "Yeah, sure." She glanced at Elaine and me. We nodded back. *Permission granted.*

Matt stood and followed Dana out the front door. I heard their footsteps on the old wooden stairs and started at the loud bark of a nearby dog.

A moment later, Elaine jumped up. "They don't have the keys," she said.

I shook my head. "I don't think they need them."

Elaine went to the kitchen, leaving me with my thoughts about Sergeant Matt Gennaro, the man I was engaged to. I was proud of the way Matt presented himself to Dana, but something gnawed at me. I wondered how long you had to be with someone before you'd seen all his potential and knew all his secrets. Was Dana hearing something I'd never heard? Or was this just Matt and Dana, ES worker to ES worker, engaged in shop talk?

Matt didn't tell me much about being in the line of fire. I could only imagine how frightening it would be to confront violence as part of your everyday work life. Had he witnessed the death of a fellow police officer? A partner, as Dana had? A criminal? I was aware of some of the crises in Matt's life. His wife of ten years died of heart disease, and he was still dealing with his own prostate cancer. What else was there? I chided myself for not being more alert.

Elaine's return and the smell of the espresso she brought distracted me from further uneducated psychological analysis.

"It'll be great if Matt can help Dana," Elaine said. "We should have thought of that in the first place."

I nodded and smiled, as if I'd done something good by bringing Matt to California just when it needed him.

When Matt and Dana returned, we decided there was time for one more round of coffee. "Then we need to let Dana get some rest," Elaine said.

It was my turn in the kitchen, and I volunteered to freshen the mugs. No one mentioned Matt's "notes," and the atmosphere had become significantly more cheerful.

"You've done a nice job with the place," Elaine said. She did a similar "nice job" of sounding sincere, considering she'd recently invested a month's pay in a new carpet because the color was maybe ten wavelengths off from matching her new couch.

We all looked around, as if to verify Elaine's judgment. It was clear that her evaluation didn't include the pots and pans stacked on chairs and window ledges, nor the unopened cartons scattered through the common area.

A laptop computer and its peripherals occupied most of the dining room table. The cord was looped over the backs of chairs and along the floor until it disappeared into one of the bedrooms, to an AC outlet, I assumed. The living room had a badly scratched bookcase stuffed with paperbacks, and stacks of CDs (the equivalent of my old crate of LPs, I told myself) were strewn around a stereo system. Two sleek, contemporary-style bicycles were propped against the wall outside one of the bedrooms.

If we'd been playing a game from a puzzle book—find the object that doesn't fit—I'd have chosen the expensive brown leather briefcase, standing in a corner next to a *Whole Earth* canvas tote bag full of recyclable cans and bottles. The case was the attaché style, thin and rectangular, with a gold spinning combination lock at the top.

"It belongs to the guy," Dana said when she caught me staring at the briefcase. "The guy Tanisha and I took to the trauma center last night—a gunshot vic. He had a briefcase plus a duffel bag."

"So the person who shot Tanisha probably just got sweaty gym clothes," Elaine said, sadness in her voice.

Dana nodded, twisting a long strand of brown hair in her fingers. "We usually make two trips into the hospital, the first one with the patient, of course, and then we go back to the ambulance, and one of us changes the paper on the gurney and cleans up whatever"—I tried not to picture "whatever" from an ambulance patient—"while the other makes a run inside with the patient's belongings. But this guy had a lot of stuff, so Tanisha said she'd run in with the big duffel bag while I checked around the back of the ambulance for anything that might have spilled, and"—Dana's voice cracked—"and then I'd take this briefcase and whatever else I found, like his wallet was on the floor, and some cards fell out and I wanted to make sure I got them all. And . . . I was sort of reading them, because it looked like there were a dozen IDs, all different. The same face. An Indian, I'm pretty sure. But different names. A lot of what looked like lab badges. I've seen a few of those. Now I'm thinking, if I weren't so nosy, if it hadn't taken me so long . . ."

Matt seemed to have unleashed a talkative Dana. A dozen IDs, that was interesting. I made up a quick story about how the patient ran an identity theft scam, then I clicked my tongue at my runaway mind. This new habit of seeing criminal behavior everywhere must be a substitute for my former theorizing days in a physics lab, I figured, when an errant data point on an otherwise smooth curve might unleash one theory per hour.

Still, the man *was* shot.

Elaine moved closer and put her arm around Dana's shoulder, handing her tissues. Matt went to the kitchen and brought back a glass of water. I sat, helpless, putting myself in Dana's shoes, rubbery yellow thongs at the moment. I could guess what she was thinking. If she'd been faster, she might have been out of the ambulance and able to help Tanisha immediately; if she'd have been alert, she might have been able to warn Tanisha; if she'd gone out first, she'd be dead and her friend Tanisha might be alive. All the ifs and might-haves of survivor guilt.

It wasn't too long before Dana was able to talk again, perhaps remembering Matt's "notes."

"I didn't know what to do with the briefcase. I mean, Valley Medical doesn't want it, right? So I called the police. I gave them all those cards that were in the guy's wallet, because I'd already stuffed them in my pocket before I heard the . . . shots." Dana cleared her throat and swallowed. "I didn't think of the briefcase. Anyway, they said they'd come and pick it up, but I don't know when."

"I'm surprised they haven't already claimed the case," I said, looking at Matt, as if he were the "they" and not three thousand miles from his sphere of responsibility. "What if there'd been a bomb in it?" I asked, and immediately regretted it. We all moved back an inch or so and then laughed.

"Too late," we all said, in one form or another.

"The cops wanted to question me at the station, so Julia, my boss, had to send a couple of people to get the ambulance back to Valley Med headquarters."

"The ambulance was not the crime scene," Matt said, as if to defend the Berkeley PD for not taking custody of a vic's belongings immediately.

Dana continued. "And this guy, Reed, is new, so he thought

the briefcase was mine." Dana slapped her forehead. "Go figure. He brought it here, thinking he was doing me a favor."

"And now here it is," I said, nearly salivating at the idea of opening it. I stared at it, and then it came to me. In our midst was a briefcase, not a duffel bag. Phil had been correct this morning when he said a duffel bag had been taken from Tanisha. But how had he known? "Elaine, didn't you say the shooter"—*oops, police talk*—"uh, the person who shot Tanisha absconded with a *briefcase*?"

"Yes, I guess I did. I must have heard Dana wrong last night."

"But at breakfast, Phil said the murderer took a duffel bag. Did you tell your dad it was a duffel bag, Dana?"

Dana shook her head. "No, I don't think I went into that kind of detail with Dad."

"I'm the one who told Phil about the briefcase," Elaine said. "Or maybe I did say duffel bag." She waved her hand. "Who knows what we said, with all this confusion." She gave me a strange look, as if to ask why any of this was important.

Matt's look, however, was quite different.

I could hardly wait for a private talk.

"I see where you're going with this, Gloria," Matt said the next time we were alone. It was late that afternoon, back at Elaine's, when she left us to make some phone calls. Matt shook his head, put his hand under my chin, and stared into my eyes. "You're as bad on vacation as when you're on the job in Revere."

At least he followed the scolding with a kiss.

"Just hear me out," I said. "Assume Dana got it right the first time and told Elaine the shooter took a duffel bag. Elaine doesn't own a duffel bag. She wouldn't be caught dead—uh, she would never own one. She thinks they're sweaty when they're brandnew. So she probably translated it in her mind to a briefcase. Then she tells us, and Phil, it was a briefcase that got stolen, but Phil knows it was a duffel bag."

"How would he know that?"

"Exactly."

Between the hearty brunch and the snacks at Dana's, none of us wanted dinner on Saturday evening, so we settled for a liqueur from Elaine's vast store. Neither Matt nor I drink alcoholic beverages, but we both feel that liqueur is more dessert than liquor. This one was coffee flavored and lovely to look at in Elaine's special crystal. I hoped I'd be able to control my clumsy fingers, more used to holding tumblers bought in sets of eight at the supermarket.

It was difficult to ply my trade in front of Matt, but I wasn't deterred.

"I know you've told me, but what exactly does Phil do again?" I asked Elaine. A casual question while sipping from a dainty glass.

"I don't know much about it, except that it's classified and has something to do with nitrogen." Elaine smiled, lifting her eyebrows slightly. "I suppose you'll want to tell us all about nitrogen, Gloria."

"Yeah, Gloria, what should we know about nitrogen?" Matt asked.

"It's the N in TNT," I said, and took another sip of my drink.

CHAPTER FOUR

Dana leaned over the basin of her bathroom sink and looked down into the bowl. She studied the chipped porcelain, the rust rings around the drain, a curvy black crack radiating from the bottom. She held her hand under the leaky faucet and watched as the drops piled up on the pad of her finger, then slipped around to her nail and dropped off, like tiny liquid divers plunging to their death.

Until yesterday the condition of the sink annoyed her; she'd finally convinced her roommates they should talk to their landlord about a new one. Now the sink seemed right, normal. The sink was like life—chipped, rusty, cracked, leaky. Why else would Tanisha be dead at twenty-six, punished for doing her job?

Dana squinted and pulled a chestnut hair from the stained basin. Hers. Long, and straight as a bullet. She thought of Tanisha's hair. Seventeen-hour hair, their mutual friends called it when Tanisha described the long process of producing an intricate design of braids and cornrows.

Tanisha's friends teased her about her car, too, an old blue station wagon, a hand-me-down from her grandfather, who'd marched with Martin Luther King Jr. The wagon sported an American flag decal and a BLACK IS BEAUTIFUL bumper sticker, both also from her grandfather.

"'African American' is too much of a mouthful, girl," Tanisha had told Dana in her rich voice. "They got it right in the sixties.

Too bad I was born so late." And her laugh, from deep in her large bosom, would fill the room.

I could have been the one to tech the call, Dana thought. *I could have made the first effects run. Why wasn't it my turn to ride in the back with the patient while Tanisha did the ring-down?*

Dana finished brushing her teeth, moved slowly to her bedroom, and flopped backward onto the pale blue comforter. She thought of Rachel, Tanisha's four-year-old daughter, with a set of tiny cornrows of her own and a dozen braids that ended in bright plastic balls. Pink, blue, white, yellow. Rachel knew all her colors.

Dana knew she needed to visit the San Leandro home where Tanisha and Rachel lived with Marne, Tanisha's mother. She shouldn't wait until the funeral. Rachel's father was a loser, out of the picture from day one of the pregnancy, Tanisha had told Dana. Dana might be able to help, maybe take Rachel for an ice cream or to the Oakland Zoo.

If she could only get out of bed. Maybe she'd had one toke too many after Elaine and her friends left. Or maybe the strain of grass was not a good one. Sometimes Kyle brought shwag—stuff Dana felt was from the reject bin in some warehouse in Colombia. It had a harsh taste and left her feeling more tired than relaxed.

For the hundredth time, Dana went over the events of Friday evening. Looking for answers? Trying to roll back to the beginning of the shift and do everything differently? Who knew why? But she couldn't stop rerunning the hour through her mind.

In her marijuana fog, Dana is back at the scene.

Dana and Tanisha are lounging in the front seats of the ambulance, having a snack. They're parked in the lot of a strip mall off I-580 in Oakland, not far from Lake Merritt. Dana is in the driver's seat.

"I love all the perks," Tanisha said. "I swear they think we're cops." They were joking about the attention they got in their black EMT uniforms and rehashing stories about the guys that hit on them regularly.

"Hey, I need resuscitation," one cute guy had yelled out his window up to the cab where Dana sat, waiting for a green light. "I'm feeling faint. What's your phone number?"

"911," Dana had yelled back as she roared away, and she and Tanisha had laughed for the next quarter mile.

Tanisha dug into the bag of chips she'd just received, gratis, from a fast-food place. They talked about the complimentary passes they got at theaters, and the free convenience-store sodas now and then, depending on the neighborhood.

"Who wouldn't think we're cops? The uniform's the same color, and we have all this stuff hanging on our belts." Dana jiggled her radio and pager, and Tanisha followed suit. They were having a good time, almost as if they'd just shared some wacky weed. No smoking on the job, though; they were together on that.

It was a quiet shift so far, and the partners continued bantering, solving the problems of the world, gossiping.

"What about those missing meds and supplies?" Dana asked. "I'll bet they try to pin it on EMTs." She was thinking of an ongoing problem with inventory—pills, drugs, needles—disappearing from local hospitals and convalescent homes.

Tanisha popped a large potato chip into her mouth and smacked her lips. "Yeah, well, you'd think they'd be going after the big guys instead of trying to track thimblefuls of medicine." She gave Dana a playful punch. "Wish we had a little thimble full of grass now, don't you?"

It was five-forty-five, near the end of the shift, when the call came.

A little action, finally. "225 responding," Dana said.

"Priority 2 out of Golden going to trauma. A GSW vic." It was the Valley Med radio voice telling them to transport a gunshot-wound victim from Golden State Hospital, off I-580, to the city trauma center in Berkeley.

Dana and Tanisha straightened up and buckled their seat belts. Dana started the engine. "225 en route," she said into the radio.

Golden State Hospital was only about a mile and a half away. Dana eased the ambulance out of the lot, down a divided road, and onto the I-580 freeway. She headed west, not the rush direction, though there was less and less difference these days as the Bay Area added one housing development after another. Dana weaved in and out, able to do seventy without her lights and siren.

They exited the freeway. Two rights, a left, and they arrived at the hospital.

"225 on scene," Dana said into her radio.

Dana and Tanisha moved their patient—dark skinned, maybe Indian, Dana thought—onto Valley Med's heavy-duty yellow gurney. No extra backboard for this guy, no scooper. Patient positioning standard. The patient had already been treated in Golden's ER; he'd been bandaged, but he needed the more appropriate facilities of Berkeley's trauma center.

"It never fails," Tanisha said, shaking her head. "People who drive themselves to the hospital always pick the wrong one."

"Right," Dana said. "They should know they're going to end up in an ambulance one way or another, so why don't they just call us to begin with?"

Tanisha took her place in the back on the gray vinyl seat across from the gurney and flipped through the paperwork from the ER. The patient had his IV drip and seemed comfortable.

Dana walked quickly to the front of the ambulance and stepped up into the driver's seat.

A normal call, Code 2.

They were on their way. So far, so good. Dana liked the rush, the feeling she got sitting up there high above even the SUVs. She was in uniform; she was in charge. So what if some jerks were still crazy enough to cut her off now and then? She'd loved the time she drove full throttle over the center divide on the freeway, flicking on the earsplitting sirens, going the wrong way for a quarter mile or so, and then jumping back on, past the stop-and-go traffic.

But this evening's patient was conscious enough to maybe be freaked out by a big fuss—he was a little looped from the morphine—so Dana decided to stay Code 2, no lights, no siren.

This time she took city streets, winding her way north and slightly east, crossing the line from Oakland into Berkeley, headed for Ashby Avenue. She knew Berkeley; she knew how to avoid the annoying streets that were blocked by makeshift rotaries, designed to slow traffic down. The array of bulky concrete slabs in the middle of the intersections reminded her of a cemetery.

Dana skirted a guy wearing a woolen cap that looked a lot like a yarmulke but was probably just another Berkeley fashion statement: *I can wear wool in June if it makes me happy.* No wonder suburbanites called it "Bezerkley."

Time for the ring-down. Dana steadied the ambulance with her left hand, held the radio with her right.

"City, this is Valley Med 225. I have a Code 2. Forty-plus-year-old male, BP 106 over 56, pulse 100, resp rate 24." The numbers Tanisha had yelled out. "ETA five to ten minutes. How do you copy?"

"Copy clear." The trauma center dispatcher, at the ready.

Seven minutes later—good timing, in spite of too many arrogant bicyclists thinking they were more important than any motor vehicle, even an ambulance—Dana pulled into the wide semicircular driveway.

Dana walked to the back of the ambulance, where Tanisha had the doors open. They unlocked the gurney and pulled it out. They wheeled it over the rough asphalt, into the trauma center.

One, two, three. Dana and Tanisha moved the patient, supported by the sheets from Golden State Hospital, from the gurney to the trauma center bed. They handed over the paperwork and left Golden State's sheets behind.

Dana and Tanisha walked back to the ambulance.

"This guy has a lot of stuff. I'll start with the duffel bag," Tanisha said. "You clean up and follow me with the rest, okay?"

"Got it," Dana said.

Or did Dana say, "Tanisha, you take the duffel bag"? Dana doesn't remember. She hopes it was Tanisha's idea to go first.

Tanisha left the back of the ambulance carrying the duffel bag. It was a gray-and-silver bag, shiny, and distended enough to strain the white zipper.

Dana stayed behind. She sprayed the gurney with a germicide from a clear plastic bottle and wiped it down. She gathered up the contents of the patient's wallet, which had spilled on the floor. She noticed multiple IDs; same face, different name. Oh well, not her problem. She stuffed the laminated cards into the pockets of her uniform pants.

She heard a noise. Fireworks already? It was barely mid-June. They started earlier and earlier every year.

Another blast. Not a firework. She stepped out of the back of the ambulance and looked toward the ER doors.

Tanisha is down, sprawled on the driveway.

Someone is running through the bushes to the left of the doors. Running away.

The old security guard runs out from the building. He yells something—it's unintelligible to Dana, who is also running toward Tanisha.

More people come. Doctors and nurses, a gurney, not rugged and yellow like Valley Med's but small and white. Tanisha's large frame fills the bed of the gurney; there's blood on her cornrows.

Dana hangs on to the gurney, walks with it, her body leaning over Tanisha, calling her name, "Tanisha, Tanisha, oh my God, Tanisha," until someone pulls her back and sits her down on the cold cement bowl of a potted plant.

Dana's ears are ringing. She tries to block the sound, but it only gets louder and louder.

The phone was ringing, but Dana couldn't find it. Bleary-eyed, she fished around under her pillow, among the folds of her tangled comforter, on the floor, under the bed. Finally the shrill sound stopped and her answering machine clicked on.

"Dana, this is Julia. It's Sunday morning. Actually, noon." Her boss's voice, sounding like she had a cold. Valley Medical Ambulance Company's owner, Julia Strega.

Dana threw herself on her back, arms outstretched, and squeezed her eyes shut, trying to force herself back to sleep.

"Just want to say we missed you today," Julia's drone continued. *"You need to come in and get debriefed and, you know, let's just talk. Call me, okay? Take care."*

Sure, Dana thought. *I'll take care.*

"Dana, Dana, wake up."

Dana opened her eyes enough to see Jen, one of her roommates, standing over her. "How come the door was wide open? I can't believe you went to sleep and didn't lock up the house."

Jen's voice was a scalpel, cutting into Dana's brain, her short blond hair a surgeon's cap. "What?" Dana managed. "I overslept."

"It's two in the afternoon. Didn't you go in for your meeting? And the front door was open to the world. My bike and Robin's are still here, thank God, but—" Jen stopped and stared at Dana. "Oh, my God, Dana, I'm so sorry. I forgot, almost." Jen sat on Dana's bed, hardly making a dent with her tiny body, and took her hand. "I just got worried when I saw the door like that. Can I get you something? How about some tea? And I see all kinds of delicious pastry out there."

Dana nodded yes to the tea and shook her head no to the pastry. She could still taste the blueberries from yesterday's scone.

She felt it was still high and heavy in her gut, which she'd known would happen, but she'd wanted to show her appreciation to Elaine and her friends.

"And don't worry, I closed the door," Jen said.

Dana had no idea what the big deal was about the door. Of course she'd locked up. Robin must have come back or something.

"Here you go," Jen said, stirring honey into a mug of hot chai. Jen had coaxed her to the living room.

Dana watched her roommate—the youngest of the three women, a junior history major at UC Berkeley—as she moved the milky liquid around in careful swirls, as if trying to make up for her lack of gentleness earlier.

Dana knew she should be grateful to have good friends and family. A lot of people were there for her. Her dad—not the warmest of guys, but in a pinch he'd come through. Well, most of the time, unless someone in China needed him. Her mom—not so much since she moved to Florida with Mike, but she'd called as soon as she'd heard about Tanisha from her dad. She was sure it was Elaine who'd suggested her dad call her mom. He'd never have thought of it. She liked Elaine and hoped her dad wouldn't screw it up as he usually did.

Her two roommates, Jen Bradley and Robin Kirsch, weren't bad, either, especially compared to some roommates-from-hell she'd lived through in college. Robin's and Jen's boyfriends were nice guys, too. If it weren't for Jen's boyfriend, Wes, who loved to cook, they'd be eating frozen dinners every night. So what if she herself was between significant others? Not a bad place to be while she thought about her life.

She thought of her good friend and sometime partner, Tanisha. *There goes the lucky feeling.*

Dana's eyes filled up; her gaze drifted past the dining room to the bikes Jen had been so worried about, to the furniture, which any thief would be dumb to steal. The only thing vaguely valu-able was the laptop, which was still in its place on the dining room table, and maybe that expensive-looking briefcase—

Dana sat up, alert. "Did you move the briefcase?" she asked Jen.

"What brief . . . oh, that one Reed brought by. Nuh-uh." Jen had eaten the rest of the blueberry scone and had started on the currants in another. Hard to believe she could stay a size one with her sweet tooth. "Maybe Robin moved it."

Dana had a vague memory of Robin's coming home while she was moving in and out of sleep a while ago. She couldn't be sure. She'd heard the dumb dogs next door bark. They yelped no matter who came or went in the neighborhood, residents or strangers. Some watchdogs.

"Yeah, maybe it was Robin. Or maybe the cops came by," Dana said, only half aloud, while she made a circle around the house. Into her room, then into the bathroom, and out through Jen's room. Checking corners, behind doors. *Did I really leave the front door open?* Skipping Robin's room, which was locked. She'd have to wait till Robin came home. Through the kitchen, into the back hallway and second bathroom. *And the cops just walked in and took the briefcase?* Back through the kitchen, dining room, living room. No briefcase.

It didn't make sense.

But then not much did this weekend.

CHAPTER FIVE

I found it hard to get away from Elaine, even for a minute. After all, I'd come three thousand miles to visit, to help with wedding chores, to gush over the antique crystal necklace her great-aunt Judith had worn. (With each wedding, Elaine chose a different "something old.") How could I tell my friend, the bride, I needed some time on her computer to investigate her fiancé?

"Don't do this, Gloria," Matt said, in response to nothing in particular. I could tell by his tone that it was only a halfhearted recommendation. Either he agreed Phil needed to be vetted, or he knew I'd do it anyway.

I started on Sunday morning by asking Elaine if I could check my e-mail.

"I didn't realize you were that connected," she said.

I was ready with a small lie. "I told Andrea I'd keep in touch; she's looking into some material I'll need for my next science class presentation at Revere High."

Half true. My friend Andrea Cabrini, a technician at Revere's Charger Street Lab, regularly checked the lab's news bulletins for topics I might use for my work with the high school science club. Okay, one-quarter true. I knew Andrea would not expect to hear from me while I was away.

Elaine looked confused. "School's over until fall, isn't it? What's the rush?"

Now what? I felt my face flush. I hoped that if my color had changed noticeably, Elaine would attribute it to her warm living room. Or to my old California allergies.

"Summer school," I said, not daring to look at Matt. I made a mental note to think things through more the next time I planned a lie.

Elaine seemed satisfied. "I need to make a run to the farmers' market," she said, showing me the canvas tote she'd gotten out. Unlike my market totes, Elaine's looked cleaned and pressed; I questioned the net energy savings. "I thought we'd shop together, but you don't really have to come, I guess." She sounded forlorn, as if she'd been so looking forward to our picking out ripe avocados and giant string beans, arm in arm. Normally I'd enjoy it also, but I had work to do, so I stood firm.

"Thanks, Elaine. I'm glad you don't mind going alone. Maybe we can skip out on Matt this afternoon and go for a walk around Holy Hill? Our favorite route, remember?"

Elaine's face brightened, and I felt the heel that I was.

Matt and I huddled over Elaine's computer. I'd assigned him lookout duty for Elaine's return, but he thought he could do it as well from her upstairs office.

Elaine's home office was as well put together as the rest of her home. Framed award certificates from the Society for Technical Communication hung on the wall behind her scanner and printer; her file cabinets were made of fine wood, as was her corner desk and shelf arrangement.

"You're as curious as I am," I told Matt, who hovered over me as I hit the keys and entered PHILIP CHAMBERS.

Matt smirked and opened his arms, palms up. "It's what I do." Detective Matt Gennaro's trademark act, the one that always made me laugh.

I had no idea that another Philip Chambers was a movie and television star, with twenty-four movies to his credit. I scrolled past his fan club sites; past links to others of the same name who were lawyers and doctors; past a well-published Dr. Philip Chambers, oral surgeon and specialist in something called maxillofacial reconstruction, which I planned to look up later; and finally arrived at a P. L. Chambers in a reference to a conference on nitrogen.

"Here's something," I said. "A paper delivered by chemist Dr. Philip L. Chambers. It's on the BUL Web site, dated a year ago. It has to be Elaine's Phil Chambers. He worked with a group developing a molecule with a combination of carbon and nitrogen, shaped like a soccer ball."

"Didn't someone already do that with carbon alone?" Matt asked. "Buckminsterfullerene, right?" He seemed very pleased with himself.

I smiled broadly and patted his forehead, which was sweaty, like mine. If I weren't concerned about California's outrageous utility rates, I'd have cranked up—or down—the temperature on Elaine's air-conditioning unit. "I love it when you remember my science lessons," I said. "Technically, any soccer-ball-shaped molecule is a buckminsterfullerene. The nitrogen version would store more energy than a totally carbon version—a tremendous amount of energy, in fact—and it's a prime candidate for a new high explosive or a high-performance propellant." I adjusted my glasses to peer more closely at the screen. "According to this, success was imminent, but they always say that. 'We've made great progress,' 'In the next fiscal year,' etc."

"I don't get why this matters," Matt said. "What's so good or bad about Phil's working on a new nitrogen molecule?"

I shrugged. How did I know? "It's just that here's a guy, Dana's transport patient, an Indian with multiple identities and laboratory badges. He gets shot, presumably over something in either a briefcase or a duffel bag, and there's Phil, who seems to know the difference between them. And . . ." I flicked my finger at the computer screen. "And here's Phil working on a potential new weapon. Something any country would be happy to have."

"Isn't this a little too James Bond?" Matt asked, with good reason.

I shrugged again. "You read the papers. Think of all the recent true-life spy stories, at the national labs, at the Department of Energy." I summarized the cases I could remember on the fly and ticked them off. The scientist who allegedly transferred American nuclear technology information to China. The supposedly accidental misplacement of a computer disk with classified data at a DOE facility. The Pakistani nuclear scientist who sold secrets to Libya, Iran, and North Korea. Even a chaplain at a military base caught selling restricted data. "And those are just the ones we know about. James Bond is all around us."

"Myself, I've been wondering about the bullet," Matt said.

"Aha."

"I'm sure the Berkeley PD will try to match the two bullets."

I hung my head. "I didn't think of that. It might not have been the same shooter for the spy and Tanisha." Matt laughed at "spy," but didn't contradict me.

"Of course, if the guy lives and knows who shot him, we may have an immediate end to our game here," Matt said.

A sound in the driveway brought us both up short. I quickly logged on to check my e-mail. I found a short thinking-of-you note from Andrea and a blank message from Rose. Her teenaged grandson William's name was in the sender line, but there was no title and no text message. Rose had never used e-mail but had promised to learn while I was away. I smiled at the image of her sitting at William's computer, annoyed at the icons and the cursor. I planned to phone her soon and talk the old-fashioned way.

We heard the sounds of the back door opening and closing, and then Elaine's footsteps on the stairs, accompanied by her cheery voice.

"Warning, you two, I'm on my way up."

I was sure Elaine meant her warning to break up a compromising position. I felt a pang of guilt that Matt and I were not under the covers but undercover at her computer.

Elaine stepped into her office, hands behind her back. "We have avocados, green beans, peaches, and . . ." Elaine pulled her arms around to the front and dangled a long, narrow package, almost hitting Matt's pronounced Roman nose. Kettle corn, one of Matt's favorite snacks. And hard to get at home in Massachusetts. Though the sweet popcorn dates back to colonial times, we'd seldom seen it anywhere but at West Coast farmers' markets.

"Whoa!" Matt said, clearly pleasing Elaine. He undid the twist-tie and opened the waxed paper bag, releasing a wonderful sugary aroma. We let him have the first handful, then helped ourselves.

"Anything from Andrea?" asked Elaine, the most well-mannered kettle-corn chewer I'd seen.

A whopper came to my lips, way too quickly for comfort. By rights, I should have choked on a salty-sweet kernel.

"An attempted message from Rose." (A truth to start with, at least.) I cleared my throat. "And also Andrea mentioned some new work on a nitrogen molecule. Maybe Phil knows something about it? Do you think he'd be willing to talk to me?"

I saw Elaine's eyes light up. At any time that wasn't two weeks from her wedding, Elaine would have balked at the coincidence— an hour after she tells me Phil is working on nitrogen, Andrea Cabrini, three thousand miles away, finds something that prompts me to have an interest in it, too? Blinded by love as she was, I thought, Elaine instead saw this as a bonding opportunity. I could almost read her mind—her best friend and her fiancé, discussing a common interest. So what if it was a molecule?

"Of course!" she said, with enough enthusiasm to power a firecracker.

I didn't dare look at Matt.

On Sunday afternoon, Elaine and I walked around the neighborhood, as promised. For girl talk, we told Matt, who was just as
happy to stay home and listen to Elaine's many jazz CDs.

"Every one of my boyfriends had a different musical taste,"
she'd told us. "And each one added a new section to my music
collection. The jazz is from Bruce, the one who . . ." Elaine waved
her hand and grinned. I thought I saw a blush creep onto her
face. "Oh, never mind. Enjoy, Matt. Let's go, Gloria."

I hoped she would *not* tell me about Bruce.

Elaine and I returned to one of our favorite routes, up and down
Holy Hill, the local name for Berkeley's Graduate Theological
Union. Nine different Catholic and Protestant seminaries and
a dozen other religious programs were centered at GTU. We
played our traditional game of picking out religion or theology
students from the other passersby. We checked out the spines
of their books, noticing their medals, pins, and T-shirt logos.
(WWJD slogans were in the lead: WHAT WOULD JESUS DO? A close
second was SHANTI, the Hindi word for peace.)

We thought the snippets of conversation were uniquely
Berkeley.

"Deepak Chopra is old news," from a young man with very
worn Birkenstocks. "I'm listening to an audiotape by Houston
Smith."

"I thought he was dead," from his female companion.

A nun in a modified dark blue habit crossed the street in front
of us. Her posture was ramrod straight; her veil hung off the
back of her head, like a fabric ponytail.

"I didn't think they wore those anymore," said I, a long-lapsed
Catholic with no factual basis for the observation.

"You see them all the time around here," said Elaine, who'd
never belonged to a major religious denomination. Unless you

counted the Spirit of Energy Church, the Breath of Life Congregation, and a few other flocks of Berkeley souls she'd joined over the years.

"For the community aspect, Gloria," she'd tell me every time she tried a new group of worshipers.

"You mean for a dating pool?"

"That, too."

On this Sunday afternoon, with a cooling breeze coming off San Francisco Bay, I should have been relaxed and comfortable. Instead, the storefronts along Euclid Avenue seemed older and more run-down than I remembered, the sidewalks more cracked and littered, the bicyclists more rude.

Or maybe I was feeling the weight of my deception. I'd researched Elaine's fiancé using her own computer, in her own home, less than two weeks before I'd stand beside her at her Rose Garden wedding. Guilt poured down my back like a stale, flat champagne toast.

Not that it influenced my behavior.

"When do you think I can talk to Phil?" I asked her.

"Oh, I already made a date. We're meeting him for lunch tomorrow." Elaine whipped off her lightweight sweater, which perfectly matched her olive green slacks, as if the thought warmed her. "You two really have a lot to talk about. You know, Phil reads lots of scientific biography, just like you. He has books on Newton's Laws, Boyle's Laws, Bernoulli's Laws, Einstein's Laws, Everyone's Laws."

"Have I taught you nothing, Elaine? Science is not about laws—"

"I know, I know, just kidding."

"You just don't want my speech about the sciences as philosophical models of the universe—"

"Anchovies," Elaine said, snapping her fingers.

"What about them?"

"Phil hates anchovies, just as you do. There's something else in common."

We laughed together, the way we used to before I suspected her fiancé of evil deeds.

I told myself I wasn't snooping. Wasn't it the duty of an official witness to a marriage to ensure there were no objections to the union? Once satisfied, I'd forever hold my peace.

Before Matt and I left Revere for this so-called vacation, Rose Galigani gave me two phone cards, each with five hundred minutes prepaid.

"That's almost seventeen hours, Rose," I'd told her. Now I thought it might take that long to finish our first cross-country conversation. We both missed our daily contact.

"There's some drama here, Gloria, even without you," Rose said. "Not a murder, though, so don't worry." I wasn't sure when, or if, I'd reveal that I'd dragged the murder MacGuffin with me to Berkeley. Not now, I decided, and settled back on the easy chair in Elaine's guest room.

"It's boring here without you, Rose," I said. "Tell me something dramatic."

She plunged right in. "Remember how Sandy Caputo died before you left last week?"

"You mean two days ago? Sure." I didn't remind Rose that I didn't know Sandy Caputo and even now couldn't remember whether Sandy was male or female. Rose, on the other hand, had lived in Revere all her life and was her own one-woman historical society.

"Well, he was scheduled for this afternoon, Parlor B, the closest to the stairway."

That I wouldn't forget—the layout of the Galigani Mortuary building where I'd lived before moving in with Matt, daily breathing in the aroma of funeral flowers, passing Parlors A and

B, and sometimes a makeshift C, on the way up to my third-floor apartment.

"You won't believe what happened," Rose continued. "The Caputo family's in an uproar. They were trying to reach Frank, but he was setting up a nun from Holy Names downstairs, and since it's Sunday, no one was in the office, and Robert was picking up the Higgins boy, who should have gone to O'Neal's in Chelsea, really, and I guess I had my cell phone off—" Rose took a breath. "Are you still there, Gloria?"

I smiled to myself. "I'm here, waiting for the punch line." I was used to Rose's story-building and had learned to follow the plotline in spite of the extraneous threads.

"They're saying Sandy's in the wrong suit." Rose's voice registered extreme stress and incredulity. "Sandy's wife says he'd never wear a yellow shirt and the jacket is way too small and not his."

"The body's in the wrong clothes? How did that happen?"

I'd made a clothing run for the Galiganis more than once, picking up an outfit from a dry cleaners or from the family of the deceased. I'd mark the bag or valise carefully before stepping out of my car with it and, holding my nose against the odors of death, would deliver it to the Galigani prep room.

In fact, I knew more than the ordinary layperson about the process of prepping a client for presentation in a casket. Rose and Frank and I had been friends from grade school, never losing touch, even when I moved to California after college and didn't return home, as Rose called it, for thirty years. Frank had been in the funeral service business forever, starting as an informal security guard for a Boston mortuary when he was a chemistry major at Boston College.

"I wish you and Matt were here to do a little investigating, Gloria." No matter that I wasn't a real detective, private or public, and that the rest of Matt's Revere Police Department was still on duty in her city.

I didn't bother to suggest that two clothing deliveries might have been switched accidentally by a Galigani employee. Frank and Rose, and their son Robert, ran a very tight ship.

"It wouldn't be the first time a grieving family got a little confused," I offered. "Or tried to take their anger out on the mortuary staff."

Frank and Robert had told me stories of spouses and parents who turned their anger on the funeral directors, as if the person arranging for the burial of their loved one was responsible for his death. It usually happened, I learned, when the deceased met an especially tragic end or was "too young to die," as we say. As if anyone were old enough to die.

"Want to know what I really think?" Rose asked, bringing me to the problem at hand. "I have an idea how it happened, but I can't prove it. I think it was Bodner and Polk."

"The mortuary chain in Boston?"

"Not just in Boston anymore. They're branching out, literally, to take over all the independents they can. I told you they made an offer to O'Neal's last month. They're working their way to Revere."

"How could they get into your prep room? Also, it's hard to imagine a big business like that stooping to a childish prank like switching clothing."

"They'll do anything, Gloria. Ralphie over at O'Neal's told me they had a similar screw-up a couple of weeks ago, right after they refused to sell." She took a breath. I knew the extent of Rose's agitation when she didn't bother to apologize for using an expression that her grandson and everyone else in Revere might use, but not her. "Screw-up" was not in Rose's normal working vocabulary. "O'Neal's van went to the wrong hospital for the Myers girl's removal, and now this? All of a sudden we're all getting sloppy? I don't think so."

I knew Rose's worries were real, and well founded. Like most other small businesses, family mortuaries were fast becoming a thing of the past. Chains were able to get bigger discounts on caskets, flower stands, votive lights, and all the fragrant chemi-cals that were necessary for business. Thus, they could offer bet-ter prices to clients. However, I decided to give Rose the upside of the issue.

"Cost isn't everything, Rose. Galigani's has a reputation for the kind of attention people want in a time of trial. The personal touch, run by a family, using local businesses for supporting ser-vices like florists and printers and—"

Rose's laughter came over the lines, as clear as if we'd been eating biscotti on her front porch. "You sound like our brochure."

"What's wrong with that?"

"I miss you, Gloria. But I hope you're having a good time. Don't worry about your newspapers and your mail. I'm picking everything up, and I'll let you know if anything looks urgent. Or interesting." Another laugh, because we were both aware that Rose's curiosity knew no bounds.

"Thanks, Rose. Bye for now."

"Oh, wait—I haven't even asked you what Elaine's fiancé is like."

"We'll go into that next time, okay?"

"Hmmm. I'll call you."

"Or you can e-mail me again," I said, with a wink in my voice.

We hung up. I felt lucky my friends tolerated my impertinence.

CHAPTER S I X

Dana checked her wardrobe for something suitable for a day of interviews. First she'd have to report to Julia Strega, the owner of the company, then she'd be seeing a counselor, then the Berkeley police.

Not a fun day, but Elaine had arranged for her to have a massage this evening. A classy lady, always doing thoughtful little things. She'd even checked to be sure Dana was okay going ahead with the wedding plans. *Totally,* Dana had told her, but she was glad she'd been asked.

She'd have to move on the wedding shower, too, which was only about ten days away. She'd offered to host a party for the bride and groom at her house, forgetting that it would mean housecleaning and food planning. But a party might do everyone some good, Dana thought.

She clicked through the hangers in her half of the closet she shared with Jen. Crop-top tees and mohair scarves; a swishy, too-short black velvet skirt from the thrift shop; a wraparound top with beaded fringe everywhere. A pathetic selection except when she was dressing for a rave. The EMT uniform had spoiled her. She hadn't needed to invest in anything vaguely adult or professional in more than a year.

The laundry basket in the back hall gave up only a bad smell. So much for Plan B. Plan C would have to be called up—borrow from her roommates.

Jen's clothes were way too small, but she could manage with Robin's longish, straight black skirt and her own Moulin Rouge shirt.

She hadn't seen Robin since Saturday morning. Overnight with Jeff again, Dana figured. She might as well move in with him and save on rent. Robin was studying for a certificate in international business at some online university. She was in the intern phase at a San Francisco financial institution. Robin loved to call herself a consultant. Though it didn't pay much, she constantly reminded them that one day it would all pay off. Big time.

Her roommates couldn't be more different, Dana thought. Jen was Wisconsin fresh, blonde, and wholesome, from the kind of family that baked cookies together on Saturday afternoons and held hands walking to church on Sunday morning. Jen wanted to be a history teacher. Robin didn't talk much about her family, which had fallen apart when her father, a Vietnam vet who never recovered, had committed suicide. Robin had been only nine years old. *Poor kid.*

Being an only child, Dana didn't have much experience with kids, but she knew Tanisha's little Rachel, and she'd done a couple of career-day talks at local schools and she knew how vulnerable kids could be. One time Dana had four junior high students on a tour of the back of an ambulance, each wearing a sticker: I'M A JUNIOR EMT. She remembered being surprised at how impressionable they'd been, in spite of their I'm-cool demeanor.

Dana supposed her family life was somewhere in the middle, between Jen's and Robin's. Not your Hallmark family, but not devastated by such a catastrophe as suicide, either. Of course, her parents' divorce had been hugely traumatic, but she always knew they both loved her. She figured she came out of it all reasonably healthy.

Back to the wardrobe search. Dana checked the door to Robin's room. Unlocked. *Great.* She must have come home sometime last night. Robin was fussier than Jen about sharing clothes and about privacy in general. She'd insisted on having the bedroom with its own door and often locked it; Dana and Jen didn't mind having a common bathroom between their bedrooms and never locked their doors.

"I hope you don't freak out that I'm in here, Robin," Dana whispered to the empty room.

Dana tiptoed past Robin's twin bed and newly painted white dresser. She always thought the photo Robin kept of her father was a little creepy. An eight-by-ten (who had those anymore?) in his military uniform, with a look so somber you almost knew he was going to kill himself soon. Jen's centerpiece photo, on the other hand, was of a Bradley family reunion, with her father wearing a chef's hat, standing at an outdoor grill.

Dana put her hand on the knob of the accordion-style closet door and paused. She looked over her shoulder and listened for a sound. She laughed at herself. She was alone in the house, and anyway, she wasn't a thief. Only a borrower, and Robin had lent Dana clothes before. Dana had never just walked in and taken something, but she felt sure Robin would cut her some slack, especially this week.

She opened the closet door and stepped back. At least a dozen new items, tags still on them, had been squeezed into the middle section of the rod. Dana flipped through them, careful not to wrinkle anything. Skirts, pants, sweaters, at least four dresses, and all looking very expensive. She scratched her forehead. None of the women could afford shopping sprees like this, and neither could Jeff, TA-ing his way through a graduate program in English lit. Dana grinned. Well, none of her business if Robin wanted to max out her credit cards.

Robin didn't hide the fact that her goal in life was to be as rich as the people she read about in all her money magazines. She'd spent about six months' pay to join a fancy tennis club.

"Volleyball is for kids," she'd said when Dana asked if she

wanted to join the city league. "If you want to meet rich people, you have to take up their sports."

Dana found the black skirt she'd come for, looking old and faded next to the new threads. She took it off the hanger and pushed the new clothing back together, leaving the rod the way she thought she'd found it. A silky spaghetti-strap top slipped off its hanger, and Dana rushed to retrieve it from the closet floor. She gave the strap a little pull toward her. With it came another item. A card of some kind. The strap had fallen around it, making an inadvertent loop. Dana picked up the card. A laminated ID for Dorman Industries. The company of consultants her dad worked for. And the photo. A dark-skinned man, fortyish, short-cropped dark hair—could it be . . . ? Dana frowned, concentrating, struggling to piece together the bits flying around her mind. The gunshot victim? Their patient when Tanisha was shot? How . . . ?

"What the hell are you doing in here?" Robin's voice was low and threatening.

Dana gasped and fell back on her butt. "Robin! I . . . I just came in to borrow . . ." She pointed to the black skirt, now on the floor next to her.

Robin, about the same height as Dana, loomed over her. Her face was red, way out of proportion to the offense, Dana thought. But not out of character. Robin had a temper and could easily blow up if she or Jen so much as dipped into her box of coffee filters. If she was going to meet her stated goal in life, to be a female Donald Trump, Robin would have to get a new attitude. *Or not.*

Dana hoisted herself from her position half in and half out of Robin's closet and, for a reason she couldn't explain, surreptitiously slid the ID card into the back pocket of her shorts.

Robin's brown eyes narrowed to mean-looking slits; her arms were folded across her chest, partly obscuring the image of a dragon on her black T-shirt. She didn't say anything further, as if she were deciding which to do battle with, her words or her fists.

"I'm sorry," Dana said. *Putting it lightly,* she thought. She offered the skirt to Robin.

Robin relaxed a little, a very little. "No, it's okay. Take it. But you know I don't like anyone messing with my things."

"I'm really sorry," Dana said again. "I have all these interviews today, and"—she threw up her hands—"nothing to wear." Risking a little humor.

Robin dropped her shoulders further and nearly smiled. "It's okay, really. I know you're stressed. I overreacted. Are you going to see that counselor?"

"Yeah, and the police after that. You didn't happen to see that briefcase I had in the living room, by the way, did you?"

"I thought you already talked to the police."

"They need a formal statement, plus I guess they have more questions."

Robin moved toward her closet, making room for Dana to walk past her, out the door.

"See you later," Dana said. She heard Robin's door click shut. She went into her own room, sat on the bed, and took a deep breath, the first one since Robin had walked in on her. She'd forgotten to return to the question of whether Robin had seen the briefcase, but no way was she going back to that room.

Dana felt the card in her pocket carve a huge question mark on her butt.

Dana sat on a broken rocker in Valley Med's employee lounge waiting for her boss, Julia Strega, who'd sent word that she'd been delayed. She stared at the walls of the faux apartment, filled with schedule spreadsheets and posters. Her favorite was the staple of EMS rooms everywhere: WE DON'T WANT YOUR BUSINESS. A few hand-lettered notes around the coffeepot and the bathroom doors made futile pleas for cleanliness. The watercooler, sink, and refrigerator that lined one side of the room, the couch and broken easy chairs, were all as familiar to her as the furniture in her own house, except this furniture made hers look like Ethan Allen. Dana was tempted to stretch out on a cot in one of the small bedrooms. More than occasionally a nap in this area was her only break in thirty-six hours.

"Hey, Dana." Tom Stewart, not her favorite Alameda County EMT, and not just because of his pimply skin and ugly Adam's apple. No chance for a nap now. Just as well, since she didn't want to mess up Robin's skirt.

"Hey, yourself," Dana said. *Go away* was what she wanted to say.

"Nasty business with Tanisha, huh?"

Dana closed her eyes and ignored him, hoping he would get the hint or think she was napping.

Tom had been an EMT longer than anyone else at Valley Med—no one knew exactly how many years, but longer than anyone in history, Tanisha used to say. An EMT stint was not usually a permanent vocation unless you bought the company as Julia had done. The job was physically too demanding and paid too little for any but the very young; most EMTs were on their way to other careers in emergency services—paramedics, cops, ER doctors and nurses. Tanisha had applied for her Fire 1 exam. Dana's chest constricted at the memory of her ambitious, hard-working friend. And here she was, procrastinating on her own alleged plans to apply to med school.

"So what happened? Did you see it all?" Tom asked, moving a chair close to Dana's rocker. He shook his head in an it's-unbelievable gesture. Dana caught a whiff and wondered when was the last time he'd washed his thin brown hair. "Must have been a totally confusing scene, huh?"

More confusing than you know, Dana thought, still trying to process the most recent scene, the one in Robin's bedroom. She had thought that Robin had taken the briefcase, or at least arranged for someone to remove it from their house, though she couldn't imagine why. Someone in so much of a hurry they left the front door open. *Now who's overreacting?* she asked herself. But the Dorman Industries ID card threw her—what was that about? Such a big company, with international consultants flying back and forth every day, most likely her dad had no clue who this guy was. Still, she'd put in a quick call to her dad, getting only his answering machine, before she left the house.

Dana wished she could disappear for a week and think about things. Not just what happened on Friday evening, and this strange stuff with Robin, but her own life. Like, what kind of doctor would she be if she fell apart when she was faced with death and trauma?

"Hey. Earth to Dana. Are you with me here?" Tom was waving his knobby hands in front of Dana's face. *Obnoxious.*

"Tom, I'm a little spacey right now. I have this interview, then counseling, and then the cops." She ticked off the appointments on her fingers for emphasis. "So I'd like a little downtime, if you don't mind." *And even if you do.*

"The cops." Tom gave a little bow, as if the idea impressed him. "Better be careful what you tell them. You don't want them following you around forever."

Dana rolled her eyes. What was that supposed to mean? She decided not to ask.

A voice rescued her from Tom. It came from a speaker high on the wall.

"Dana, come on back. Sorry to keep you waiting." Julia Strega, and not a moment too soon.

"Gotta go, Tom."

Dana took a seat opposite her boss. Outside Julia's unadorned, metal-framed window was a bustling industrial district off University Avenue, a major thoroughfare in Berkeley. The loud noises from trucks, heavy machinery, and crowds of loading-dock workers surprised Dana, and she realized she was seldom in the neighborhood during normal working hours.

"You're all dressed up," Julia said, folding back the cuffs of her Cal Bears sweatshirt. "For me?" Her voice still had the remnants of a cold or allergies.

Dana smiled. "I guess you haven't seen me in a skirt since my job interview, right?"

For everyday reporting, Dana had a supervisor—Doreen, now on maternity leave—but Julia was also heavily involved in day-to-day operations, more than was usual for a company owner. Though it was still considered small compared to other ambulance companies in Alameda County, under Julia Valley Med had grown to nearly two hundred employees with all levels of EMT support from basic to full paramedic, with nurse-staffed critical care transportation.

Business was good, but nothing like what it would take to get a company so big so fast, and Dana figured Julia pumped a lot of her own money into it. Now she was talking about extending the business into other counties in the Bay Area. Julia had been hinting to Dana that it would be nice to have an experienced EMT transfer to a new operation in Contra Costa or San Mateo County.

"Let's get to it," Julia said in her no-nonsense way. She pulled a folder from the piles of papers on her desk and put on wire-rimmed half-glasses. "Getting old," she muttered.

Dana felt she was supposed to contradict her boss—*no, you're not old*—but in fact, Julia was old in Dana's mind. At least as old as her dad, her very red hair notwithstanding. Julia was as trim as any of her EMTs, but there was no denying the deep wrinkles in her face. And her lipstick was starting to spread into the little crevices around her mouth.

"I have some forms here, so I'll just run down this list of questions. It's all routine," Julia said, half of her words buried in the tissue she held to her nose.

Routine. The word bounced around Dana's brain. *Not quite.*

Julia buzzed through a set of more or less factual questions, most of which she could have answered herself. How long had Dana been on the job? (Fourteen months.) Had she ever been involved in a critical incident? (Yes, one mass casualty on I-580, but nothing this personal.) Ever had CISD? (Critical incident stress debriefing. Yes, one session, after the I-580 MCI.) Did the current CI involve damage to the ambulance? (No, the ambulance came out alive.)

Dana had downloaded the Valley Med form from the Internet and checked all the boxes next to the stock questions. Then she typed in her own report with the particulars of the incident that took Tanisha's life—the time of the call, the trip with the GSW vic, all the details that Dana had run through her mind over and over since Friday evening. Robin had offered to change the cartridge and print out the report while Dana got dressed, probably to make up for her bad behavior earlier.

"Here you go," Dana said, handing the pages to Julia.

"Thanks. I'll let you know if we need anything else." Julia leaned over the desk and offered Dana a sympathetic look. "Please take all the time you need to decompress, Dana. You know you'll have to sign up for the CISD sessions?"

Dana nodded. She knew how it worked. The county participated in a national program for ES workers, in which severely stressful job-related incidents were discussed with peer counselors and mental health professionals. The death or serious injury of a coworker in the line of duty was high on the list. She'd be expected to show up at a meeting at least by tonight. Fortunately, she had a relaxing massage coming, too, thanks to Elaine.

"And you're scheduled to see Dr. Barnett today?"

Another nod.

"Good. You know that seeing a counselor one-on-one is part of the comprehensive critical incident stress management system . . ."

". . . recommended for emergency services workers," Dana finished. "I know the drill. I'm good to go." She tried for a don't-worry-about-me tone.

Julia pushed back from her desk. The wheels of her chair rumbled along the linoleum. "One more thing, Dana. Be careful what you tell the cops today."

What was this? Everyone seemed concerned about her interview with the Berkeley PD. Maybe she should be more worried herself.

"I'm not suggesting you lie, of course," Julia continued. "Just, you know, we want to avoid anything that would reflect badly on the company." She flipped her short too-red hair, as if making sure her own appearance would give a good impression of Valley Med.

"Okay," Dana said, without the slightest idea what Julia meant.

CHAPTER SEVEN

Early Monday morning Matt and I sat side by side on the gold jacquard loveseat in our room. Elaine was down the hall, still asleep—or preparing her face for public view, but quiet at any rate—so we'd brought our mugs of coffee and two lemon biscotti back to the bedroom. The perfect breakfast.

Sunlight came into the room with great effort, having to first pass through Elaine's elaborate window treatment and a hexagonal piece of stained glass, in gold and blood-orange hues, hung by an invisible cord.

"I've been patient," I said to Matt, "but I need to know."

"What I said to Dana on Saturday."

A statement, not a question. No wonder I loved him. No games, no making me beg.

I hoped I wasn't motivated by idle curiosity or, worse, by jealousy that another woman might know something about Matt that I didn't. I was reasonably sure this need came from loving him and wanting to understand the highs and lows of his life before I met him. I'd thought about it off and on for two days, and I felt more and more certain he'd shared a significant occupational low with Dana.

Unlike our friends Rose and Frank Galigani, childhood sweethearts, now married more than four decades, Matt and I had met as adults. We carried baggage and emotional histories, both positive and negative.

I hadn't needed to tell Matt much about my first and only other fiancé, Al Gravese. Matt was a rookie cop at the time and knew before I did that Al was "connected" and that the car crash that took Al's life three months before our wedding wasn't an accident.

I hoped I was less naive now than I had been then. I'd never questioned where Al got the rolls of bills he carried around, and felt proud when he'd tear off a fifty and give it to my father. I remembered his deep voice and his flashy style: *Get yourself some butts, Marco.*

I'd pieced together a picture of Matt's first wife, Teresa, from what Rose and Frank told me about her low-key personality, her work with special-needs children, and her long illness. One evening after Matt and I had been seeing each other regularly for a couple of months, he took an album from a desk drawer. We went through it page by page, photo after photo: birthday parties; sailing trips around Nantucket Sound with Matt's sister, Jean, and her family; Fourth of July barbecues; Thanksgiving turkeys; Christmas trees. His life with Teresa.

"Remember the time you shared your Teresa album?" I asked him now.

He took a sip of coffee. "I do."

"I loved that moment." I cleared my throat and tasted lemon frosting. "Do you also have a police album?"

Matt laughed and took my hand. A noble gesture since it meant he had to sacrifice half a biscotto for the time being.

"First, you know I love you, and I would never keep anything from you deliberately, to deceive you or to—"

"It's not about that."

He nodded. "I believe it."

The house was very quiet, except for what I thought might be Elaine's hair dryer, down the hall. Matt kept my hand in his lap but stared straight ahead, where a framed art print of sunflowers hung on the wall. I couldn't name the artist, which would sadden

Elaine, who'd tried to fill in the gaps in my very technical educa-tion. The lines in the painting were curvy, and I thought I re-membered that feature went with van Gogh. Or Cézanne. Matt seemed to be tilting his head to figure it out himself.

I sensed rather than heard the hard swallow that preceded all his serious disclosures. Some were upsetting: *My wife died ten years ago today.* Then, later, *I have cancer.* And some were thrilling: *I love you, I want us to be married.*

I knew this one would be difficult.

"It was my worst moment," he said. "On the job, anyway. I wasn't much older than Dana. Kenny was a dispatcher I knew very well; I'd gone to school with him in Everett. We'd been at a retirement dinner at a hotel on Route 1." Matt took a long breath. I felt him pull back to that day. "We're walking to our cars to-gether."

I squeezed his hand. "If you'd rather not . . ." *Fine time to be magnanimous,* I thought.

He shook his head. "If you ever want the illusion of safety, put yourself in a banquet room where more than half the people are cops and firefighters. We're physically fit and highly trained in self-defense. We're armed and tough. We're essentially a para-military corps. We're used to being in control. People expect us to be confident, take charge. Nothing can touch us, right?" He sighed. "I think it's called denial."

I thought it was the longest speech I'd ever heard from Matt. Eventually he got to the story itself.

"We're down in the garage, we say good-bye at Kenny's car, and I split to go to mine. I'm about two cars over when I hear a kid yell, 'Gimme me your wallet. Hand it over. Gimme your keys.' I turn and the kid has a gun under Kenny's chin. I had a split second to decide what to do. I remember thinking, *How dumb is this kid?* But we're in civvies, and he couldn't have known that we were law enforcement and about a hundred cops were twenty feet above him on the ballroom floor."

"I can't imagine," I said, weak from picturing myself in that garage.

"I yell, 'Police, freeze.' But even before it's out I know this kid doesn't care. He swings his gun around to me, giving Kenny a chance to reach for the kid's neck, and I hear two shots. One is mine; one is the kid's. I can't tell you how long it took me to figure which bullet went where."

A light knock at the door. Elaine. "Hey, you two. Thanks for making the coffee." I knew she'd be impatient to get on with the day's business. A trip to the caterer was on the list, and then our eagerly awaited nitrogen lunch with Phil.

"Give us ten minutes," I said.

"I'll warm up the car."

Matt gave me a questioning look.

"Our little joke, about how that's not necessary in California, and how that's why I should never have moved back to Massachusetts."

Matt kissed my cheek. "I'm glad you don't mind a little cold weather."

Elaine's knock had broken his rhythm, perhaps fortuitously. He'd returned to the present, ready to wrap up the story.

"So, bottom line. I'd shot the kid in the chest. The kid got Kenny through his thigh. The kid died. Kenny had a limp for the rest of his life, until he died a couple of years ago. It didn't matter that the kid had a record a mile long. He was nineteen years old and I killed him."

"You had no choice, Matt. And you saved Kenny's life."

"You always have a choice. But I know what you mean. For months I had nightmares. One night it would be that the gun failed on me. The next night the gun wouldn't stop firing."

I was stunned by the whole story, and by Matt's revelations—his thoughts and his feelings about the seamy side of his job. I understood why his sharing this with Dana might help her. He hadn't seen his partner killed, but he'd lived through a traumatic incident and gone forward in his profession.

In the end, I could only be thankful that neither of the bullets got Matt. Not physically, anyway.

Waiting for Elaine to fix her face, as she termed it, I sat with my notebook, doodling, my usual process when I was working on a case, real or imagined. I was prepared to give Dr. Philip Chambers a second chance to show himself a worthy fiancé for my friend, with no involvement in the nefarious events of the weekend. *Wouldn't he be thrilled if he knew of my generosity?* I mused.

I'd never been so ill equipped for a meeting of this kind—the kind where I'm ostensibly having a friendly visit but in my mind conducting an interrogation. In this case, I'd managed to inflate the facts of Phil's condescending attitude and what might have been a simple error—duffel bag or briefcase?—into a full-fledged *Murder One* scenario. The possibility that I was way off base was enormous.

I had no forensics information about the actual crimes—the shootings of Dana and Tanisha's patient, and then Tanisha. Even with my special brand of cajoling, I hadn't been able to persuade Matt to present himself to the Berkeley PD and learn the inside scoop. I'd had to rely on the newspapers, which I knew not to trust for full disclosure on an open case.

We did learn that the victim of the first shooting had died at the trauma center. The newspapers said more or less what we knew from Dana, that he was Indian and carried multiple ID cards. Police determined that he was "really" named Lokesh Patel, in this country as a visiting scientist. They didn't mention the existence of the other IDs. He'd been working on a project with scientists at BUL and local consulting firms. There was no apparent motive for the killing. All the authorities could glean from the records at Golden State Hospital, where he'd driven himself from someplace in Oakland, was that he'd been shot in the chest. The victim had said nothing about where the shooting took place, other than "in the parking lot."

The obituary was only slightly more informative: Patel had no family in this country; he was an upstanding citizen, a member of the Claremont Tennis Club and a volunteer with charitable organizations throughout the Bay Area.

"No dying declaration," Matt had said, reminding me how handy it would have been if Patel had, number one, known he was dying; number two, named his killer; and number three, then died. One of the more compelling pieces of evidence in a murder case. When I'd once asked Matt how come, he'd told me the traditional wisdom was *If you know you're going to meet your maker, you're not going to try one more lie.*

Tanisha's death in the line of duty didn't buy much space in the Bay Area papers. On the first day, one of them had carried a photo of Tanisha with her daughter, Rachel, blowing out candles on a birthday cake, a happier time. After that, there were no reports of the second shooting.

The papers quoted the police as saying the two incidents appeared to be unrelated, but I guessed that was a misstatement on the part of some journalist. If Alameda County was anything like Suffolk County in Massachusetts, the ballistics report would be a long time coming, since this was not a high-profile case.

I tried to think of ways to insert myself or Matt into the Berkeley PD files, but the only cop I'd met, Inspector Dennis Russell, wouldn't be happy to see me, I knew. I'd had a not-so-pleasant interaction with him the last time I'd visited. I'd thought I was helping his investigation into the death of a former colleague of mine; he'd thought I was meddling. Matt did promise to keep his eyes open when he accompanied Dana to the police station later in the day. That would have to do.

Along with these limitations, I was hampered by having to hide my curiosity and suspicions from Elaine. Fortunately, her computer was in an office, separate from her bedroom, and I was able to sneak in after she'd gone to bed. I hoped she wouldn't think to track the most recently accessed URLs on her browser. She'd count a half dozen nitrogen- and weapons-related sites. It was all I could do to remember not to bookmark them.

The elements of the physical universe always amazed me, especially how different forms of the same one had such widely varying properties. Nitrogen, the seventh element on the periodic table, was a perfect example. A two-atom form of nitrogen was the most abundant element in our atmosphere, making up nearly 80 percent of the air around us and found in all living systems. We breathed in nitrogen safely every day.

A three-atom form of nitrogen, however, was highly explosive.

Even the explosive form had a spectrum of uses. Nitrogen gas exploded in air bags to save lives; it also exploded in events like the Oklahoma City bombing.

At the last minute, just as we were about to leave for our lunch date with Phil, Elaine had a call. I gathered from her side of the conversation that something logistic was not going well. By the time she hung up, Elaine had an exasperated look.

"My florist," she said. "I'm going to have to go down to the shop and choose another color scheme."

"With three thousand blooms in the Rose Garden, you need a florist?" I asked. "That's probably seventy-five thousand petals."

Elaine laughed. "Leave it to you to find a way to do arithmetic, Gloria. We still need bouquets, corsages, centerpieces for the tables at the reception." She gave me a hopeless look as she prepared a beige leather purse, almost as large as my carry-on, for departure. Of course, she had on beige shoes. "I can see that you'll need me when it comes to planning *your* wedding."

I choked. On nothing but my own breath. Matt and I hadn't talked about a wedding date. Or a wedding at all. I didn't see why we couldn't stay engaged forever.

Elaine patted me on the back. "Don't worry. I'm too caught up in this wedding to worry about anyone else's. But after our honeymoon, I'm linking up with Rose, and we have major plans for you and Matt."

Scary as that thought was, I at least had a reprieve. I blew out a breath.

Elaine looked at her watch. "The bad news is I'll have to skip lunch with you and Phil. The good news is you and Phil get to bond without my being in the way."

"Is that a deliberate pun?"

Elaine frowned, then raised her neatly drawn light brown eyebrows. "Of course. I meant, like nitrogen bonding."

I'd taught my friends well.

CHAPTER EIGHT

The bonding lunch suffered from another last-minute change. A call from Phil, his cell phone to mine, brought me to a bagel place near his work site, a few blocks from Bette's Diner. He had to give a presentation to some visiting consultants at Dorman Industries, he'd said, and needed to keep his lunch hour short. Typical bureaucracy, I thought, where consultants have consultants.

The bagel shop was in the same block as Berkeley's Breathing Institute. I smiled as I passed the recessed, glassed-in doorway. *Ah, Berkeley, the city that trains you to breathe.*

I remembered the year Elaine signed up for breathing classes. To stop her nagging, I'd agreed to give it a try and accompanied her to a session. About a dozen of us sat in a converted kindergarten classroom on tiny wooden stools—already a hindrance to good respiration, in my opinion—and chanted the vowel sounds, one after the other, using all the possibilities. Short *a* (aaaaaaaah, as when the doctor says, "Open wide"), long *a*, middle *a*, long *e*, short *e*, and so on. That had been enough for me, and I dropped out. It hadn't been as easy to drop off the mailing list, however, and for several years I received invitations, on recycled paper, to their events and holiday parties. My favorite was the flyer inviting all to BREATHE IN THE NEW YEAR CORRECTLY!

I approached the bare-bones bagel shop at the same time as Phil, who was accompanied by a tall, white-haired man. I thought he was the same man who'd picked Phil up outside Bette's diner on Saturday.

"Dr. Gloria Lamerino," Phil greeted me. "Dr. Howard Christopher, my boss at Dorman." Phil seemed enamored with the titles, nearly bowing when he uttered them, the way we used to bow our heads at the name of Jesus when I was a little girl in Sunday school.

"I'm glad to meet you," I said. "Will you be joining us?" Over the odor of fresh bagels, I smelled a golden opportunity to quiz two Dorman employees at once.

"I'd love to," Christopher said, "but duty calls."

"Some other time," I said.

Christopher pointed his index finger at me, in the gun-shooting position. "You bet."

I almost "shot" him back but thought I'd behave, for the time being.

Neither Phil nor his clothes showed any signs of being affected by the heat. He wore a silver-gray shirt and a light blue jacket, the best-dressed person in the shop.

I'd pinned to my summer shirt a blue-and-gold seaborgium pin, a small replica of a block on the periodic table assigned to element 106, named after Berkeley's Glenn Seaborg. Common ground, I figured. Who hadn't loved Seaborg, Nobel-winning scientist and devoted educator? I was proud of myself for the gesture, honoring a chemist.

"Your bride has a flower crisis," I told him.

He threw his head back and laughed. Elaine was right; he was handsome. "If it were up to me, we'd be married in a judge's office and have dim sum afterward. But I'm happy to let her do what she wants." Two points for Phil, I thought. His idea of a wedding matched mine, but he'd given in to my friend's wishes.

"Thanks for meeting me here instead of a place with cloth napkins," Phil said. "Not elegant, but it's close to Dorman. I'm on a short track for a deliverable."

I translated mentally: *My funding sponsor wants a report immediately, and I have no data.* But I had to admit, Phil was charming.

"I love bagels," I said, calling up my own charming side.

"Thanks for saying that. Elaine says you're doing some teaching—I've thought about that, too. Maybe someday when I'm not as critical to these projects, when I really retire."

Uh-oh, minus a point. As if teaching were not a valid career choice for the nonretired. I'd always considered it part of a working scientist's responsibility to inspire youth . . . I turned off the recruiting brochure in my head. When would I stop trying to mold Phil and every other scientist into my picture of what they should be?

I settled for "Actually, I've always done volunteer work in the schools."

Phil made a good-for-you gesture, with a wink and a nod.

Phil scored another point by noticing the book I'd brought, a new biography of Galileo. He'd already read it, he said, which added value. We chatted for a few minutes about whether the great Renaissance man sincerely recanted or pretended to, all the while using Church resources to further his own theories. A Galileo enthusiast in the family, so to speak, would definitely be a plus.

I was dizzy trying to keep score. One moment he was Phil the Charming—he'd shaken my hand warmly, laughed at my joke about Elaine's flower crisis, and allowed me to rave on about Galileo. The next minute he annoyed me. Phil the Supercilious, making it sound as if he were too important to teach.

At least I could get something out of this bagel lunch, I decided. "I'm interested in your nitrogen work," I said. "I like to be sure my Revere High classes are getting up-to-date material. Maybe you could give me a quick overview of your projects?"

"Well, most of what I do is classified, as I think Elaine told you." Phil had a pleasant smile, but I read his face: *So this is really a waste of time.*

"I've been reading about a nitrogen fullerene molecule, where some of the sixty carbon atoms are replaced by nitrogen atoms. This gives it much more explosive power, of course." I took a sip of coffee. "Is that part of your work?" I asked. I meant *Are you working on explosives?*

The appearance of our lip-ringed waitress gave Phil time to think, though I was sure he'd been preparing since Elaine set up this meeting. The young woman, in black jeans and turtleneck despite the lack of air-conditioning, set down the toasted bagels we'd ordered at the counter.

"My project deals with computer modeling to determine the stability of energetic materials," Phil said.

Energetic materials. I smiled at the euphemism, but Phil remained straight-faced. We talked for a while about the various possibilities of inserting nitrogen subunits into an otherwise carbon fullerene. All very interesting, but not moving me toward the connections I sought among Phil, the Indian scientist, and a certain briefcase.

With a mental picture and my creative X-ray vision I saw through the leather briefcase to a computer disk or DVD storing classified data. Phil's spy-partner had messed up the assassination of Lokesh Patel, followed the ambulance, killed Tanisha, and run off. But he took the wrong bag. Phil knew this and was now desperate to get his hands on the briefcase. My scenario was so real, I was surprised to hear Phil's voice out loud.

"I have something for you," he said. He reached into the pocket of his jacket, now hanging on the back of his metal chair. "I brought an article that might interest you, on some of our modeling work. It includes some new work on boron doping as well."

I marveled that he'd brought a report. I'd been correct to figure that Phil was much more prepared for this meeting than I was.

I was losing ground. I had to catch up.

"I read about plans to develop TATB even further, to make it more insensitive. Are you involved in that at all?" I hoped Phil wouldn't challenge me to recite the composition of TATB; I remembered only that it ended with trinitrobenzene, and I wasn't sure I could find the URL again since I'd had to refrain from bookmarking Elaine's browser with my revealing choices.

"You know I couldn't tell you even if I did know anything about it," he said. "Our funding sponsors keep their cards close to their vest."

I love gambling metaphors almost as much as sports metaphors. More minus points for Phil. As he ran his fingers through his dark brown hair, I glanced at his fingertips for signs of dye.

"Dorman seems to be a match for BUL as far as its security and funding," I said, honestly wondering why our government wouldn't keep classified work on its own sites.

"Yes, indeed," Phil said. "You must remember what a complicated org chart BUL has, as far as funding."

"Money from the government, oversight from the university or private industry," I added.

"And your annual raise determined by no one who ever saw your work."

I nodded, sensing a bonding moment. "Does Dorman have the same Big Brother physical safeguards around the building?"

"Not quite that bad." We laughed at the reminder of the barriers around BUL's site. About half a block from the checkpoint was a STOP sign. If you decided not to stop your vehicle and accelerated as you approached, a four-foot metal barrier buried in the ground would rise from the asphalt.

"At one point in my career, I had fourteen passwords," Phil said. "One to get into a VTR—you probably know what vault-type rooms are—and then thirteen others to access all the different computers and storage areas once I was inside. On a given day, I'd use at least eight or nine of them. And they'd change every six months. It's definitely not that bad at Dorman."

"I recall a lot of inconsistencies," I said. "Your briefcase might be searched on a random basis, but never your coat pockets, for example."

"You bet," Phil said. "Or how about this—no cell phones or personal laptops in the VTR, but you can keep your PDA handy."

Phil's expression turned serious, and he seemed concerned about the illogical procedures, as I used to be. "And download anything you want into your address book," I added.

Personal digital assistants weren't around when I was working. I suspected it took management a while to catch up with all the new technologies that threatened the security of a classified system. Maybe Phil remembered the old days, as I did, when everything was on paper, to be hand-carried from one facility to another. I'd had a little white card in my wallet authorizing me to carry classified material.

"Remember when you couldn't keep a classified file with you in a hotel room overnight?" I asked.

"Oh, yes. No matter where you were, you had to find a government field office and deposit the material in a safe, and then go and pick it up in the morning for your meeting."

Since we were doing so well, I told Phil my favorite security story. I was leaving BUL on my bicycle, in the days when commuting by bike was a treat for me, with a large tote bag in my wire basket. I was due for a change of office, and the tote was full of material I'd cleared out of my desk—periodicals and files I wouldn't need on a daily basis. My bike was so old and beaten up, it looked like it belonged to the fleet of bikes BUL kept on site for travel among its spread-out buildings.

At the gate, the guard stopped me.

"Is this a lab bike? You can't take a lab bike off the property," he'd said.

I assured him it was my own personal bike, but he kept me a good five minutes while he searched the entire frame for a hidden government serial number.

"He even tipped the bike upside down," I told Phil, "while I stood to the side, holding the tote bag, obviously overflowing with goods. Then he let me go."

"He never bothered to check the tote? You could have had a couple of line-up lasers in that bag," Phil said, laughing. "I have to remember that one. Well, this has been fun, Gloria. Tell you what—maybe next time I'm in your neighborhood I could visit your classroom myself. I love to talk to kids, and I go to MIT now and then."

I straightened my shoulders, alert. MIT, in Cambridge, Massachusetts, less than ten miles from Revere. "And you've been to the Charger Street Lab in Revere, I presume?"

"Uh, once or twice."

Aha. Lucky guess.

Phil seemed to have been caught off guard. I guessed he'd kept this from Elaine, who, I was sure, would have told me if she'd known Phil was in Revere. I wasn't easily offended, so the fact that Phil might not want to spend time with his fiancé's friend didn't bother me. The good news was that I'd be able to sic my favorite lab technician, Andrea Cabrini, on the case. My girl in the field, I thought.

What case? I asked myself. *What field?*

No time for self-doubt; I decided to press my luck.

"Did you work with Lokesh Patel?" I asked, neatly spreading sun-dried tomato cream cheese on a jalapeño pepper bagel. Phil had opted for plain all around, probably better suited to an afternoon of work to follow.

Phil gave me a quizzical look, raising eyebrows almost as neat as Elaine's. "Should I know him?"

"He's the man Dana was transporting when her partner was killed," I said.

"Oh, yes, I think I read his name in the *Trib*. I doubt Dana knew him."

Not a smooth move: answering a different question, one he couldn't be expected to know the answer to. "I meant—" I started. But I'd observed no sign of nervousness or discomfort when I mentioned the gunshot victim, so I decided I'd gone down a fruitless road. I told myself I should be thrilled to find Elaine's fiancé free and clear of wrongdoing. It was time to drop the whole idea of the briefcase/duffel-bag murder and get into a wedding/vacation mode.

Phil checked his watch, stood, and pulled his jacket from the chair. "My people will be looking for me. I'd better get back. Can I walk you to your car?"

I showed him empty palms, as if I'd have been holding a car in my hands if I had one. "Elaine dropped me off, and Matt and Dana will be picking me up. He went with her to her counseling session."

"I heard that. It's quite handy that he's around. I appreciate all he's doing. I know Dana admires him a lot."

I nodded at Phil the Charming. "He's happy to do it. He'll go to the police station with her also."

Phil stopped midsleeve, a frown crossing his wide brow.

"But don't worry about me," I went on. "I have my book, and if I get impatient, I'll catch a bus up University Ave."

If that's what you're worried about, I thought.

"Right," Phil said, favoring his bandaged hand while adjusting his jacket. Maybe he wanted me to remember the lovely hors d'oeuvres platter he'd given blood for. "Well, good-bye for now, Gloria."

I thought back to Phil's slight hesitation at the mention of police. Was that the slip I'd been waiting for? How desperate was I to incriminate Phil in something?

I ordered another coffee and took out my notebook.

Contact Andrea, I wrote.

CHAPTER NINE

Ne 10 20.1797

My next contact was not with Andrea but with Matt's voice mail. I called his cell phone and left a message that I wouldn't need to be picked up. I walked from the bagel shop to a branch of the Berkeley Public Library, staying on the shady side of the street as long as possible. I enjoyed the odors that reached the sidewalk from Berkeley's many ethnic restaurants. I passed a Black Muslim bakery (bean pie?), a Thai café (lemongrass soup, I decided), an Indian eatery (curry, for sure), and a French bistro (the strong coffee that I loved), all in the same block.

I began to resent the simple bagel lunch forced on me by Phil Chambers.

I arrived at the library tired out from the hot weather and the slight incline of the streets I'd covered. I made another of my heat-of-battle resolves to exercise more, but a blast of air-conditioning and a long drink from a water fountain helped immensely, and the image of a Nautilus machine faded from my mind.

I was eager to log on to the Internet without looking over my shoulder, worried about whether Elaine would catch me in the act of Googling her fiancé.

As with the Revere Public Library, computer monitors, though welcome in my life, seemed out of context with the décor of the beautiful old building. This Berkeley branch had dark wood bookshelves along each wall, intricately designed stained glass lamps hanging from the ornate ceiling, and a circulation desk so large that it appeared to have been ensconced on the spot before the building went up.

The library was crowded this Monday afternoon. My guess was that many of the older people browsing the magazine and newspaper racks were there as much for contact with society as for reading material. And I would have bet my latest *Dictionary of Scientific Biography* that it was cooler here than in their apartments and houses. The myth was that the cities and towns immediately around the bay, like San Francisco, Berkeley, and Oakland, never got very hot, so air-conditioning was unnecessary. It was true that there weren't as many ninety-plus days as out in the valley towns, but when the heat waves did hit, the days were just as miserable, and no one was prepared.

I e-mailed Andrea, using the sloppy grammar and punctuation we'd all gotten used to in the electronic era. I felt a sour sundried tomato taste as I remembered lying to Elaine about nonexistent e-mail correspondence with Andrea over the weekend as an excuse to use her computer system. *This will make it right,* I told myself.

I hit the keys.

```
Andrea: M. and I having a great time out here. weather is *hot*
but supposed to break well before the wedding. Wondering if u
can look up something for me . . . anything on the nitrogen
fullerene, and find out if anyone knows a Dr. Philip Chambers or
a Dr. Lokesh Patel who might have visited "your" lab. not a
rush, but if u have a minute, it would help greatly in my class
prep. hope things are good with u and T. love, G.
```

T. was short for Thaddeus Jin, Andrea's new boyfriend, also a technician at the Charger Street Lab. Some giggled at the notion of XL-sized Andrea at the movies sharing popcorn with the very small-framed Chinese-American Jin, but I was delighted they'd hit it off and that Andrea was more and more confident in her attractiveness as the wonderful person she was.

Not that I'd been quick to notice Andrea's personal qualities myself. At first I'd seen her as my surrogate with a badge, helping me gain access to the personnel and informational assets of the Charger Street Lab. I now thought of her as my friend and not simply a resource.

Except for today, when getting information was at the front of my mind. I checked the time—almost five o'clock on the East Coast. Andrea would be heading home. I knew most of her e-mail activity was business related, but with me here on the West Coast, she might check for a message when she got home. In any case, I'd have something from her in the morning. If I could only get to a computer to access my e-mail without a major lie.

It was too long a walk and there were too many hills between the library and Elaine's. I called to see if she could pick me up.

"Of course," she said. "The flower emergency is over. You can come with me to check out the table linens for the reception. I'm not convinced they understand the colors I need now that my flowers are all different."

"Table linens. Fantastic."

Elaine laughed. "It'll be fun, Gloria. There's a great new coffee place right nearby. I'll be at the library in about twenty minutes." She took a breath, and I imagined her tucking strands of gray-blond hair over her ear. "Oh, and did I tell you? I found a new wedding book at the florist's. I hope I don't see anything in it it's too late to do. Oh, that was a bad sentence, but you know what I mean. See you!"

I punched END and sighed. Bad sentences from BUL's best technical editor? Where was my friend Elaine who subscribed to *The New Yorker* and read all the fiction and nonfiction nominated for book awards, who had season tickets to the San Francisco Symphony and Berkeley Repertory Theatre, who'd dragged me to museum exhibits on both sides of the Bay Bridge? She seemed to have disappeared into a shower of filmy white lace and linen. I wouldn't have been surprised if she'd ordered a plastic bride and groom for the wedding cake.

I clicked my tongue and opened the article Phil left with me. "Stability for the Nitrogen Fullerene."

Finally, something interesting.

The article Phil had brought me was a general, nontechnical piece on nitrogen, covering all its uses. It included everything from research on synthesized new forms of nitrogen fullerenes to the presence of nitrogen as a detonation product of a high explosive—bomb, to the layperson. Nothing I couldn't have found with a good search engine, but it was interesting background nonetheless, with up-to-the-minute descriptions of supercomputers used in modeling events. Even before I'd retired from physics, computer modeling had become prevalent. Better to input equations and test an explosive on a screen than in someone's backyard.

I read the special section about insensitive high explosives, materials that are remarkably insensitive to high temperatures, shock, and impact. These features improved the safety of explosives while they were stored and transported. Though I'd never worked directly with weapons at BUL, I'd spent enough time around weapons scientists to be immune to the euphemisms— "energetic materials" instead of "bomb constituents"—and the seeming oxymoron of "weapons safety."

I tapped my fingers on the attractive figures in the article, colorful simulations of different experimental geometries for the molecule on one page, surreal close-ups of TATB crystals on another. I decided Phil had chosen this article more to distract me than to illuminate his work. I was about to fold the pages up— maybe even toss them into the nearby wastebasket—when I noticed the fine print at the bottom of the last page. The article had been distributed by the National Nuclear Security Administration, the people in charge of maintaining the country's weapons arsenal in the program called Stockpile Stewardship.

So what? I asked myself, but I stuffed the article into my bag and went outside to watch for Elaine.

The linen lady (Ms. Colbert? Ms. Corbett? Elaine had said her name just as a fire truck screamed past us on busy Shattuck Avenue) had about her a faux sweetness that I guess had developed over thousands of hours interacting with brides. She was wizened and hoarse, and I pictured her lighting up a cigarette at every opportunity, but never in front of a bride. On the way across town to the shop, I'd wondered why Elaine had to take care of this in the first place.

"Doesn't the club have its own linens?" I'd asked, remembering how excited Elaine had been when she'd been able to book a country club in the neighboring city of El Cerrito.

She gave me another of her poor-unenlightened-Gloria looks. "Their linens are . . . ordinary. Wait until you see what Ms. Colburn offers."

Now, in Ms. Colburn's shop, I saw how many different shades and textures of blue there were. I even felt a twinge of understanding, putting myself in a similar situation, but in a lab supply warehouse, like the kind I'd visited in my grad school days. Instead of swatches of cloth, I imagined row upon row of meters and scopes. Voltmeters. Ammeters. Fluke meters for all applications. Oscilloscopes, large and small. Instead of brocade or not brocade, I'd have to choose between analog and digital.

"Did you have a nice lunch with Phil?" Elaine asked. We were waiting for the linen lady to reappear with a corrected invoice. Not Queen Anne blue but Parisian blue, it would say.

"Yes, we did," I said, as smoothly as I could, given the lack of honesty in my answer.

"I know you didn't take to him right away, Gloria."

I said something like "Pshaw" and waved away the idea. I was glad Elaine had turned her back to sign the reprinted form.

"He's a wonderful guy. He's wonderful to me."

"I'm glad to hear that. Did Dana live with him, growing up?" I asked. I needed to ease us off the Wonderful Phil topic.

"Phil and Marilyn split when Dana was about eleven, but she stayed in the area, so it's not like Phil ever lost touch with Dana. Then, when Dana started college at Cal, Marilyn moved to Florida with her new husband. I think his family's out there." She cocked her head and smiled at me. "She won't be coming to the wedding, in case you're wondering."

I realized I knew few wedding details. I was embarrassed to ask, in case Elaine had already told me the vital statistics by phone or e-mail. How many guests? What time of day in the Rose Garden? Who was performing the ceremony? I knew Dana was Phil's "best man," but were she and I the only attendants?

But more than wedding data, I wanted to know what was going on at the Berkeley PD. I knew Matt had called ahead to tell— warn?—Inspector Dennis Russell that he'd be accompanying Dana. I imagined Russell welcoming Matt graciously. *Let me show you the files,* I heard. *And please bring Gloria to help us with the investigation.* My imagination wouldn't quit these days; the California sun was doing strange things to my brain.

I couldn't wait for the fog to roll in.

We skipped the idea of sitting in an un-air-conditioned coffee shop and drove directly from the linen lady's shop to Elaine's. I headed straight for the pitcher of iced coffee in the refrigerator and poured us each a glass.

Elaine's answering machine was blinking 4. The first call, from a colleague at work, annoyed her.

"*Elaine, this is Dave Hamill. I need to talk to you about some of the edits you made to my input for the annual report. I don't think we need to spell out those acronyms. Everyone who reads this will know what they stand for. If they don't they should be taken off the distri-bution list. Anyway, call me back . . ."*

"Typical," Elaine said. "I'm on vacation," she shouted to the machine, giving the NEXT button a sharp push.

Dana called to say thank you for the massage, claiming to be *totally* looking forward to it and to being *so not ready* to just go back to work.

Two messages were for me, from Revere. Elaine and I stared at the machine as we heard Rose, in a panic over an explosion. Someone had planted a bomb under a hearse belonging to O'Neal's Funeral Home in Chelsea.

"It's terrible," she said. *"At least the vehicle was empty, but these people will stop at nothing, and I just know we're next. Frank and Robert are with the police now, to see if there's anything preventive we can do."* A big sigh. *"Well, I'm sorry to be always bringing bad news. I'm sure everything there is rosy and beautiful and I wish I were there, or you were here, not that I'd want you to miss the wedding . . ."*

Rose rambled for a few more seconds. Ordinarily I would have called her back immediately upon hearing something so dramatic as an exploding hearse in my hometown. But the next message on Elaine's machine precluded that.

It was from Andrea, and it caused an explosion between Elaine and me.

CHAPTER TeN

D ana plunked down on a comfortable chair in Dr. Ann Barnett's waiting room. The office was in a modern building by the bay, the décor a welcoming pale green with soft lighting and ferns that were the healthy version of what hung in her house. A big improvement over Julia Strega's industrial digs. Not for the first time, Dana wished Valley Med would spring for an upgrade to the EMT lounge.

Matt arrived a few minutes after Dana. HAVE A SUPPORTER ACCOMPANY YOU TO THE SESSION, TO BE THERE FOR YOU WHEN THE SESSION IS OVER, the pamphlet said, in deep blue. No one had asked her, "Why Matt, whom you've known all of two days?" But she knew everyone was wondering, why not Dad, or Elaine, or one of her EMT friends?

For one thing, Matt was also an ES worker, in a sense, but not another Valley Med employee. His telling her about his own CI when he was a rookie had moved Dana. Matt had been so open, though he'd just met her, and she knew he was sincere, not playing a game to make her feel better.

Also—and she had to admit this was a big factor—in a couple of weeks, Matt would be three thousand miles away, unable to embarrass Dana or remind her of this ordeal.

They greeted each other with a hug, like old friends or father and daughter. Dana inhaled deeply and relaxed as Matt took a seat across from her.

"I'm really glad you could come, Matt. I know you must have a gazillion things to do with Elaine and Gloria."

Matt crossed one leg over the other. Short legs, Dana noticed, compared to most of the men in her life. "Think about it. Would I rather be helping them choose shades of lipstick?"

"Dana got it. "No, but you could be wine tasting. The famous Napa Valley's not that far away."

"I don't drink alcohol. So, you see, this is a real break for me."

Dana smiled, grateful he was making this so easy for her.

The waiting room seemed unnaturally quiet. Not just because there were no other patients. It was as if the building were wrapped in a huge emergency kit blanket insulating it from outside noises like traffic or barking dogs. No piped-in music, either, or blaring TV, though there was a small set high in one corner of the room.

Dana drew a long breath. "Can I tell you something?" she asked, almost whispering.

Matt opened his palms. *Anything.*

"I wish I'd been able to kill the guy who shot Tanisha."

"You'd be feeling a lot worse right now, believe me."

Dana sat back. She knew he was right, that he spoke from experience; she couldn't figure why she'd even needed to hear it and was amazed she'd expressed herself out loud. She looked around the room as if she might find a device that brought out secret thoughts. She saw only warm landscapes in simple wooden frames, a magazine rack, large lamps with ceramic bases, and the door to the doctor's office.

"Did you have counseling after your incident?" Dana asked.

Matt shifted in his chair and shrugged his shoulders. "If you could call it that. Internal Affairs ruled it a good shoot; the department shrink asked me if I was okay; I said sure; and my captain said, 'Okay, then, take a couple of days R&R and we'll see you on Monday.'"

Dana laughed. "I guess counseling wasn't a big deal back then. Maybe there's too much made of it these days."

"Who knows?" Matt said. "You just work with what you have and do the best you can."

Dana loved Matt's honesty. She tried to imagine what her dad would have said. She heard his deep, confident voice, lecture-style: *Follow the rules, Dana, they're for your own good, and you'll be glad later.* A not-so-subtle difference. Matt wasn't giving her any guarantees. If she didn't know before last Friday night that life promised nothing, she knew it now.

Her eyes were tearing up again. It didn't take much. Dana fished in her purse for a tissue and felt the edge of the ID card she'd found in Robin's closet. She couldn't fathom the connections—the Indian gunshot victim, the consulting firm her father worked with, and her roommate. She toyed with showing the card to Matt, but he was a cop, after all, and Dana wasn't sure she wanted to get the police involved. Even the Massachusetts police. She tried to figure why not. Was she afraid they'd investigate *her*? And find her small stash and pipe?

Before she had to decide, Dr. Barnett's secretary appeared at the door and, with a sweeping wave, invited her in.

Dana tried to pay attention to Dr. Barnett. The therapist's pageboy and blue-and-white seersucker suit were from another era, as if she'd had been called forth from a simpler time. The doctor's questions seemed simple, but to Dana they were complicated.

"Any physical signs of stress?" *How can I tell? I'm on edge most of the time.*

"Headaches?" *Yes. But more than usual? I don't know.*

"Changes in sex drive?" *Ha, no way to tell. I haven't had sex since Scott left.*

"Dizziness? Changes in eating habits? Sleeping?" *Yes. No. Maybe.*

"Poor concentration? Problems making decisions?" *What else is new?*

"Dana? Dana." Dr. Barnett's voice was sharp, bringing Dana back into the room.

Dana had no idea how her verbal responses had compared to her mental reactions, but Dr. Barnett's look said her out-loud answers had been garbled at best.

"Is there anything you'd like to ask me, Dana?"

Dana frowned and tried to focus. She smoothed Robin's skirt and wished she had a joint, or better yet her pipe, a present from Scott Gorman during happier days. She pictured the swirls of green and orange and purple on the beautiful glass bowl. "I can't seem to forget," she said. "I remember every detail, like in slow motion, Tanisha walking toward the building, falling. Then on the ground."

"You can't heal what you can't remember, Dana. So you're doing well."

Dr. Barnett sat back and folded her hands on her lap. She seemed pleased with herself, as if she'd just delivered a favorable verdict.

"Okay, then I'm on track," Dana said.

That seemed to be what Dr. Barnett wanted to hear.

Maybe things hadn't changed all that much since Matt's early days.

"Two down, one to go," Dana said to Matt as they drove in Dana's brown-and-cream Jeep to the Berkeley PD.

"This should be easy," Matt said. "Cops are the good guys."

Dana turned to see how serious Matt was, and caught his grin.

The scene in the Berkeley PD building reminded Dana of a coloring book she'd had as a child. The pages had line drawings of uniformed men and women in working poses. Handcuffing a bad guy, seated behind a high counter answering a phone, tapping away at a computer terminal, handling a drug-sniffing dog, closing a barred jail-cell door.

No insulating blanket around this building, Dana noted, as the sounds of the busy street outside competed with those within. Phones, pagers, printers, fax machines, clacking keyboards. Dana picked out angry, loud voices and guttural human sounds, like the kind you heard from the homeless on Telegraph Avenue and around the Shattuck BART station. It was expensive to ride the Bay Area Rapid Transit system but cost nothing to sleep in its stairwells.

Matt seemed right at home, leading her up a wide staircase to the offices, and she remembered he'd been here before. She noticed he'd put on a sports coat. Professional courtesy, she figured, but it was a weird shade of blue that looked awful with his maroon polo shirt.

Dana expected a lengthy delay, but a young female uniformed officer was waiting for them at the top of the stairs and ushered them into a long, narrow room. *Even the walls in this room are busy,* Dana thought. They were covered with maps and flyers and pushpins, not limited to the framed bulletin boards.

Inspector Russell, whom Dana recognized from Matt's description, sat at the end of the room behind a desk that was too small for his tall frame. His feet stuck out past the edge of the desk, into the area where Dana and Matt would be sitting. He pulled at the sleeves of his sports coat, slightly too short, and drew in his legs as they approached. If med schools rejected her, Dana decided, she'd investigate a career in personal shopping for cops.

Quick handshakes all around, and Russell got down to business. He put on half-glasses like Julia's, minus the comment about getting old, and lowered his head to a sheaf of papers in front of him. Dana thought she'd never seen a pointier chin.

"I have your statement from last Friday evening, Ms. Chambers. At that time you indicated that your partner, Tanisha Hall, was not a drug user." Dana gulped. She remembered the question, remembered deciding that a toke now and then, and a pipe at parties, did not constitute "drug use."

"That's correct," she told Russell, clutching her purse to keep from wringing her hands.

"Well, that's what I thought you said." Russell leaned back in the chair until it hit the wall behind him. His head landed next to a poster on crime prevention. Bold letters and bullets shouted safety tips and information on burglar alarms, senior safety, holiday safety, personal security, domestic violence . . . the rest were hidden behind Russell's broad shoulders. "But see here," he said, holding up a fax, "this report you submitted to your supervisor says different."

Dana shrank back, feeling her stomach clutch; Matt shifted closer to Russell's desk and made a motion to view the fax. He looked more like her lawyer than a friend, and Dana wondered if she did need an attorney. She thought of the countless *Law & Order* reruns she'd seen and how "lawyering up" was a big deal.

Matt put Dana's report on the table between them, so Dana could see the copy of what she'd given to Julia only a couple of hours ago. Dana remembered downloading the form from Valley Med's Web site and filling in the blanks on the screen. At the bottom of the page was room for a brief summary of the CI, and she'd typed that in also. She'd assumed no one outside Valley Med would see it, certainly not the police. *What would I have done differently if I'd known it was going to end on a cop's desk?* Dana asked herself, and thought, *Nothing.*

Matt pointed to QUESTION 10: TO YOUR KNOWLEDGE, WERE DRUGS INVOLVED IN THE CI?

Dana was startled by an X beside YES. She was sure she'd checked NO. What was this? A slip of her fingers? She'd have to explain.

"Uh, I'm sorry, this is an error. I meant to check no. Neither of us was using drugs." That should clear it up, Dana thought, but still felt her mouth go dry.

"Not as simple as that," Russell said. "Especially since we found rolling papers on her body."

Rolling papers. Dana thought back to the convenience-store stop they'd made on Friday afternoon. Tanisha had bought a packet of her favorite, environmentally friendly papers, no flavored dyes or toxins, no glue. *What did all that health consciousness get her?* Dana thought.

"Papers are not illegal—" Dana began.

She stopped when Matt put his hand on her shoulder.

"Do you have anything else?" Matt asked Russell.

Russell smiled. Not a friendly smile, more like a "gotcha" smile. "As we speak, we're searching the Hall residence in San Leandro."

Dana's throat closed up. She had no idea where Tanisha kept her stash, except far from where her daughter or her mother might come upon it. *It's just weed,* she thought, but she didn't dare say anything.

Some nonverbal communication that Dana missed had taken Russell and Matt to the side of the room, out of her hearing.

Inspector Russell's briefcase stood under the small table. The soft-sided kind, not at all like the briefcase the Indian scientist left in her ambulance, but it reminded Dana of the one missing from her house. The police seemed to have forgotten about the Indian's briefcase. No way was she going to bring it up now.

She thought back on her interview with Russell, and remembered Tom's admonition: *Better be careful what you tell them.* And Julia's warning: *Avoid anything that would reflect badly on the company.* She hoped she hadn't said anything against that advice. Most of all, however, she wanted to get out of there without handcuffs.

Matt took Dana's arm and led her down the stairs to the front door, a gesture Dana would never have accepted from a date, but one she welcomed now. Her legs felt like two elongated gel packs, and she wanted to leave the building quickly. She knew she wouldn't draw a decent breath until the last uniform was well behind her. She didn't like the feeling; she'd always worked well with the cops she'd met on the job, who'd helped her with a few difficult transports, and she'd dated a rookie, Derek, a reasonably fun one-monther. Quite different being on the other side of them.

"What did all that mean?" she asked Matt, safely in her Jeep. "And why aren't I in jail?"

"*You* weren't found with drugs. They have to accept your explanation for now, that you made a mistake, but if they find anything at Tanisha's, they may call you back."

"So are you the reason they're not holding me now?"

"Maybe."

"Thanks." A weak voice, and a word that hardly covered her feeling of gratitude.

"Will they find drugs at Tanisha's?" Matt asked.

Dana sighed, annoyed now that she felt free of the police building. "Maybe a couple of ounces. Or less. Just some grass, absolutely nothing else. It should be legalized anyway. Something like 80 percent of Americans favor legalization." How many times had she and her friends had this conversation, thought about getting involved with activist groups trying to change California laws?

"But it's not legal now, Dana, though I'm guessing the Berkeley PD has more to worry about than a toke or two. They're on a fishing expedition. They're looking for something to close this case. How do you think it happened that your report gave them the opportunity they were looking for?"

"I don't know. I've been pretty upset. I could have just hit the wrong box."

"Was the report in your custody until you submitted it to your boss this morning?"

Custody was such a formal word, like her parents' custody

fight when they split, or when they asked you at the airport if your luggage has always been in your custody. Dana's first thought had been to say "of course" about the report—until she remembered that Robin printed out the report for her. Robin, who suddenly had a whole new wardrobe fit for a luxury cruise. Robin, who had the dead man's ID card in her closet.

Dana fished inside her purse, stuffed between her thigh and the door of the Jeep, and pulled out the laminated card. She turned to Matt.

"I have something to show you," she said.

CHAPTER ELEVEN

23
50.9415

A ndrea's voice message started out benignly enough.

"Hi, Gloria and Elaine, this is Andrea back here in Revere, where it's very hot and humid. Ugh. I hope everything's going fine with the wedding plans. I can't wait to see some pictures."

But the message took a turn that ruined my day, and then some.

"Gloria, I happened to be hanging around here late and had a chance to look up the names you gave me. I figured I'd just call you. I'm not sure what you had in mind for your class, but I found a lot of papers written by those two guys you wanted me to look into. Looks like Philip Chambers and Lokesh Patel have worked together a lot."

I could have sworn Andrea had put undue emphasis on "Philip Chambers." Elaine looked at me as if she'd just been wounded but couldn't figure out where, nor where the blow had come from. I knew it wouldn't be long before it was clear to her.

Andrea's voice continued.

". . . a list of about six papers, the most recent that they coauthored, with some other guys, on nitrogen fullerenes, high explosives, that kind of stuff, definitely weapons related. So just let me know what's next. I'll have to dig out the unclassified versions in hard copies, and then I can fax them to you, or mail, or maybe scan and attach to an e-mail, whatever. Hope this will help your class prep. Any crime-busting adventures out there, by the way?"

Here Andrea laughed, and I nearly cried.

"You know I love to help. Bye for now."

By the close of the seemingly endless message, Elaine knew exactly who had struck the blow. She shot me a look of pain and consternation. Her eyes narrowed to slits focused on me. She leaned one elbow on the kitchen counter, between her answering machine and her blender; her other arm hung by her side. The sloppiest posture I'd ever seen on her.

How could I have been so dumb as to forget to tell Andrea to use my cell phone number? I'd given no thought to how Andrea might respond to my e-mail request from the library. A bad detective, and a worse friend. I was hardly able to stand up myself without leaning on the counter next to Elaine and her immaculate toaster oven.

Where to start? "I'm sorry, Elaine, I—"

She held up her hand. Clearly, that was not a good beginning. Elaine turned and left the kitchen. I heard her footsteps on the stairs. I heard her bedroom door slam. In my mind, I heard her call a cab to take Matt and me to the airport.

I left the house almost immediately so Elaine wouldn't feel like a prisoner in her own home. I'd slipped a note under her bedroom door. I sensed no movement inside, probably because she'd heard me pound my way up the steps.

Elaine, I'm going for a walk. I know I have a lot to explain and hope you will allow me to. Love, G.

Fortunately, in Berkeley, there's always a coffee shop within walking distance. I took a table at the one nearest Elaine's, at the edge of Holy Hill, and tried to regain my composure enough to formulate a plan. I was tempted to order from the impressive collection of Italian sodas but thought I'd fare better with another dose of caffeine.

I called Matt first, to head him off. He answered from Dana's Jeep.

"We're on our way back. Dana's going to drop me off at Elaine's," he said. "We're about five minutes away."

Close call. "Can you meet me at the Heavenly Cup instead?" I asked. "It's the one near Hearst and Euclid."

"Something wrong?" Did he know that I'd nearly blurted out, *No, no, don't go to Elaine's!*

"I'll explain when you get here."

"You're okay, though, right?"

"I'm okay."

"So, you in trouble?"

I looked at my cell phone and could almost see Matt's grin on the screen. The image relaxed me enough to take my first good breath since hearing Andrea's message.

While I waited for Matt, I called Andrea and thanked her for finding the papers I'd asked for, trying to put only a positive spin on her efforts, in my mind as well as with my words. There was no way I could blame Andrea for this. She wouldn't have recognized Phil's name. Nor would she have thought I'd be so low as to investigate Elaine's fiancé.

Without telling her why, I asked her to use my cell phone number for all future communication.

"Oh, right," she said. "I should have known not to tie up Elaine's line. Wedding calls galore, I'll bet."

"That's it." I didn't mention that I might be going home sooner than planned. "I can't really talk now, Andrea, but I'll call later with a fax number for the nearest copy place."

"Okay." Then, "Oh, wait, Gloria. One more thing before you hang up." Andrea sounded out of breath, as if she'd had to run to catch up with me before I clicked END. "There was an explosion in Chelsea today. O'Neal's—"

"O'Neal's hearse." I'd forgotten about Rose's crisis. One too many for me at the moment. "I know. Andrea, will you do me a great favor and call Rose? Tell her my battery is—" It was a measure of my distress that I resorted to a trick as old as telephone wires. I punched numbers at random, hoping the sound would convince Andrea that I was losing my battery power. Not to say my mind, but Andrea might not be able to figure that one out. Then I punched OFF and put my cell phone in my purse, out of service.

"Are you okay?" The young waitress who put a double espresso in front of me seemed concerned. I wondered what I looked like to prompt the question. I hadn't realized I was crying.

Dana stopped only long enough to drop Matt off. I was glad she didn't join us for coffee. After all, the man whose life I'd been snooping around in was not only Elaine's fiancé but also Dana's father.

Matt greeted me with a look that warned of major teasing. "Dana's going for a nice massage now. Arranged by *Elaine*. She's such a good friend to all."

Matt knew how to get to me. It was a good thing he loved me.

"How did you know? That I was in trouble with Elaine?" I asked him.

"It was bound to happen. You're living in Elaine's house and investigating her fiancé. It's a no-brainer."

"A no-brainer? I can tell you've been hanging around with the twenty-something set."

The twenty-something waitress brought a latte for Matt and added regular coffee to my tiny espresso cup. The young woman's T-shirt bore a yellow-and-black diamond-shaped design with the words JESUS AT WORK. A reminder that we were in the Heavenly Cup on Holy Hill. I felt anything but saintly.

"I feel awful, Matt," I said. "I don't know how I'm going to fix this. There's probably nothing to investigate in the first place, and here I am—"

Matt put his hand on mine. I stopped speaking and allowed myself to feel the warmth. Not molecular heat, which I had plenty of myself, but the warmth of his touch. Understanding and supportive.

And, this time, validating.

"Turns out you were right to be suspicious, if that makes you feel any better."

"Yes and no, I guess."

At that moment I wished I could have gone to Elaine, confessed to being disoriented by hot flashes, or just an old, bungling retired physicist, and beg her forgiveness for the silliest suspicions in history. But I already knew from Andrea's message that at the very least Phil had lied about not knowing a dead Indian scientist whose duffel bag or briefcase might have something to do with Tanisha Hall's death.

Now I had to decide whether to back off completely, in spite of confirmed suspicions, and crawl back to Elaine, or to crawl back to her with evidence that she would thank me for later. *When has that ever worked?* I asked myself. The messenger is rarely greeted with gratitude and open arms.

I convinced myself that my friendship with Elaine would survive on its longevity and its own merits.

"Tell me more," I said.

He laid out what he'd learned from Dana and the Berkeley PD, not necessarily in concert, he pointed out.

Russell hadn't been willing to share much except the negatives: The duffel bag did *not* have anything important, just tennis balls and gym clothes. The ballistics results were *not* in, but, because of the drug issue, they were going with unrelated shootings, just as the newspapers reported.

"A crimp in my conspiracy theory."

Matt nodded and replayed for me the scenario that had Dana mistakenly checking the YES box for drug use. He seemed to doubt it, and I was inclined to agree. I was dismayed that the police now had a reason to write off Tanisha's death as one more drug-related shooting in the African American community.

I was most intrigued by the strange surfacing of Lokesh

Patel's Dorman Industries ID and by the triple threat of Phil/Lokesh/Robin.

"How long has Dana known Robin?" Matt asked, not because he thought I knew but as part of our working routine—asking questions without answers, throwing out theories without thought of logic. The first data dump.

"How neat it would be if Dana's father introduced her to Robin," I offered.

"It seems likely that there was classified stuff in the briefcase," Matt speculated.

"And where is that briefcase?" I wondered aloud. A belated response to Dana's report to Matt about its being missing from her house.

Over unidentifiable rock (maybe) music from Heavenly Cup's speakers, I could hear the James Bond theme song. "Phil Chambers and Lokesh Patel are involved in espionage, and the CIA goes after one of them, and Tanisha Hall gets caught in the crossfire."

"Or vice versa," Matt said.

"Tanisha was CIA?"

"Maybe this is a good stopping point," Matt said.

Matt and I left the coffee shop to find a copy place with a fax machine. We walked around the edges of the campus, using city streets, passing buildings and landmarks I knew and loved from my days as a Berkeley resident. I pointed out places I'd frequented—small parks, restaurants, bookstores, produce stands. It occurred to me that with this walking tour I was constructing my own visual "album," like Matt's Teresa album, to share my past with him in a tangible way.

When Matt's cell phone rang, at least three other people checked pockets and backpacks to see if the call was theirs. In some ways, Berkeley wasn't that different from Wall Street.

"Hi, Rose," Matt said, looking at me. *Do you want to talk to her?*

he mouthed. "You tried calling her? I guess her battery's dead." He grimaced, as if ruing the day he got involved with me and my lying ways.

I couldn't put Rose off any longer. I took the phone. "Rose, I got your message. Tell me what happened." I tried to sound wildly interested. A crisis that was a full continent away was low on my priority list, but I didn't want to lose another friend.

"There's never been anything like this, Gloria." Rose's voice was high-pitched, sounding as panicky as if the explosion were happening in front of her. "John showed us the photo the *Journal* is going to carry on the front page. He's not covering the story. He gave it to a new guy. That's how John is, you know, always looking out for the younger reporters."

Rose took a breath. Across the miles, I heard her mind clicking away, telling herself her mother's pride had taken her off track. I felt a rush of affection and wished I were next to her on her wicker-laden porch. The feeling was intensified by my awareness that I'd effectively banished myself from Elaine's porch.

Matt and I sat on a short bench meant for bus riders. We were in the shade of a tall old building with ornate carvings around the high windows and tantalizing falafel odors emanating from a street-level restaurant. I was still hot, however, and eager to move into the next air-conditioned place. I hesitated to cut Rose's call short and searched my mind for a question that might express concern and enthusiasm for her tale.

I looked at Matt and asked myself what he might care about. "Who's on the case at the RPD?" I asked Rose.

"Michelle Chan was the officer at the scene. I don't know who else. She cut her long, beautiful hair, you know. Looks a lot older. Frank and Robert are down there now, and Robert is thinking of hiring a private security service for us. Everyone in the business is sure Bodner and Polk are behind this."

"The mortuary chain? Is there any evidence?"

"I don't know from evidence, but Frank's hoping to get a copy of the police report. I'll send it to you, and maybe you and Matt can take a look at it. William says there's a way to send these things by e-mail."

Uh-oh. I knew that Rose's grandson, like most teenagers, was more than capable of attaching a document to an e-mail, but I couldn't risk further aggravating Elaine. Besides, I might never again have access to Elaine's computer.

"A fax is better," I told her. "In a few minutes I'll have a fax number you can send to, right down the street from Elaine's."

"Okay, I can do that myself. Gloria, that hearse was a black, black, black . . . shell. Can you imagine if anyone had been in it? The family would be devastated." As usual, Rose worried about the dear departed and their families. She continued, "I wonder if that would be a homicide if the person killed was already dead? Matt would know."

"I'll let you ask him." I gave Matt a smug smile and handed him the phone.

While Matt—such a good sport—talked to Rose about intent to kill and felony murder, I was free to pursue the thoughts cluttering my mind.

We found a twenty-four-hour copy shop in the next block. I took the fax number and called Rose. I was able to get off the line quickly by letting her think we were just sitting down to dinner. Not that it showed in her size-six body, but Rose Galigani took mealtime very seriously.

I called Andrea next.

"You got a new battery," she said.

"Oh, uh, everything's all set." Lies always come back to haunt you, I remembered, and my punishment for the battery fib was my stuttering over Andrea's comment. Anyone but sweet, naive Andrea would have seen through me, even without being able to see the flush in my cheeks.

"It'll probably take me an hour or so to get these ready, Gloria.

I have to copy them here, and then go back to my office and get the fax code, because all the secretaries have left, and then—"

"Don't worry. I completely forgot how late it is there. I don't expect you to do it immediately. Even tomorrow would be fine." Not fine, exactly, but here was another friend I needed to hold on to. I didn't have that many left.

"No, no, I can do it," Andrea said. "Call me back in an hour and I'll let you know how it's going, okay?"

"That sounds good. And let me give you Matt's number in case you need to reach me and this phone isn't working."

"Oh, good. I know I shouldn't call the bride, right?"

"That's the idea," I said.

It was after six o'clock, many hours since my bagel with Phil Chambers, colleague of the deceased Lokesh Patel.

Matt and I sat at a table in a small Japanese restaurant on Shattuck Avenue. I wasn't sure about Matt, but I wondered less about what I'd order for dinner—crabmeat with wasabi mayonnaise or shrimp tempura?—than where we'd be sleeping that night.

CHAPTER TWELVE

The hour after dinner was an active one. We collected faxes from Andrea and Rose and walked to the UC campus library, open later than the public library branches. I was able to use my BUL retiree card to gain admittance, once I'd extricated it from deep in my purse and detached it from the sticky wrapper of an old cough drop.

UC Berkeley had overlapping summer classes, guaranteeing that the campus walkways and libraries would be busy in all seasons. Whether a sign of the times or of California, the students we passed were all ages and ethnic groups. Even with our mature body shapes and graying hair, Matt and I blended in with the mixed population. We might have been administration-of-justice majors, I mused.

Matt picked a dog-eared copy of the Berkeley yellow pages from its place in a row of phone books that seemed to cover all the counties of California. "We should think about renting a car," he said. "And maybe a room."

My meddling ways had brought me problems before this, but nothing that left me homeless. "And a Laundromat," I said, returning his smile.

I was grateful for Matt's presence; I knew I wouldn't have found humor in the situation if I'd been facing it alone.

I took my cell phone from my purse and laid it on the metal table.

"In case she calls before we get to that point."

We'd agreed to read the faxes and then make a decision about where we'd sleep.

Matt took Rose's fax, relieving my feelings of guilt over not paying much attention to her plight in the last couple of days. If he was stunned that I didn't quickly grab at an official police report, he didn't show it.

"I'm not sure what we're supposed to do with whatever information is on that report," I said. "It's not as if we could investigate, even if we were home."

Matt kindly did not point out that nothing so trivial ever stopped me before. "I think Rose just misses us," he said.

"Maybe we should go back where we're welcome," I said, close to tears.

Matt took my hand. "It'll work out, Gloria. You and Elaine have been friends too long for it to end like this."

I wondered if Elaine would agree. I tried to imagine what she was going through, whether she felt betrayed or angry, or both. I couldn't guess.

I straightened the pages from Andrea and retreated to a safe nitrogen-rich environment, free of human miscommunication.

Phil Chambers and Lokesh Patel had collaborated on a number of weapons-related papers. The unclassified versions Andrea had sent were more or less status reports, as opposed to detailed technical documents, and I longed to see an equation. There's nothing like a reaction expressed in symbols to bring home the essence of a piece of theory or experiment. The distinction between what can be distributed broadly and what is designated one of the many classified levels is generally a question of quantification—equations and numbers. Even the composition of a high explosive may be spelled out in open literature, but the specific amounts and arrangements of each chemical in the mix make all the difference.

"Like a recipe," Matt said after I briefed him on my faxes. "It's okay if the competition knows you use tomatoes, garlic, and basil in your gravy, but the amounts and how you cook them are held back."

I had a flash-forward to a time when I'd be wearing a flowered apron, making spaghetti for Matt, waiting for him to come home from work. How desperate was I for a crisis-free life? I recovered quickly. "And in the case of explosives, the specific amounts play a big part in whether you have a Fourth of July firecracker or a nuclear fission bomb. The firecracker travels only a few hundred meters per second. The explosion could reach a million meters per second."

Matt waved Rose's fax at me. I saw the familiar Revere Police Department letterhead. "I guess what blew up O'Neal's hearse would fall somewhere between the firecracker and the atomic bomb. At those speeds you don't need to translate the meters into miles per hour for me," Matt said. "Well over the speed limit. And I'm no longer surprised that you'd know these numbers off the top of your head."

"Just ballpark guesses," I said, with a modest shrug.

This must be the silver lining, I thought—Matt and I with another opportunity to learn from each other. I loved sharing the elements of science with him, and when the occasion arose, he introduced me to the intricacies of human behavior, police procedure, and the administration of justice.

To prolong our pleasant interaction and avoid our current predicament, I was inspired to write my own version of what a nitrogen-containing high-explosives equation might look like. I knew I couldn't write an exact, balanced equation, but I did remember the general energy reaction for one of the most commonly known explosives, trinitrotoluene—TNT. I took out my notebook and pen and enjoyed trying to figure out reasonable—that is, scientific—behavior. *Unlike the human sphere.*

I played with the left-hand side of the equation, knowing

only that the reaction involved a combination of nitrogen, carbon, hydrogen, and oxygen. Then it dawned on me that I was surrounded by the resources of the UC Berkeley library.

"I'll be right back," I told Matt, and headed for the science section.

It felt good to be up and moving, and researching, if only in a basic chemistry book. I found the formula for TNT: $C_7H_5N_3O_6$— a benzene ring with a methyl group attached, and three nitro groups in the form of nitrogen dioxide. I read more than I needed to, of course, indulging myself in pages on the structure of the molecule and the dynamics of an explosion—essentially a regrouping of all the elements, as with any chemical or physical reaction. Another marvel of science. No new atomic particles added or subtracted, just a reorganization that converted a benign configuration into a lethal one.

I headed back to the area where I'd left Matt, my arms full of books, prepared to lecture, as he called my explanations, on the conversion of nitrogen dioxide to nitrogen gas.

I was within a few yards of Matt when I noticed he wasn't alone. He was deep in conversation with a tall, thin woman who sat on the chair next to him.

I stopped short and thrust my head forward to see more clearly, though I had little doubt who it was. The woman, wearing an olive green skirt with sandals to match—the only person in the school library dressed for tea—was Elaine Cody.

My unsettling first thought was that Elaine had our luggage out in the trunk of her car. My second was that Matt must have called her as soon as we arrived in the building, on his alleged restroom trip.

I had no time to decide whether that should annoy me or thrill me. First Dana, now Elaine. Matt seemed to be headed for a career in HR, taking over the human relations part of this trip.

I dropped the books on the nearest table and walked toward Matt and Elaine. I was prepared to drop the whole business, too, if that's what it took, if that was the price of repairing our friendship.

I greeted Elaine with a hug that threatened to wrinkle her white sleeveless shell.

Matt stood by as we uttered mutual apologies and forgiveness. If any of the other library patrons noticed the display, they gave no sign.

When Elaine stepped back, she dabbed at her eyes with her left hand and held up her right, in the halt position. "Before we go any further I need to tell you really what brought me here." She looked at Matt. "Besides Matt's phone call."

Uh-oh, I thought, *the bags* are *in her car.* "Elaine, I promise—"

She shook her head, causing her long gold and green-glass earrings, which I'd sent for her birthday one year, to swing. "I went to Phil's place as soon as you left the house, Gloria. I needed to talk to him or just . . . I needed him. He didn't answer, so I let myself in, thinking he was upstairs in the back, in his office, where he might not hear the bell. Well, he wasn't home, but you'll never guess what *was* in his office."

With her rambling sentences, she sounded more like Rose than the old Elaine, a sign of her high stress level. Then it hit me. I had a pretty good idea what she'd seen in her fiancé's office.

"The briefcase," I said.

Elaine nodded; her eyes filled up.

"We're going to figure this out," I said. "Now that we're all together."

Back in Elaine's living room—never was there such a welcome sight—I tried to express my regrets once more about my inappropriate snooping. I didn't want Elaine to think I was happy to have been correct about Phil's involvement, however slight it might turn out to be, in the deaths of Tanisha Hall and Lokesh Patel.

"There may be a perfectly innocent explanation," Matt said. I agreed, showing more enthusiasm than I felt. I'd learned my lesson.

"Right now, I just want to help straighten all this out," Elaine said.

Since she didn't believe Matt and I could have had a satisfactory dinner, Elaine had laid out a spread of berries, California cheeses, and small cocktail breads. I'd long ago decided that food eaten under stressful conditions didn't count as caloric intake. I cut into the white slab of Monterey jack, decorated my dessert plate with strawberries and a handful of See's chocolate-covered raisins, and settled into one of the burgundy leather easy chairs.

"We have some questions," Matt said, arranging snacks on his plate. "Could help clear things up. First would be, do you know how Dana met Robin?"

Elaine's red-rimmed eyes widened. "Robin Kirsch? Dana's roommate? Is she involved in all this?"

Matt updated Elaine on the few scattered facts we had: the deceased Lokesh Patel's Dorman Industries ID card, found in Robin's closet; her expensive new wardrobe; the slew of coauthored scientific papers showing that Phil had lied to me about his association with Patel, the topic of those papers being weapons research; how Robin most likely altered Dana's report concerning drugs being involved in the incident that took Tanisha's life; the missing, now located, briefcase.

"What if Phil and Robin are . . . *involved* involved?" Elaine asked, placing her mug on the coffee table. She hadn't taken any food from the lovely three-tiered serving set, though I was sure she hadn't had dinner.

I saw that Elaine was still operating on the personal level, as if she preferred that Phil turn out to be a traitor to his country rather than an unfaithful fiancé.

"It might be bigger than that, Elaine," I said. Another blunder, implying I didn't think her engagement to Phil was a big deal. I hurried to add, "I mean it might have to do with national security."

Elaine sighed heavily. I regretted every complaint I'd uttered, albeit to myself, about her bridelike demeanor and wished I could get it back for her. Maybe if instead of nosing around I'd offered to tie little ribbons around delicate, lacy favors, Elaine wouldn't be in this predicament. But Lokesh Patel and Tanisha Hall would still be dead, I reminded myself.

"Someone at work, I think his name is Tom." Elaine seemed to have pulled a name from a high corner of her newly furnished living room.

Matt and I looked at each other. *What?*

"You asked how Dana and Robin met." Elaine managed to make "Robin" sound not like a lovely bird with a red breast but like an ugly witch to be reckoned with and from whom you needed to protect your family. "An EMT, Tom something, introduced them."

"Okay, now we're getting somewhere," Matt said, rubbing his hands together. Exactly where, I wasn't sure, but I admired his technique. *A cop is always a cop,* I thought, *even on vacation in sunny California.* "Did Phil ever talk about working with a scientist from India?"

"He works with people from all over the world, all the time. And I know he can't talk about his projects, so I don't question him about them."

Unlike me, I thought.

I took a few minutes to explain to Elaine the importance of the work Phil was doing.

"Insensitive bomb materials? I remember seeing something like that in BUL's annual report, the glitzy version they send out to potential funding partners. I thought it an oxymoron."

"The term refers to how easily an armed and ready package might go off." I reached over to an end table and lightly tapped one of her Hummels, a little girl with a red bow in her hair and a book on her lap. Elaine flinched, then gave me an I-trust-you smile. "You don't want detonation at the slightest jiggle," I said. "Insensitive explosives resist shock and temperature changes, making them safer. Insofar as an explosive can be safe."

"She makes it sound so easy, doesn't she?" Matt said.

I looked at the ormolu clock on Elaine's mantel. Almost eleven o'clock. "Is it too late to go over and check out that brief-case?" I asked Elaine.

Elaine cleared her throat. "The briefcase is empty," she said.

CHAPTER THIRTEEN

I thought about the ideal vacation Elaine, Matt, and I had worked out before our visit. On this Tuesday morning we'd be packing for a trip south, to Monterey and Carmel. I wanted to show Matt the Carmel Mission and the oft-photographed Lone Cypress Tree on the touristy Seventeen Mile Drive down along the Pacific coast. Over the past weekend, we would already have picnicked in Muir Woods, called "the best tree-lovers monument that could possibly be found in all the forests of the world," by conservationist John Muir, and Elaine would have coaxed us into San Francisco's downtown Museum of Modern Art.

As it was, between our arrival on Friday evening and now, we'd breathed neither salty ocean air nor fragrant redwoods. Instead of wandering the shops of Carmel (no great loss for me, I reminded Elaine), at one o'clock on Tuesday afternoon, we were climbing the steps of Dana's Oakland house.

We'd agreed to go together to Tanisha's service. Dana was feeling remorseful about not visiting Tanisha's family in the days since her death.

"I'd like some company, if you don't mind," she'd told Elaine on the phone.

We both knew she meant Matt.

We'd had a roundtable discussion in Elaine's living room before we left for Dana's, still trying to settle on a strategy. To tell Dana about her father's work with Patel, or not? Matt and I were *pro*, since Dana had already seen a Patel ID card for Dorman Industries. Elaine was *con*, arguing that we shouldn't upset Dana any further "until we know what we're talking about."

I found it interesting that no one suggested inviting Phil to our meeting.

As I'd have predicted, Matt wanted to adopt a show-all/tell-all philosophy, including full disclosure to the Berkeley police. I knew he was uncomfortable withholding even the little information he'd picked up from Dana. This was a double homicide, and he had to have been putting himself in Inspector Russell's shoes. I had the sense he'd call Russell no matter what, and that he was simply waiting for Elaine and me to come to the same conclusion.

"Matt would be able to find out if there's any progress on the Patel murder investigation," I said, bolstering Matt's case. "Unless Russell found a package of rolling papers in Patel's pockets, too."

Matt gave me a look. *You've made your point.*

We developed a plan. Matt would set up an appointment with Russell for Wednesday morning. He admitted he had nothing concrete enough to warrant immediate disclosure. Everything we had was circumstantial, all our theories hypothetical in the extreme. In the meantime, we'd go to Dana's and continue to brainstorm.

"This evening's news might even tell us the case is solved," Elaine had said. The red rings around her eyes gave away her true state, but she'd attempted a lighthearted tone.

We'd all nodded. Why not?

It had been almost a whole day since the last time Elaine brought up wedding trivia. I'd gotten my wish, but at a great price.

Now, at Dana's, we focused on helping her through whatever stage of grief she'd reached. She looked more relaxed than the first time I saw her, dressed in black pants and a sheer black blouse over a white tank top. Ready for a wake. The heat wave had broken, making it useful to open the Oakland house to the outside, and a breeze ruffled Dana's long, fine hair as she sat next to a window.

"I had such a great massage last night," Dana told us. She picked up a basket full of small bottles of different colors and sizes and held it out to us. "And they gave me all this cool stuff—samples of oils and lotions. It made going to that mandatory group counseling so much more palatable. Thanks again, Elaine."

Elaine smiled, seeming happy to have something go right.

We'd decided Matt would take the lead in introducing a list of things we thought Dana could help clear up. After a suitable time for small talk, he started.

"Have you heard from your dad?"

Dana fiddled with the tiny bottles of toiletries. Her long fingers were unadorned, her nails short and unpolished. "No. I left a message for him yesterday. It usually takes him a couple of days to get back to me."

"I know what you mean," Elaine said, surprising me.

Almost from the beginning of our relationship, Matt and I had seemed to know how much or how little distance we each needed. We had talked frequently during the day, before we lived together, and now it was still the norm for us to check in by phone every few hours. I couldn't imagine going twenty-four hours without a call. Quite a turnaround for someone who'd spent most of her adult life living alone.

From what I knew of Elaine in her relationships, she was more likely to be a call-every-hour partner, and I wondered how that played out with Phil Chambers.

No one had seen Phil since he left me on Monday afternoon. Was I that hard on him? I wondered facetiously. It hadn't even been twenty-four hours, but I realized if I hadn't heard from Matt in that long, I'd be frantic.

"Is Phil likely to work long hours and not call?" I asked, before thinking ahead to whether I should probe.

Elaine gave a resigned sigh. "He's likely to fly to Hong Kong and not call until he gets there."

Dana threw up her hands and nodded in agreement. "That's Dad."

I would have thought that between his imminent wedding and his daughter's troubles, Phil would be checking in more frequently. But Phil Chambers's women, it seemed, had acquiesced to his style.

"Elaine says you met Robin Kirsch through another EMT in your company, right?" Matt asked. He was moving on.

Like the rest of us, Matt looked significantly more cool and comfortable than he had over the weekend. He'd ironed a pale blue cotton shirt and wore it under a light sports coat. My mind drifted back to his regular workweek in Revere, where Tuesday was brown suit day. Except for his casual clothes, Matt's week was turning out to be "regular" in some ways.

"Yeah, Tom Stewart introduced me to Robin at a party," Dana said. "She was an EMT a couple of years ago and worked with Tom, who was born at Valley Med, as Tanisha used to say." Dana paused for a heavy breath. "This was maybe three months ago, when Jen and I lived in a small apartment and were thinking of moving into a bigger place." Dana frowned, as if remembering an unpleasant smell or taste. "Tom's not my favorite partner, in case you haven't guessed."

"I thought Tanisha was your partner," I said.

"We rotate. Not like cops." She gave Matt a glance I'd have classified as just short of adoring. "We might have a different partner every shift. Some you get close to, some you don't."

"Okay, we know it's likely that Robin doctored up your incident report yesterday." Matt crossed one leg over the other. He kept his voice casual and wrote no notes. "But before that, did you have any reason to think Robin might be involved in something squirrelly, or have something to hide?"

Dana wrinkled her brow, as if trying to focus all her energy into answering Matt. "She's always been more private than Jen or me, but I assumed it was because she was an add-on, sort of. Jen and I have been roommates forever. Robin's doing a lot, I know, so she's stressed. She's going to school online, and she has this intern position at a bank that doesn't pay a lot—hardly enough for her tennis club dues—so she moonlights doing some kind of work on her home computer. Says she's 'consulting,' whatever that means."

"What about her boyfr—" Matt began, then stopped at a noise. *Clump. Clump. Clump.*

It sounded like someone wearing tap shoes on his way up the front steps. We all turned to the door as a tall young woman came through, carrying a skinny bike in one hand, its frame resting on her slim shoulder. Not your mother's bicycle, I thought, remembering the Monarch I'd had as a child, with its balloon tires, thick handlebars, and heavy metal chain guard. This bike seemed as light as the pair of titanium earrings Rose's daughter had in her collection, all thin wires and spokes. Its largest component was a plastic water bottle buckled to its frame. A crystal pendant hung from one of the handles, reminding me of people who draped such items over the posts of rearview mirrors, distracting themselves and other drivers. At least Robin's crystal wasn't at her eye level.

"Robin!" Dana said. I wondered if she always greeted her roommate so enthusiastically, or only when caught talking about her in an unflattering and accusatory manner.

I had to stop myself from staring at Robin's outfit. Brand-new? Expensive? An unobtrusive look said no, although they were serious bike-riding clothes—black spandex pants and a tight rubbery jersey, topped off by a helmet with hot green and yellow stripes. She propped her bike against the outside living room wall. Her shoes made tapping noises on the wooden floor around the area rug; evidently bikers had special shoes, like golfers and bowlers and tap dancers. Not so in my Monarch days, when thin white Keds ruled.

Dana introduced us, nicely recovering from the blush I'd seen. Robin's smile was pleasant but lacked warmth; she made no eye contact that I could tell. She wore fingerless gloves—as a bike fashion statement? for protection?—and there was no handshaking.

"Won't you join us for coffee, Robin?" I asked, boldly taking over hostess duty. I felt entitled only because Elaine and I had brought the coffee and miniature biscotti now filling the small metal table.

"Thanks, but I need to change," Robin said. She was about as tall as Dana, and I could see how they'd be able to share clothes. Her hair was darker brown, shorter, and thicker than Dana's but had the same shiny quality.

"Robin doesn't like to be seen in her bike clothes," Dana explained.

Robin shot her a look and a twisted grin. She took a key from what looked like an impossibly tiny fanny pack strapped to the back of her bike, unlocked the door to her bedroom, and disappeared.

We sat like four guilty gossipers, at a loss for conversation since our most recent target was within earshot. It didn't seem prudent to bring up Dorman Industries, either, with Robin in the house. Everyone reached for the biscotti plate at the same time, fingertips and knuckles bumping, prompting a round of soft chuckles.

"Is Robin planning to attend Tanisha's service?" Elaine asked in a near whisper, though the question was quite harmless.

"No, she only met her once, I think. But Tom'll be there. You'll have that pleasure," Dana said. She brushed crumbs from her shirt, as if she were dismissing her unappealing sometime partner from her lap.

We shared another awkward round of eating and sipping; then Elaine suggested it was time to head to San Leandro for Tanisha's service. A rather loud collective sigh and we were on our way, leaving Robin Kirsch and some unanswered questions behind.

On the road, with four of us in the green Saab, Elaine tried to reach Phil on her cell phone. She left a message, during which Matt, Dana, and I chattered, to give her some privacy. But sitting up front, I couldn't block out Elaine's voice entirely. I heard "Hutton Funeral Home; call me either way" and "even if you're in Tokyo," followed by a nervous giggle and a sign-off click.

The streets of San Leandro, a Bay Area suburb, were sunny and lively. We passed an elementary school in time to see children rush out like atoms escaping a container, creating high entropy conditions on the sidewalks and crosswalks. I marveled at the large number of vans with momlike drivers jockeying in and out of the school's parking lot. Didn't anyone walk to school anymore? And didn't kids stay after school and help the teachers, as we loved to do?

I was impressed by the rows of neat houses, many of them with senior citizens in bright straw hats bent over colorful front-yard gardens. On one corner, a small park was busy with the stroller crowd. Tinny, excited voices came in through the open windows of Elaine's car.

But once we entered Hutton's, dark and quiet prevailed, overlaid with the flowery smell that signaled a potentially sickening odor just below the cold surface.

It was strange to be in a funeral home that wasn't, one, the Galigani Mortuary in Revere and, two, downstairs from my living quarters. When I first returned to Massachusetts, Rose and Frank offered me the apartment on the top floor of their building while

I decided whether the move would be permanent. The conveniences were many: a lovely living space, without house hunting, less than a mile from the Atlantic Ocean, plus the world's best "landlords." I quickly got used to the distinctive smells and sounds of the business of death, but not to the daily reminder of mortality.

We fell silent as we signed in at Hutton's guest-book stand, then entered the parlor, crowded with nearly equal numbers of African American and Caucasian mourners. Some sat on straight-backed chairs; others gathered in small circles along the sides of the room.

I couldn't help comparing Hutton's décor with that of the Galigani Mortuary. Not as different as I might have expected. With its dark mahogany paneling, Hutton's felt solemn enough to be transported to an old East Coast community like Revere. No bright lighting or pastel carpets, as I'd seen in other West Coast mortuaries. Not the cheerful look that marked the more modern funeral parlors, but heavy and serious.

I thought Rose would have placed the gladioli closer to the ends of the cherrywood casket and would have chosen a smaller, more discreet cross for the curtain behind the tableau. Hutton's cross—or maybe it belonged to the Hall family—was enormous, an elaborate gold affair with sparkles and flourishes on each arm.

Both Rose and Frank would have approved of the music, fitting the deceased. The Galiganis had been known to accommodate everything from grand opera for the late president of the Sons of Italy to band music for a teenage member of the Revere High marching band who died in a drowning accident.

For Tanisha Hall and her family, soft gospel music filled the room at Hutton's. Here and there a row of guests swayed to the soothing rhythm, one or two mouthing the words.

I need Thee every hour, in joy or pain;
come quickly and abide, or life is vain.

I heard a tired sigh from Dana as she preceded us into the parlor, as if she'd just single-handedly lifted someone as heavy as me onto a gurney. She walked down the long aisle toward Tanisha's open casket and took a place on the maroon velvet kneeler.

Tanisha's face appeared natural in death, and I heard Frank Galigani's approving voice in my mind. A jeweled, multicolored striped hat covered the top of her head; her braids were draped over her shoulders, falling on a bright orange, black, and green tunic top. Tanisha looked colorful and at peace, but mostly, she looked very young.

I guessed Tanisha Hall was Catholic, though I couldn't have said for sure that other Christian denominations didn't use kneelers. I pictured Protestants more like Martin Luther, standing strong, taking on the kneeling Roman Catholic hierarchy.

Matt, Elaine, and I followed Dana from the kneeler to the front row of visitors, where a thin, dark-skinned woman with straight black hair sat in an overstuffed armchair, the kind of chair the Galiganis reserved for the principal mourners. In her lap was a small girl, perhaps three or four, in a loose navy blue dress and tights. Tanisha's mother and daughter, Marne and Rachel Hall. The ends of Rachel's neat braids were folded into dark blue beads.

As Dana approached Marne, the woman stood, reaching eye level with Dana. Dana had said Tanisha's mother was only forty, having given birth to Tanisha as a teenager, but tonight Marne looked every bit someone's grandmother. She bit her lip; her fist tightened around a white handkerchief.

I waited for the tender embrace, the soft words, comforting pats on the back. Instead, Marne put her hands on her hips and thrust her face close to Dana's.

"You have a nerve coming in here," she said. Marne's voice was low but sharp, her attitude unmistakably irate. Rachel had slipped off her lap and now leaned against a bent, elderly woman in the next seat.

Dana stepped back. We followed suit, nearly tripping over each other in the awkwardly narrow space between Tanisha's casket and the front row of chairs. In the dim light I couldn't see the expression on Dana's face, but I imagined she was surprised at the angry reception. The soft music continued—*Thou art the potter; I am the clay*—and it appeared that only a few people were aware of Marne's hostility to Dana.

"What—" Dana began.

Marne kept her hands in place, on her hips. "Did you bring the police here, like you sent them to my house?" She said "he-ah" for "here," as I used to, before I lost my Boston accent, and she stretched out "police" until it was a long hiss. I glanced back at Matt, experiencing a fleeting moment of worry that she'd see through his civilian clothes and recognize him as the poh-leesss.

"I didn't send—" Dana sputtered. She put her hand on her heart, ready to utter an oath.

"Not what I heard. They about tore my house apart. Rachel was there. And her friend, for a sleepover. How could you do that?"

Before Dana could answer, if, indeed, she had a response, a large black man in a dark suit stepped in and gently took Marne's arms from their stiff akimbo position. Another black man handed her an opened bottle of water. I had the useless thought that Rose would have had a crystal glass at the ready.

"Trouble, Mrs. Hall?" the first man asked, guiding her back to her seat. He turned his head toward Dana, his thick neck suggesting considerable muscle mass at his disposal.

Marne relaxed her posture but still glared at Dana. "No trouble. This lady and her friends are leaving."

Matt and Elaine and I filed around to the side aisle, dismissed, not stopping to speak to Marne or other family members in the front row. I saw that most of the guests had become aware of the drama. They strained their necks, shook their heads, and whispered. I had a rare feeling of alienation from my surroundings.

Wounded and weary, help me I pray, the music continued.

I couldn't imagine what Dana must be going through.

I glanced back at Tanisha. She seemed at peace, unlike the rest of us.

CHAPTER FOURTEEN

Dana felt confused and dizzy. Her eyes stung and her stomach hurt. She'd had nothing to eat all day except some crumbs of biscotti to please Elaine, and they weren't sitting well. And now Gloria was hovering over her as she leaned back on the couch in Hutton's lobby. Elaine was off in the corner, on her cell, probably trying to reach Dad. At least Hutton's goons hadn't forced them outside the building.

What had gotten into Marne? Dana had barely heard the words. Something about sending the police to Marne and Tanisha's home. She wanted to go back into the parlor and take Marne aside, find out what was going on.

A dozen questions about her current state were being pummeled at her.

Do you need some air?

Are you dizzy?

Do you feel nauseous?

"I'm okay," she said to no one in particular, hoping to cover all the questions.

Dana took a deep breath and a sip of the water Matt had miraculously produced. It seemed years since she'd signed the guest book, years since she'd looked at Tanisha in the casket.

She'd nearly fainted on the kneeler, even before Marne lashed out at her. Seeing Tanisha like that, so beautiful. But so dead. Dana had always admired how Tanisha could pull off the head-turning, flamboyant look. Next to Tanisha, Dana felt boring, with her middling-brown hair, only occasionally brought to life when she bothered to add a little red; her drab wardrobe; her uninspired accessories. But Tanisha had a way about her. She'd sashay into a room, wearing wild jungle-print tights or bright red shoes with enormous platform heels, full of confidence and optimism.

Dana's head hurt, but she tried to focus on what might have upset Marne. Somehow she must have found out about the mix-up on the report and thought Dana really accused Tanisha of being a druggie. But Dana couldn't believe the cops would bother unless they thought Tanisha was a dealer. And there was no way they could twist Dana's words into that.

"What happened in there?" Dana heard.

A familiar voice. Her boss. Julia Strega had joined Elaine, Gloria, and Matt. Tom Stewart was right behind her. Tom and Julia must have already been in the parlor when Dana arrived.

"We wondered if you'd even show up, after . . . you know," Tom said.

"No, I don't know," Dana said, alert now. Leave it to Tom to get her juices going, queasy or not.

"We heard the story on the local news this morning, plus all the gossip."

Dana hated Tom's stupid grin and bobbing Adam's apple and the way he always acted as though he had some secret you were dying to know. She wouldn't give him the satisfaction of asking what the story was. Luckily, Julia was aware of the ongoing tension between Dana and Tom and paired them only when she had no other choice.

"Could you get me some more water?" Dana asked Matt.

Tom screwed up his mouth, defeated.

"Sure," Matt said. His look was understanding, but Dana knew he wondered why she had let herself get drawn into this infantile game.

As Dana would have guessed, Gloria took Tom's bait.

"What was on the news that we should have heard?" she asked.

Julia broke in to answer. "It was about the search of Tanisha's house." Julia's hair looked especially red today, a poor match to the peach-colored shirt under her jacket. "They, uh, found incriminating stuff."

"Heroin," Elaine said, sounding in the know, holding her cell phone in a position to be answered immediately.

"Nuh-uh," Tom said, clearly pleased with himself. "Supplies."

"Supplies?" Gloria asked.

"Medical supplies," Julia said. "And meds."

"The ones that were stolen," Tom added. His thin lips disappeared into his cheeks.

Tanisha had the stolen medical supplies?

Tom licked his lips, his tongue just missing the pimples at the corners of his mouth. It turned Dana's stomach.

Dana ran her hand across her forehead; her palms were sweaty. She watched the room spin in front of her, as if she were in the middle of the centrifuge in her college biology lab. Flowers, chairs, people, purses all flew out from her. Elaine, Gloria, Matt, Julia, Tom, flung to the edge of her vision. Colors mixed, becoming white; the music faded.

Pass me not, O gentle Savior; hear my humble cry.

HAPTER FIFTEEN

The last person who'd passed out in front of me was Matt, early in his cancer treatment program. That ordeal came rushing to my mind as I saw Dana, white as the covers of Elaine's wedding books, slump to the side, her elbow landing on the arm of the couch, as if she'd made an effort not to fall to the floor.

Julia Strega took over. No one else tried to help, deferring to the expertise of the veteran EMT. Even Tom stepped back, his movements edgy, more nervous than his own emergency services training would dictate. I wondered if his petulance around Dana might be due to some unrequited affection for her.

In the space of a few seconds, Julia had loosened Dana's clothing, thrown her own jacket over Dana's upper body, and held Dana's limp wrist in position to take her pulse. I wondered idly if Valley Med's owner had driven to the service in an ambulance. Maybe she drove one on her daily errands. I tried picturing the small, wiry woman behind the wheel of a massive, screaming van.

Elaine asked, "Where's Phil?" in an exasperated whisper, as if her fiancé should have been at his adult daughter's side. *Her* side, was more likely what she was feeling.

Julia's words to Dana were inaudible, except for their soothing rhythm. When she stood up to address us, she seemed satisfied with her impromptu patient.

"She's breathing fine, coming around," Julia said. "Temporary blackout. She's probably dehydrated." Close up, past the red hair, Julia looked my age. I pulled at a strand of my unruly, graying waves and reminded myself that it was possible, if I so desired, to revisit the black hair of my youth.

Matt, who'd left the group when Dana fainted, now handed Julia a bottle of water. "The ambulance is here," he said.

So Matt had been busy; he hadn't left the scene from squeamishness as I nearly had. I didn't often get to see Matt's emergency skills at work. I allowed myself a pleasant moment, imagining Matt in his uniform days, learning and administering first aid.

Dana was awake enough to try to reject the gurney ride, but by then two middle-aged men—Hutton Funeral Home employees, by their stiff dress and manner—had arrived and reinforced the notion that Dana needed formal medical attention. I saw fears of liability in the wringing of their hands.

In a massive regrouping outside the building, Julia and Elaine (by special concession, Julia said) rode in the ambulance with Dana; Tom was to drive Julia's car; and Matt would drive himself and me in Elaine's Saab. We'd all end up at the nearest hospital in San Leandro.

As the red-and-white Valley Med ambulance pulled away, I had a better idea.

"You and Julia came together, right?" I asked Tom.

Tom nodded, bouncing from one foot to the other, his muscular arms waving slightly, in time with his head. A whole-body nod.

"Why don't I drive you home, Tom? You don't really need to go to the hospital, do you?" A bright, generous offer from me, followed by a spirited affirmative shake of Tom's head. "Matt, you can take Julia's car. I'll take Tom home in the Saab and then meet you at the hospital."

Matt's smirk told me he saw right through my tactic. "Sounds like a plan," he said, as we exchanged keys.

I couldn't wait to get to know Tom Stewart better.

I let Tom tell me his life story. The only son of a doctor; three older sisters; grew up in rural Arnold, California; award-winning quarterback in high school. He explained how the quarterback had to be very bright, as so many male colleagues had tried to convince me over the years. *"Bright" is not playing a game requiring body armor,* I'd respond.

Tom shared with me how he always wanted to be in a helping profession and had thought of med school himself.

"But, too much time and money," he said. "And I wanted to, you know, be able to get in there and do my job." Tom mimed tossing a football for emphasis.

"No waiting in the dugout for Tom Stewart," I said, buying into his sports metaphors.

"That's baseball," he said.

"I knew that."

As we shared a laugh, Tom seemed to me a sweet, pathetic creature, and I wondered why Dana disliked him so intensely.

We rolled west along San Leandro streets toward the I-880 freeway and Tom's home. Head for Jack London Square, he'd told me. I apologized to Tom for the fitful starts I made after traffic lights and stop signs. I hadn't driven Elaine's car in a long time.

"I'll bet you're a great driver," I said, "having to maneuver an ambulance all day. I'd never be able to do that." *Too obvious?* I wondered. But Tom's proud expression said I was doing fine.

"You get used to it. The worst part is backing down a long driveway or something, but I'm pretty good in reverse, except one time, I hit a rock, and my partner in the back didn't shut the door good, and all these rubber gloves fell out and onto the ground."

Ah, the segue I'd been waiting for. "Say, what about those medical supplies?" I said, clicking my tongue. "They actually found them in Tanisha's house? Rubber gloves and things?"

"Ha," Tom said, "not rubber gloves, you better believe. Think needles. And meds. All kinds of meds, from nursing homes mostly. You'd be surprised at how often they use morphine in those facilities, for any kind of pain, for mechanical ventilation, for respiratory failure, for arthritis. You'll even see Roofies. You know, the date-rape drug."

I knew. "I'm surprised. Morphine is at least legal. But Rohypnol? Why would a nursing home have the date-rape drug?"

"They use it as a mild anesthetic, like maybe pre-op, or even a cure for insomnia."

"So, someone"—I did not say "Tanisha"—"steals a nursing home drug and then sells it to someone else?"

"Yep. There's been lots of other stuff missing for a few months now, here and there, and everyone was wondering. EMTs always get blamed, you know, and I guess this time they were right."

"Why would she steal the meds? Is it that easy to sell them, do you think?"

I caught Tom's face, raised eyebrows and crooked grin. "Hello? There's certainly a market out there."

"Really?" From a wide-eyed old lady. "Where?"

Tom made a sputtering sound to go with his *duh* attitude. "You can go to any street corner in Oakland, for one thing."

"That seems dangerous, and not very efficient. Walking around from one corner to the next selling . . . what? Roofies?"

"There's also morphine, remember—a standard supply in a SNF."

"A sniff?"

"S-N-F." Tom spelled it out. "Skilled nursing facility. Plus you'll have psychotherapeutics, hypnotics, lots of stuff."

"Wouldn't there be a more organized way to distribute all these meds?"

"Yeah, well, I couldn't say."

I wondered.

Matt called my cell phone to tell me Dana had already been released from the hospital. She'd been given a shot of nutrients and told to take care of herself. The consensus was that we needed to take her home to Elaine's and give her a decent meal. The Italian solution.

"How was it with Tom, by the way?" Matt asked, as if he'd feared for the young man who'd been in my clutches.

"Interesting," I said, glancing over at Tom.

I'm still with him, said my tone, but one look at Tom, his head leaning on the side window, either nodding off or pretending to, told me I'd gotten all I was going to get from him for now.

As far as I knew, Elaine Cody had no Italian blood, but you couldn't tell from the meal she'd prepared. Pasta with a clam sauce, a side dish of sautéed zucchini and mushrooms, and large amounts of focaccia, olive oil, and salad. Maybe it had been Matt Gennaro's influence in the supermarket they'd stopped at on the way home. My contribution was a stop at a local ice cream parlor to pick up a quart of spumoni and a half pint of their chocolate sauce. It was hard to beat an Italian menu when it came to fattening someone up.

Dana was a good sport about eating a little of each course while we watched and pretended to count her calories.

"I'm fine, really. They gave me B-12 at the hospital. I think it was just . . . everything, you know. Seeing Tanisha, then Marne coming after me like that. And then the supplies." Dana's voice got higher with each item she ticked off. "No way in hell did Tanisha steal supplies. She was studying for the firefighters test."

I failed to see the connection, but I wanted to believe Dana's judgment of her friend and partner.

I'd thought about going up to Mrs. Hall at the service, to see if I could find out more about the search of her home and what led her to believe Dana had prompted it. But what would I have said? *I'm with the woman you just threw out.* I hoped there'd at least be an opportunity for Dana to talk to her.

I looked across Elaine's red-and-white bistro tablecloth at

Dana Chambers. Except for her stature, she didn't resemble her father, and I wondered if her mother had the same classically pretty features, with a small nose and perfect teeth. She seemed outwardly to be doing well, but I sensed a deeper discontent.

Elaine had thrown herself into meal preparation, but it was clear that she was upset about Phil's absence. She'd put her cell phone on the kitchen counter while she was cooking, then carried it to the dining room table. I decided to let her bring it up first if she wanted anything from me.

Another thing about Italian meals, besides the fattening effect, is that they make everyone sleepy. We all turned in early, including Dana, who accepted the invitation to sleep over on the twin bed in Elaine's office.

No Internet access tonight, I thought.

Matt and I had managed a quick debriefing before falling asleep, but there wasn't much to report on either side. Matt thought it would be a good idea to go to Phil's house in the morning, and I agreed. My only offering was a bit of detail from Tom Stewart about the stolen medical supplies, and a hunch that he knew more. But a hunch was just that—conjecture, speculation, gut feeling. Nothing I'd built my career in science on.

I expected to be the first downstairs to make espresso, early on Wednesday morning, but I could tell by the aroma that Elaine had beat me to it, except she'd made regular coffee.

"Now my espresso machine is broken," she said. "What else?"

I understood the stress that would lead her to equate a faulty kitchen appliance, easily replaced, with a missing fiancé.

She picked up her landline phone—checking for a dial tone, I assumed.

"Still can't get Phil?" I asked.

She shook her head, close to tears. She reached into her pocket for a tissue and dabbed at her eyes. She was dressed casually, which for Elaine meant neatly pressed khakis and a knit crewneck shell. She'd set out four matching mugs with modern geometric designs in muted colors.

"No answer at work, or home, or cell. I talked to his secretary, but she couldn't, or wouldn't, put me through to Phil's boss. I have half a mind to go over there."

"Didn't you say he sometimes has to fly out of the country on short notice? Couldn't this be one of those times?"

"He'd have called by now. It's been almost two whole days. And he promised me he'd be around the next two weeks. I keep thinking about that briefcase I saw in his office."

"You said it was empty, right?"

"Yes, but I didn't look for secret compartments or anything."

I rolled my eyes and screwed up my mouth. Had I done this to my friend? Seeing my clownish look, Elaine came up with one of the first smiles I'd seen in a while.

Elaine sat on a counter stool and rotated slowly, ninety degrees, back and forth. "What if he just got cold feet, Gloria?"

The thought stunned me. That my confident, intelligent friend worried about being jilted also surprised me. Though she went in and out of relationships frequently, none of Elaine's breakups had been dramatic; certainly no last-minute dropouts, on either side.

And Phil didn't seem the cold-feet type. I phrased it differently for Elaine, however. "I think if Phil had problems he'd have told you straight out."

"You think?"

I reached out to Elaine. Our hug was interrupted by the swinging door between the kitchen and dining room. Matt, probably needing that first sip of caffeine that seemed to lift the bags under his eyes.

"Worried about Phil?" he asked.

I gave him a nod that asked, *Can you help?*

He pulled Elaine away from me and put his arm around her. "Listen, do you want me to see what I can do?" he asked.

The response was what I wanted, but at the same time, it unnerved me. It made Phil's absence more serious, not just a temporary lapse from a busy guy who lost track of time, or whose cell phone battery was low. He might be in serious trouble or danger.

I knew that Matt already had an appointment with Inspector Dennis Russell to lay out the flimsy information we had that might be new and useful to the Berkeley PD. My biggest expectation had been that Matt might be able to coax the police into considering Tanisha Hall a murder victim, instead of primarily a drug user or thief who'd been killed.

Now I had another agenda, which was to find Phil Chambers. I had no idea what the law was concerning missing adults. I could imagine the police declining to put much effort into locating a healthy, strapping man who was known to be a frequent international traveler and who was destined for the altar in less than two weeks. I suspected that, like Elaine, they'd first latch on to the cold-feet theory. But Phil was also a scientist working on a classified, security-related project. Shouldn't someone care? Maybe Matt's presence, as one of their own, would help.

Apparently Matt's offer unnerved Elaine, too, since her tears started flowing.

Right then Dana appeared in the kitchen wearing a lavender chenille robe I recognized as Elaine's. Her arrival made things worse, as it seemed to occur to all of us at the same time that Phil's daughter needed to know why Elaine was crying.

I knew Dana's short period of grace, which had brought color to her cheeks, was about to end.

CHAPTER SIXTEEN

We dropped Matt off at the Berkeley PD—*lots of luck,* I thought, glad I wasn't the one headed up the imposing stone steps to the front door—then Elaine, Dana, and I drove to Phil's house in Kensington.

The FOR SALE sign on the lawn reminded me how glad I was that Elaine had convinced Phil to move to her house after the wedding, instead of her moving in with him. Elaine's neighborhood was physically almost an extension of the UC Berkeley campus, a significantly more diverse environment than this small, affluent, mostly white community in the hills to the north. Of course, I reminded myself, Phil hadn't yet made the move.

"What are we even looking for?" Dana asked as Elaine produced a key. She scanned the house and grounds, seeming less concerned than I expected that no one had heard from her father for almost two days. Probably because they weren't in daily contact. Neither Elaine nor I wanted to disabuse her of the notion that there was really nothing to worry about. I also had the thought that Dana couldn't admit yet another crisis into her consciousness this week.

"We're going to check out the briefcase," Elaine said.

"And try to find his calendar," I added. "Or just a telephone number or note that might give us a start to figuring out where he went."

"And see if his suitcases are missing." Elaine was still on the he's-having-second-thoughts theme, I noticed.

Dana shrugged. Tall as she was, she looked like a child who'd been dragged on a family outing.

Once inside Phil's home, I had second thoughts about big, sprawling houses in the hills. The real estate agent's flyer, prominent in the high-ceilinged foyer, promised *lavish living room suite w/balcony and magnificent gg bridge view*—not an exaggeration. An enormous redwood deck offered panoramic views of San Francisco Bay and the Golden Gate Bridge. Also correct was the description of the state-of-the-art kitchen with cherrywood cabinets, granite counters, hardwood floors, and exquisite light fixtures.

Beautiful as it was, however, the house had an eerie feeling, partly because it was unnaturally neat—to impress prospective buyers, I guessed—and partly because I knew its owner might be missing. I sniffed the air, as if to test for human presence, alive or dead.

"It's creepy in here," Dana said. Her sigh sounded nervous to me, as if she dreaded what we might find. "Like his cleaning lady just came through and sucked up everything with the vacuum. Let's get some sound at least."

"Judy Collins is in the CD player," Elaine said. "We play it all the time, once we found out we were both at a concert she gave in the seventies in the Greek Theatre."

Dana uttered a disgusted grunt, plucked Judy Collins from the player, and tossed her carelessly onto the couch. "That's so last century," she said.

A new side of Dana Chambers. Now I was sure she was more stressed out than she let on. She pushed the radio on, scanned around the frequencies, and settled on something loud and jerky.

I resigned myself to the fact that we'd be searching the three thousand square feet quoted in the broker's flyer to the strains of something I'd never be able to hum.

"Evanescence," Dana said. I wasn't sure if that was the artist or the song. She moved her body to the rhythm. Elaine and I tried to follow suit and were rewarded by a full-throated laugh from Dana. Mission accomplished.

Our plan: Elaine would take the more personal areas of the house, Phil's bedroom and office; Dana and I would comb the downstairs rooms.

"Look at this," Dana said, pointing to a photo mounted on Phil's refrigerator. "It's me and Scott. I guess Dad's not up-to-date." The photo was of Dana and a young man with hair almost as long as hers, both in serious hiking clothes. A rectangular magnetic frame held the photo to the refrigerator door. Next to it, in a similar frame and aligned with the edges of the door, was a snapshot of Phil and Elaine, with the same misty mountainous backdrop. Not like my fridge photos, which were askew, precariously held at their corners by clunky decorative magnets. A Cape Cod lighthouse, Paul Revere on his horse, the Golden Gate Bridge, and a miniature bumper sticker—TRUST ME, I'M A SCIENTIST—stuck at a forty-five-degree angle to the floor.

Dana removed the photo of her and Scott, folded it, and put it in her pants pocket, leaving the magnetic frame empty. I had a feeling its life was over. I caught a snippet of the Evanescence lyrics, something like *fifty thousand tears I've cried.* By actual count? The scientist in me wondered.

A cork bulletin board was bolted to the wall over a small desk in the kitchen. Dana and I reviewed the contents together. A fractals calendar, for looks or reference only, apparently, since there were no appointments listed. A postcard from Hawaii—from a cousin, Dana said. A list of speakers for the BUL chemistry department colloquia. An agenda for the next department meeting. A two-dollars-off coupon for a pizza.

On the counter was an old book, verification of Elaine's claim that Phil loved science history as I did. I picked it up and breathed the slightly musty smell of its worn brown cloth covers.

It was dated 1919—a treatise on the manufacturing and testing of military explosives. Not "regular" history, as I called it, with stories of kings and queens and one country invading another that left me cold. Scientific biographies and early science texts, on the other hand, intrigued me. This old book, by John Albert Marshall, described work he did for what was then the War Department.

I flipped through a chapter on the history of nitrogen as a component of explosives, first suggested in 1890. I smiled at the description of TNT as "resembling powdered maple sugar" and wished current texts would be so easy to read and so accessible to the layperson.

It made sense, I thought. Phil Chambers, working on nitrogen in the twenty-first century, would do as I would—go back to the beginning, for interest and amusement, if not critical information.

I was starting to like Phil again, but that might have been because he was missing.

When my cell phone rang, Dana and I jumped. Not that we were on edge. I checked the caller ID: the 781 area code, followed by Rose Galigani's phone number.

I'd put Rose off long enough. "I'd better take this," I told Dana. She gave me a salute and disappeared into the living room.

"Gloria! I can't believe you're there."

Rose's exclamation was suited to a long separation, and it had been only Monday evening that I'd talked to her. I realized I'd given no more thought to her faxed police report on the blown-up hearse, and hoped she hadn't called to quiz me on it. I decided to tell her right up front.

"I haven't had a chance to look at the police report—"

"No, no, don't worry about it. There's been no further action takeover-wise, but we're all walking on pins and needles waiting for the next little prank. But I've been thinking—I've been so selfish. You're the one on vacation, so I'm really calling so you can tell me everything *you've* been doing."

"Well, we're dealing with two murders, a theft of drugs and medical supplies, secret nitrogen files, and a missing person."

Rose made no attempt to contain her laughter. "I know you hate wedding things, Gloria, but stop wishing for calamities."

"Just kidding," I said, making a quick decision, too emotionally drained to do anything but let Rose keep her illusion that Matt and I were enjoying a relaxing prewedding vacation. "Everything's fine."

"Did you buy your shoes yet?"

Shoes. The last thing on my mind. "Not yet."

"Elaine has hers, I'm sure. How's it going with Phil's daughter? Is she nice?"

"She's very nice." *She's currently searching her father's house for a clue to his whereabouts.* I needed a diversion, lest I break down and tell Rose the truth. "Has Frank persuaded everyone to take the trip to Houston?" I asked her.

"You know Frank. He can talk his family into an igloo in the heat."

I had a passing thought that she meant "cold," but Rose had her own versions of figures of speech. The important thing was that she was ready to take off with her own agenda. She updated me on Frank's latest project—organizing a family vacation to the National Museum of Funeral History, in Houston.

"They have an exhibit of bizarre caskets, Gloria. People who've had different shapes to go with the spirit of their lives, like one fisherman was buried in a casket shaped like a giant marlin."

I rubbed my forehead, parallel to my frown lines. "Fascinating."

The only way I'd be able to handle this conversation—I knew Rose would roll right through the whole family now—would be to multitask. I carried the cell phone to the island in the middle of the kitchen and started opening drawers. Maybe Phil had a junk drawer, as I did, where a scribbled note might land.

While Rose told me about her lawyer daughter-in-law Karla's

newest case, I shuffled through serving spoons, spatulas, and long forks, careful not to make too much noise.

"Karla's doing so well," I said, feeling that would cover anything I missed.

When Rose moved on to John, son number two—"He had another date with Denise on Sunday. She's old man Mattera's granddaughter, you know"—I'd moved to the counter.

I quietly pulled the appliances out from their positions against the wall and checked behind the toaster, blender, can opener, mixer, bread box. Not a crumb. Phil's cleaning lady had done a perfect job. Not a clue, either, however, and I wondered what we were doing there. Maybe with two hands free, Elaine and Dana were doing better in other parts of the house.

"John will find the right woman, in his own time," I said. Another platitude to the rescue.

By the time Rose started her report on her teenaged grandson, the e-mail whiz William, and his success at basketball last night, I'd covered the whole kitchen and the half bath between the hallway and the family room.

I turned back to the kitchen and caught a side view of the bulletin board. Its wooden frame wasn't flush with the wall at the bottom, as if something were pushing it out. I walked up to it for a closer look and saw that the bottom bolt was loose. With a pair of scissors from a drawer, I fished around in the gap at the lower edge. I wedged the phone between my jaw and shoulder and tried using the scissors and my fingers to pry the gap into a reasonable size.

"William's a natural," I said. I'd heard Frank use that phrase when William took off on his first set of Rollerblades; I hoped it applied to all sports.

With my head pressed against the wall, the phone in the crook of my neck, and my arms contorted to hold a gap open, I noticed the corner of a piece of white paper hanging below the bulletin board, partially obscured by the pizza coupon.

". . . in the next couple of months," I heard. Rose was now talking about her youngest, Mary Catherine, my godchild, who was living in the mortuary apartment I'd abandoned to live with Matt.

"So MC is moving out?" I hoped I got that right.

"No, Gloria. This must be a bad connection. I have your mail here. Is this a good time to go through it? Lots of catalogs and junk mail, but there are a couple of first class pieces."

A long distance reading of my mail was so far down on my list of priorities, it reached the status of contemporary poetry.

"Rose, I hate to go, but Elaine is waiting, and—"

"Oh, you should have told me you were busy. Sorry, Gloria. I wish I could go shopping with you two. We'll finish later. Miss you."

I hung up and went to find Dana and Elaine. I needed help with some carpentry.

"Nothing missing that I can see," Elaine said. She'd already come down the stairs. "His closet's full. His large suitcases are there. I can't speak for his carry-ons—he has so many. And there might be a few missing shirts and pants."

"Did you find a calendar or date book?" I asked.

"Nothing."

"How about his computer?" I asked. "Did you look through the files?"

"As many as I could access, which was most of them. Nothing."

"I have nothing, either," Dana said, looking as though she needed a nap.

"I might have something," I said.

Thanks to Dana's familiarity with her father's garage and tools, in a few minutes the bulletin board was off the wall and standing against an island cabinet. The bolts that had held it to the kitchen wall rolled around the ivory granite of the island, surrounding the pile of business cards from the real estate broker.

As the only one who'd turned up anything vaguely useful, I was assigned the task of extricating the several eight-and-a-half-by-eleven sheets from the back of the cork panel. They were unbound and had been held in place by masking tape. What I'd seen during my acrobatics was the page closest to the panel, which had slipped a bit from the package.

We spread the pages—five in all, obviously photocopies—on the island and peered at them. Elaine had made coffee, decrying the lack of snack food in Phil's cabinets or refrigerator, as well as the absence of an espresso machine.

"Not that I've rushed out to replace mine," Elaine said. Her voice sounded wistful, full of nostalgia for her normal life.

"I don't get this," Dana said. "These are Valley Med invoices. What are they doing in my dad's house?"

"And why would Phil hide them?" Elaine asked. I wondered if she was at all relieved that we hadn't uncovered evidence that indicated a cold-feet theory might be in order—a perfumed love letter, perhaps, or a note saying *Thanks for last night.*

"This is a laugh," Dana said, pointing to the letterhead: VALLEY MEDICAL AMBULANCE COMPANY, and under that, ACCOUNTING DEPARTMENT. "Julia *is* the accounting department."

We continued to stare at the invoices, as if the words were one half of an equation, about to rearrange themselves into the other half, making the whole understandable, giving us a reason why Phil had the copies in the first place, and then thought it necessary to hide them.

The suite of Evanescence songs ended, emphasizing the silence that settled over us, the excitement of finding "something" overshadowed by "so what?" The last words I heard as the music came to a halt were *bring me to life.*

"Not bad," I told Dana as a commercial for a tranquilizer replaced the music. "Not Tony Bennett, but not bad."

In the short-lived thrill at finding the invoices, I'd forgotten about the briefcase, which I now noticed standing in front of the oven.

"It was in the same place," Elaine said, in tune with my gaze. "Still empty. I thought we should take it with us this time."

I nodded agreement. I was sure Matt would want to take it to Russell, though by now there'd be a sufficient number of overlapping fingerprints to make it useless, I guessed.

"Wait a minute," Dana said, waving an invoice in our direction. Elaine and I put down our mugs and gave Dana our full attention. "There's no Schnur Convalescent Home in Alameda County."

"You mean you've never heard of it?" Elaine asked.

"I mean there isn't one. I know them all. Hospitals, senior centers, convalescent homes, trauma centers, you name it. I *have* to know them all." Dana picked up the sheet and held it closer to her face, studying it. "Here's another one. A bill for a pickup at a Mattson Assisted Living Center. That doesn't exist, either." Dana ran her fingers down the page. "Okay, okay, okay," she said, apparently giving approval to some of the listings. A little more than halfway down the page, she tapped her finger and shook her head. "Absolutely no Jacobs Home in Alameda County. I don't believe this. There must be at least six care centers listed on this page alone that don't exist."

"Maybe some of them are new?" I asked. "Or really small facilities, so you might not have made a pickup?"

Dana placed the invoice on the island counter so we could see it. She stepped back and folded her arms across her chest. "Then how come I'm listed as the driver?"

With a highlighter from Phil's kitchen-drawer collection, Dana marked the nonexistent facilities Julia had billed, all with post office boxes as addresses. We examined the pages, shuffling them among us, one or two at a time.

PATIENT ID	FROM	TO	DRIVER	$COST
04435678	SCHNUR CH	TC	CHAMBERS	450
04435679	TC	SCHNUR CH	HALL	360
04436780	GGH	TC	STEWART	350
04446781	OAK H.	TC	HALL	350
04472382	MATTSON ALC	OAK H	LANGLAND	575

Dana gave us a quick rundown of the acronyms for sites such as convalescent homes, assisted living centers, and the trauma center, and the patient codes that included dates and insurance IDs.

It was obvious that Julia was running some kind of scam, laundering money through services she never rendered.

"These billed amounts are all different," I said.

"The basic cost of transport is three hundred dollars, then on top of that there's fees if we need equipment or supplies." Dana ticked off the list. "Like oxygen, cannulas, bandages, dressings. That's all extra." She looked down the list. "Say there's about six or seven fake trips a week here. She could be hiding, like, ten thousand dollars a month."

"Somehow Phil uncovered this swindle," Elaine said.

Or was part of it, I didn't say.

"This is a new one on me," Dana said. "I've heard some worse things, though, like beating old people so they'll need the ER and more money comes in from their insurance. Then the ER and the home split the reimbursement."

"What?" Elaine seemed stunned, as I was. It made taking extra pens and pads of paper from the lab supply room seem not worth noting.

"I wonder how Phil discovered this," Elaine said, still on her Phil-is-one-of-the-good-guys tack.

"Dad met Julia once or twice, but he doesn't know her well, and I'm sure his only connection to her is through me," Dana said.

"And Robin," Elaine said. This time the lovely bird came out as a growl. When we looked doubtful, she elaborated. "Robin used to work for Julia at Valley Med. Robin had a badge in her closet from the company Phil works with. The briefcase was in Robin's house, then Phil's."

A little loose and haphazard, but I could almost follow Elaine's thinking, although she'd skirted two murders.

"What if Dad's in danger?" Dana's voice cracked as she uttered what we were all thinking. "There's a lot of money involved in this, if it's ongoing. Dad might be—"

"The cookies are here!" A cheery voice from the foyer broke into our high-level meeting, just in time. An energetic fifty-something woman, in a red-and-black power suit and pumps, despite the heat, burst into the kitchen. "Sorry I'm a little late, but Brokers' Open House is now officially under way."

The woman tore plastic wrap from a plate of chocolate chip cookies; they smelled warm and homemade.

We dug in, ready for something sweet and simple.

CHAPTER SEVENTEEN

It didn't help that there was a stack of wedding presents waiting for us on Elaine's doorstep. A UPS truck seemed to have dumped half its load of cartons, large and small, meant to cheer and honor the bride and groom. But the pile of boxes was simply one more reminder that, instead of happily anticipating and celebrating a joyous event, we were accumulating one mystery after another.

Rose's gift had already arrived, even before Matt and I did. On our first evening in California, Elaine had shown me the beautiful hand-fashioned wine set—eight glasses, a decanter, and a tray, all in bold stained glass colors.

Matt and I had yet to decide on a present. I'd tried to get a hint from Elaine, but she refused to give one, claiming our trip was present enough.

"Anyway, if I ask for something, it'll be too much like registering at some mall store, which I hate," she'd said. "A gift should be a gift. Whatever moves you."

Matt arrived soon after Dana, Elaine, and I reached home. His step seemed lighter now that he'd communicated with Russell, his fellow law enforcer.

"Phil is still among the missing," Elaine said, by way of a greeting to Matt. From her tone she might have been a hostess checking off guests invited to a party. Or a wedding. I wondered if she felt an obligation to appear strong for Dana.

It had been more than forty-eight hours since I'd watched Phil walk out of the bagel shop, the last of this immediate circle to see him.

In a movie, I'd be the prime suspect.

Dana briefed Matt on the situation with the phony Valley Med invoices. She'd noticed that Julia Strega's fictitious driving duties rotated among two dozen or so EMTs.

"Probably to avoid tax problems," Matt said. "This way no one individual EMT's tax returns are going to be flagged as not matching the company's statements."

"Also, there are some fake EMTs here," Dana said. "I don't know absolutely everyone in the company personally, but I'm pretty sure I know all the names, from seeing the schedule in the lounge, and from talking. You know, who's a good partner, who's an a—" She flushed. For whose benefit had she cleaned up her vocabulary? I wondered.

"A what?" A tease from Elaine, one of few light moments lately.

"A jerk," Dana said with a smile. She ran her fingers down the list. "Gary Langland, Marcia Streich, José Williams. Who are these people?"

"Julia would sprinkle phony names among the real ones, again, just for cover," Matt said.

"This could be why Phil is missing," Elaine said. "What if someone is holding him . . . hostage"—her voice cracked; she glanced at Dana and continued—"because he uncovered Julia's scam?"

I mentally amended her statement, pending some explanation Julia might give, to *alleged* scam. Hanging around Matt will do that to you.

Inspector Dennis Russell had not been impressed, according to Matt. Not by Robin's taking over the printing of Dana's incident report, and certainly not by her new wardrobe. Russell took custody of the Dorman Industries ID Dana had found in Robin's closet, but without comment. He had listened to a description of Phil's connection to Lokesh Patel through Dorman Industries, but again without interest.

"Unless we're ready to report Phil missing," Matt said, with a look around the table.

Elaine gave me a helpless look. "Not yet," she said. "It's still sort of within the window . . ."

I gathered Phil had done this before—that is, be even less considerate than Elaine had made him out to be. *Not my problem,* I told myself.

"Russell did say he wanted the briefcase immediately," Matt said, "and that we were not to fiddle with it."

"Fiddle?" I asked.

"His word."

"I'm surprised he didn't detain you until he took custody of it."

"I told him it was at Phil's house, so they're headed over there." Matt was not about to encourage a joke at the expense of a fellow officer.

Elaine looked at Dana, and they both looked at me. "The briefcase is here," we all said, out of synch.

"What will they do when they get there and no one's home?" I asked Matt.

"Except the cookie lady and her open-house guests," Elaine reminded me.

Matt frowned. Thinking. "Well, in a situation like this, no urgency, I'd call his office. If that didn't pan out, I'd ask around at the neighbors, see if anyone knows when he's due home. They won't have a search warrant, and, remember, technically Phil is not missing unless and until we make a report. So they're not going to go busting in."

"And eventually they'll call . . . whom?" Elaine asked.

"I gave them this number. By rights, I need to call them now and tell them the briefcase is here."

"By the time you look up the Berkeley PD number in the phone book—" I began.

"Russell gave me his card."

"But you still have to find it in your pockets. How much time do we have?"

"For what?" Elaine asked.

"For fiddling," Matt said, and left the room to make his call. His back was to me, so I couldn't determine what level of humor, if any, was in his remark.

Elaine brought the briefcase to the living room and set it on the coffee table, pushing aside her bride books in the process. I regretted every derogatory remark I'd made, to myself and others, about the various planning and make-your-day-special volumes. She flipped open the briefcase.

"It wasn't locked when I opened it the other day, either," she noted.

We peered in and scanned the beige leather lining, as if it would take more than a fraction of a second to determine that the roughly two-hundred-cubic-inch briefcase was empty.

We each took a turn fiddling with the briefcase. Elaine ran her fingers around the inside edges, trying to pull up a corner. Nothing. Curiously, Dana lifted the case close to her nose and sniffed. She shook her head. A silent *Nothing.* I manipulated all the metal parts. The hinges, the decorative buckles on the sides, the lock. Still nothing.

Matt might as well have brought the cops with him to pick up the briefcase.

To report or not to report Phil missing?

"What do you think, Matt?" Dana asked.

Matt scratched behind his ear. I knew he'd already given this matter some thought. He took his time giving his opinion.

"Can we talk about Phil for a few minutes? When did we see him last, for example."

He addressed Dana and Elaine, but for some reason I raised my hand slightly, reminiscent of seeking permission to go to the girls' room at Abraham Lincoln Elementary School in Revere, circa 1955.

"I had lunch with him on Monday," I said. A confession, but no one seemed to notice. We'd gathered in Elaine's living room, our seats in a conversational arrangement I was sure was meant for her book club, not a brainstorming session on the whereabouts of her fiancé.

"I talked to him Friday night, after Tanisha . . . we talked about Tanisha," Dana said. "That's it." She rubbed her hands together, as if she were applying lotion. But I knew there was nothing soothing in the gesture.

"I haven't talked to him since Monday morning." Elaine's voice was controlled and weak.

"And ordinarily, would you talk to him every day?"

"Not me," Dana said.

"Not *every* day," Elaine said. "But he wouldn't just disappear."

It was hard to tell whether Elaine was trying to convince us or herself.

Dana stood up abruptly. "Maybe this is a clue," she said. "Before I left for my interview with the police on Monday, Julia told me to be careful—like, don't tell them too much, or something. Maybe she was afraid they'd start looking into stuff and find her scam." She snapped her fingers. "And Tom, too, he said sort of the same thing. Maybe he's in on it."

"Don't forget Robin," Elaine said. I knew she was speaking from her fear of an involvement between Phil and Robin. "She had that ID."

"Okay, we're getting somewhere," Matt said.

I raised my eyebrows. *We are?*

"This is just a long shot, but does Phil have any hobbies that might put him in danger? Like—" Matt began.

"Scuba diving? Rock climbing? Hang gliding?" I filled in with some of my top candidates for dangerous pastimes.

Elaine shook her head. "Not unless you think handball is dangerous. And I did call Barry, his gym buddy. And I told you I spoke to his BUL administrator, Penny Thomas, since he checks in with her now and then. And also to Verna Cefalu, his secretary at Dorman. Phil was there for a presentation Monday, but that's the last she saw of him."

I had a thought. "Phil's last words—" *Bad choice.* "Phil was on his way back to Dorman Industries to give that presentation when he left me after lunch, and he did show up there, evidently. Let's start from there and see if we can pick up the trail." *The trail?* It made me nervous that I slipped into cowboy talk so easily when I was out west.

"Would you be able to go there, Matt, and ask some questions?" Dana asked.

"You, too, Gloria, in case there's some . . . nitrogen . . . involved," Elaine added.

I couldn't have said it better.

We reached consensus that once we determined Phil's movements when he left me, we'd make a decision about whether to make a formal police report. Matt had explained that in cases like this—an adult with no history of criminal behavior, not falling into any special at-risk category, like a person with Alzheimer's—we could expect the police to enter a bulletin and a photo of Phil into their MUPS system within four hours.

"Missing unidentified persons," Matt said. "It got started nationwide in the seventies after a particularly bad case where the police dragged their feet on an MP report, and . . . it didn't turn out well."

I could see that Matt was sorry he'd referred to a case with an unhappy ending.

"What will they do with the information?" Elaine asked. "Go out looking for him?"

"The system is monitored by investigators, maybe from the state, the DA's office . . . I'm not sure how they do it in California. But, within that four hours, they'll start the process. They check to see if he has outstanding warrants, for example, and if maybe he's in custody somewhere." Elaine smiled at this, but I couldn't see how we could rule anything out. "Then they'll start calling hospitals, ERs, and so on."

I figured "and so on" meant morgues.

I looked at Dana and felt sure she had the same thought.

"How awkward is this going to be?" I asked Matt on the way to Dorman Industries. After a too brief respite, the heat wave had returned, and even in the late afternoon we needed the Saab's air conditioner. I raised my voice to be heard over the noisy fan. "I'm sure when Elaine queried the secretaries she did it in a way that didn't reveal she's essentially lost her fiancé."

"I think we just ask the questions and accept that this might be embarrassing to Elaine or Phil."

Though I was driving Elaine's car and not mine or Matt's—our usual classroom venue—it seemed the right time and place for a nitrogen lesson. We'd had some of our best tutorial sessions in our cars, riding to or from an interview—and once or twice on a stakeout.

"It makes the science seem less of a commitment," Matt had told me. "And it's less likely that there'll be homework or pop quizzes."

I ignored the slur against science education.

"The two most common forms of nitrogen are N_2, which is the most abundant element in our atmosphere—"

"And number seven on the periodic table."

"Very good. And the second form is N_3, which is highly explosive. A nitrogen fullerene—sixty atoms of nitrogen arranged in the shape of a soccer ball—would be an oddity, but a welcome one."

"Because . . . ?"

"Because nitrogen bonding is so tight, when it's broken, the explosive power of the molecule would be dazzling."

"Did you know that there are some people who use the word 'dazzling' to describe a piece of jewelry, or the performance of an Olympic-medal-winning skater?"

"Would you rather be with one of those people right now?"

"Not on your life."

Keeping my eye on the road, I was sure I'd missed a *dazzling* smile.

"As I told you in lesson one the other day, the energy released this way could be the basis for either a new weapon or a really novel nitrogen-based fuel—think supersonic transport. Either way, there'd be a lot at stake in the competition to produce this molecule."

Matt reached over and put his hand on my knee. He'd waited till we were stopped at a light on University Avenue. Not to disturb my accelerator foot, I guessed.

"Do you think all lovers talk this way?" he asked.

I felt my face flush, and nearly missed the green light, but didn't stop the lesson.

"Last I heard, people were working on the possibility of joining six ten-atom nitrogen molecules into the soccer-ball shape. We'll have to check on the progress next time we're online."

"This is sounding like homework," Matt said.

I smiled, and reluctantly gave up on the nitrogen tutorial when we saw the address we were looking for on a large white stucco building. Various signage indicated that Dorman Industries and several other consulting firms had quarters in what looked like a restored factory building. We were in the neighborhood a few blocks north of Bette's Diner, an area that had once been a bustling manufacturing center. It was heartening to see that many of the structures had been converted to useful space for retail outlets, offices, and artists' studios.

I pulled into a slot right in front of the building—a miracle in Berkeley, where even residents had restricted parking permits.

"About that 'lovers' comment," Matt said, as we opened the frosted glass door to the lobby. "Pretty soon we'll be able to say 'husband and wife.'"

"Uh-huh," I said.

And then I tripped on the edge of the carpet.

"Okay," Matt said. "'Wife and husband.'"

I regained my composure and gave him a loving smile.

Our worries that Dorman consultants would overreact to our questioning presence were put to rest when we met the imposing, white-haired Dr. Howard Christopher, whom I'd been introduced to at the bagel shop the day Phil and I had lunch. The day Phil disappeared.

Christopher's manner was stiff, like his modern office décor, and his responses were brief and factual.

"Chambers came to the meeting around one-thirty on Monday. Right after that lunch with you, Dr. Lamerino." He nodded at me, as if to shift blame for any upset. "He gave a presentation to the senior staff." Christopher leaned back in his black leather chair, keeping his hands in his jacket pocket.

"Anything you can talk about?" Matt asked.

"Not really."

"Understood."

"Was there anything unusual about the presentation?" I asked. A weak attempt at a cop question, though Matt and I had decided not to play up his RPD credentials. He was, after all, three thousand miles from his jurisdiction. We'd made it clear to Christopher that we were on a personal errand, on behalf of Phil's family.

Matt and I had discussed the near certainty that Inspector

Russell had visited Dorman to inquire about Lokesh Patel, the firm's recent gunshot victim, but so far Christopher hadn't mentioned an onslaught of "investigators" at his office.

"Nothing out of the ordinary," Christopher answered. "As usual, Chambers had some, uh, charts, and some, uh . . ."

"Data?" I offered.

"Right." Christopher's voice was deep and resonant, reminding me of a network news anchorman whose name escaped me. *Elaine would know,* I thought. She watched all the Sunday morning political talk shows and was always up on current events. I felt a shiver of distress at her current plight. And maybe Phil's.

"That's it?" Matt asked. "Nothing you can tell us about his manner, or his mood?"

Christopher shook his head, sending a shock of white hair to his forehead.

I wasn't sure why I didn't believe him; maybe because, except for his hair color (that is, not colored), he reminded me physically of Phil, whom I'd never gotten to know well enough to trust.

With a matronly body much like my own, Verna Cefalu, one of the consulting firm's secretaries, managed considerably more animation than the tall, fit Dr. Christopher.

"What's this about?" she asked. She raised her eyebrows, revealing more of the pale blue eye shadow that matched her sweater set. "Has something happened to Dr. Chambers?"

"Ms. Cefalu, did anything unusual come up for Dr. Chambers, say, on Monday afternoon? Something he might have needed to pay attention to unexpectedly?"

"Nothing." Ms. Cefalu twisted a button on her cardigan. "Well, except for that urgent phone call."

I gasped, but internally.

"I see. Can you tell us about that?" Matt asked, with a restraint I wouldn't have been able to summon.

"Once in a while he gets these calls, from the same man, I

think, and then he has to leave in a hurry. He got one on Monday. I had to call him out of his meeting. Should I have done something different?"

I was distracted by the thought that Howard Christopher hadn't considered it important to mention the urgent call that took Phil from his meeting. I knew I'd been right not to trust him. Not that I was quick to jump to conclusions.

"Do you remember exactly what the caller said?" Matt asked.

I loved listening to Matt *not* answer questions. One more way that his training differed from mine. Scientists tended to answer questions directly and literally. Like children, sometimes. I thought of a typical telephone dialogue I'd had with Sophie, my cousin Mary Ann's five-year-old grandniece.

"Is your aunt home?"

"Yes."

No offer to call Mary Ann to the phone, as an adult would. Children had no context for social dialogue; scientists had context trained out of them, to better prepare them to attack each question or problem with rigorous logic.

With Matt, it was all context. He understood layers of meaning, and often answered a question with one of his own when on the job. The subtext: I'll ask the questions; your job is to give *me* information. Pleasantly administered, but a firm and effective policy nonetheless.

I wondered what Ms. Cefalu's training was.

"The caller said for Dr. Chambers to meet in *one* hour at the usual *place*." Ms. Cefalu emphasized her answer by crossing her right index finger over her left for "one hour," and then over two left fingers for "place." "This time he said it was urgent."

"Did you recognize the voice?" Matt asked.

Ms. Cefalu pulled at her skirt to take it to the tips of her chubby knees. I could relate. "Only that this same person has called before. A man, middle age, I guess. I mean not a kid, you know, or an old, old man. No accent or anything."

Ms. Cefalu had led us to a small grouping of chairs between her desk and the entrance to the building. The setting spoke of a woman's touch, unlike Christopher's office. Or mine, I realized.

We were interrupted by a Type A scientist or engineer who handed Ms. Cefalu a stack of papers—I recognized the familiar style of bulleted vu-graphs—with a curt, "Twenty copies by COB."

"Close of business," Ms. Cefalu said to us. Her way of apologizing for the man's rude behavior, I sensed. She checked her watch unobtrusively.

"Does Phil ever seem upset when he gets these messages?" Matt asked.

Ms. Cefalu bit her lips, bottom over top, then vice versa. "Not usually."

"But on Monday?"

"Well, he did rush out. Of course, the caller doesn't always say it's *urgent*." She made a cross with her fingers again, and I got the idea that Ms. Cefalu was a very organized, logical person, with mnemonics and tickler files to help her get her job done.

"When did these calls start?"

Another lip-biting session. "I'd say, about two months ago."

"And he didn't leave word with you about where the meeting was, or a phone number where he could be reached?"

"No. I was in a hurry because my son's babysitter called. She got a flat tire, and I had to pick him up from school and take him to day care." I pictured a minivan with juice boxes in the backseat. "Then I came back to work, but Dr. Chambers was gone by then. But Dr. Chambers never would give me details when these messages came. Like when he'd be back or anything."

I heard panic and guilt in Ms. Cefalu's voice. Was she to blame for not getting a forwarding address? Did her lack of attention to detail cause a problem for Dr. Chambers?

"That's good to know," I said, by way of positive feedback.

"Can you tell me—is Dr. Chambers missing? I mean really missing?" she asked.

I figured Ms. Cefalu meant milk-carton missing versus a-half-hour-late-for-a-tux-fitting missing.

"Thanks for your help, Ms. Cefalu," Matt said, standing up.

She followed us to the door. "I mean, first Dr. Patel, the poor man, and now Dr. Chambers." She pulled her cardigan across her chest, as if to protect herself from being the next to fall.

Matt shook her hand. Warmly, but not budging as far as imparting any information. "We'll get back to you as soon as we know anything."

This time I felt genuine sympathy for Ms. Cefalu, so cooperative, yet not getting even a tiny hint of an answer to her questions.

I hoped Matt never pulled his cop Q&A training on me.

CHAPTER EIGHTEEN

Thursday was a dry, warm day. The kind Dana thrived on. She walked briskly, making a conscious effort to feel her muscles work and to breathe deeply, clearing her head. A trip to the farmers' market, where she bought a single large sunflower, a bag of long green beans, and a scoopful of dried cranberries, had brightened her spirits.

Dana had been born in Silicon Valley, but she loved living close to Berkeley. *All the Berkeleys,* she thought. She could ride her bike up in the hills behind the university campanile or down in the flats by the marina. If she felt like a successful professional, she could put on her Eddie Bauer shorts and a crisp white shirt and join the yuppies with their Cadillac baby strollers on Fourth Street. If she felt retro, she could join the hippie crowd— she'd thread a multicolored cotton belt through the loops of a pair of worn jeans and cruise the vendor tables on Telegraph Avenue. Berkeley had something for everyone.

Today Dana wore a gauzy shirt with an African motif, in honor of Tanisha Hall. On the way home, she stopped at Dziva's, a women's bookstore-café near the Oakland/Berkeley border, and sipped Rooibos, Tanisha's favorite African red bush tea. She thought of her friend and favorite partner and tried to replace the image of Tanisha in a silk-lined casket with that of the vibrant woman who made everyone listen to her daughter's knock-knock jokes.

Dana closed her eyes and remembered.

"Knock, knock," Tanisha says.

"God, not again," Dana says, grinning in spite of herself.

Tanisha nudges her. "Come on, Dana. Knock, knock."

Dana sighs. "Who's there?"

"Jamaica."

"Jamaica who?" Dana holds back a laugh.

"Jamaica cake today?" Tanisha belts out a laugh; Dana gives in and joins her.

Dana ran her tongue around the rim of the handleless ceramic cup, savoring the sweetened tea, and smiled at the memory.

A group of rowdy kids from the junior high school across the street entered the shop and headed for Dziva's famous oversized snickerdoodles. Dana couldn't remember having a ten o'clock cookie break when she was in junior high, but the interruption was just what she needed to shake her into the present.

Julia wasn't being pushy, but Dana knew she couldn't put off work forever. She needed to be doing something, not dwelling on this last, upsetting week. As if it weren't bad enough to lose her friend, there'd been a murdered patient, too. Plus the stolen medical supplies in Tanisha's home, a dead man's ID in Robin's closet, and Julia's questionable billing practices.

And now her father might be missing. Dana's head hurt. To think, a few days ago she'd considered working and getting ready for a wedding a lot of stress.

Now, work was the answer to relieve stress, even if it meant partnering with Tom Stewart for a while. She wished Tom would get over being nosy about her personal life and, more important, the idea that he and Dana could be an item. When she'd broken up with Scott—five minutes after she realized he had a "best friend" on every shift—Tom had seen it as an opportunity. *In his dreams.*

Matt had convinced Dana to say nothing to Julia about finding the phony invoices, and Dana was just as glad to let him handle it with the Berkeley PD. She knew she'd miss Matt when he went back east. Hanging around with him made her realize how totally young and immature all her boyfriends had been. Matt was out of circulation, but there might be other guys her father's age Dana should consider. Or maybe Dana would wait until *she* was her father's age before getting involved again.

Thump. A backpack swung into Dana's arm, rattling the small black metal table and sending her cup to her lap. The few drops left of her tea spilled onto her jean shorts.

"My bad," said the kid attached to the pack. He and his buddies sauntered away without looking at her.

Dana packed up her tote and went out into the bright sun. Julia had told her to come by anytime and pick up a shift, whenever she was ready.

It was time to go back to work.

Dana had so much energy, she offered to help change the oxygen tanks in the ambulances that were on-site at Valley Med. Julia played it straight when it came to this kind of regulation. She'd trained her EMTs to follow the strict fire department guidelines and not let the tanks go below about five hundred psi of oxygen.

"Are you sure you want to do this?" the rookie Melissa asked her. "The dirty jobs are supposed to be for newbies."

"Just this once," Dana said. She gave the young woman's back an affectionate pat, remembering her own first days on the job. Melissa was hardly any bigger than Jen, but Dana knew better than to judge someone's strength by appearance.

The two women opened the side door of the first ambulance. Dana turned off the valve and unscrewed the head, and she and Melissa lifted the nearly empty five-foot tank from the cabinet behind the backseats. The tank was covered in dust, which was immediately transferred to the women's black uniforms.

"Good thing dirt is sexy," Melissa said with a smile, as she and Dana inserted a new tank. "Two thousand psi and ready for action."

They worked together, checking that all the ambulances had small tanks attached to the gurneys, plus the larger ones needed for longer transports. As Dana had guessed, Melissa was quite able to handle her share of the physical load.

"I'll take the old ones to storage," Melissa said, but she didn't budge. She cleared her throat, and Dana felt something heavy in the air. Sure enough, it came out. "I know it's none of my business, but I just want to tell you, I don't believe the stories about Tanisha."

"What stories?" Dana asked.

Melissa put her hand to her head, shading her eyes, pulling at her wispy brown bangs. "Well, the coke and the meds and—"

"Good. Don't believe them," Dana said. She brushed off her uniform and stormed into the building, heading straight for the employee lounge, no doubt in her mind who was operating the rumor mill.

She found what she expected: Tom Stewart was stretched out on the couch, the TV remote in his right hand, a large soda cup in his left. Dana reached from behind his head, grabbed the remote, and clicked the TV off. His cup fell to the floor, spilling reddish liquid on the couch. *No one will even notice the extra spots,* Dana thought.

"Hey!" Tom sat up. He smiled when Dana came into his field of view. "You want my attention?"

"Yes, you wank." Dana strained to keep her voice low. No use waking the EMTs grabbing some Zs in the bedrooms. "Since when does a little grass become coke? I'd appreciate it if you did not mess with the reputation and the memory of my friend and your coworker."

She had a good mind to grab the long-handled brush in the corner and whack him. Maybe that would also remind him to take his turn washing the outside of the ambulance once in a while.

Tom kept his smile in place, calling attention to an especially large pimple near the corner of his lips. "Not my fault. The cops came to search Tanisha's locker. We all saw them."

"And you saw *coke?*"

"Maybe not coke . . ."

Dana's jaw muscles tightened, the beginning of a serious headache. "So, I'll expect you to spread the truth around just as loudly, or—"

"Pickup at No Name 5 in Emeryville." Julia's voice boomed over the loudspeaker, in time to break up the argument. Dana wondered if their boss had the employee lounge bugged. She wouldn't put anything past Julia after seeing the fake billing lists.

"No Name" was Valley Med's jargon for the many skilled nursing facilities in the area that were regular homes, with three or four bedrooms, in residential areas, with no sign in front. No Name 5 was on a quiet Oakland street not far from Dana's own house.

"That's us," Tom said. "Lucky me. I get to hear you bitch some more. But I don't mind. You're so hot when you're—"

"Cool it, Tom. Let's just do this job, okay?"

Dana tore out of Valley Med's driveway before Tom was fully buckled in. This was her first call since Friday evening. *This is my job,* she thought, *the same as before.* Most of their calls were pretty ordinary, Dana reminded herself. Only a few stood out.

"Remember the last time we partnered?" Tom asked, apparently also in a reminiscing mode. "The kid with his eyeball popped out?"

Dana would never forget the little boy who'd been hit in the eye by a swing on the school playground. By the time they picked him up, he'd been bandaged, with a small paper cup taped to his face to hold the eye in place, but the trickles of blood were creepy to see.

Today's No Name call was a wait-and-return. Dana and Tanisha had transported this patient several times before. Maria Santiago was recovering from spine surgery for scoliosis, about halfway through her rehab at No Name 5. She'd be getting an X-ray at the trauma center, where her insurance card would be accepted. It wouldn't take more than a half hour, so it was easier for the EMTs to wait around and take her back.

The big question was how Dana was going to get through the half-hour wait with Tom. Usually that wasn't a problem; partners would go to the cafeteria and chat over free food, or they'd finish up paperwork together.

Dana had a flashback to similar waits with Tanisha and longed for a knock-knock joke.

At No Name 5, a pale pink stucco home with a neat lawn, Dana switched with Tom, letting him drive while she got in the back with Maria. She admitted to herself, but not to Tom, that she wasn't ready to face turning into that trauma center driveway again so soon. She'd have to deal with it later, but not today.

"I like to talk to Maria," she'd told Tom as they climbed the few steps to the front door.

"Practicing your Spanish?"

She glared at him and rang the doorbell.

Maria needed spine precautions, so Dana and Tom stuck a board under her on the gurney. She looked less than comfortable. This was a routine Code 2, and Dana went through the questions on the PCR, the Patient/Customer Care Report.

"Any pain today, Maria?"

"Yes," Maria said, pronouncing it *jes*. "A little."

"Is it radiating?"

"No." A short *o*.

"Can you rate it for me?"

"A five," Maria said. *Fi*. Halfway to excruciating.

Dana took Maria's pulse and blood pressure and reported them to Tom, who'd be doing the ring-down when they got closer to the trauma center. To get Maria's respiratory rate, Dana resorted to the usual trick.

"I need to take your pulse again, Maria," she said. Dana folded Maria's arms over her chest and counted her breaths. She'd been clued in on the technique by older EMTs: If you told patients you wanted their resp rate, they'd get nervous and throw off the reading, so you'd let them think you were doing a pulse check. She looked at Maria's gentle face and wondered if she'd caught on by now.

Dana heard Tom through the window between the cab and the back of the ambulance.

"ETA five to ten minutes. How do you copy?"

When Tom steered the ambulance into the driveway about eight minutes later, Dana drew a long breath. She held it and held it until she was satisfied there'd be no gunshots.

Evan Harvey, a resident, was on duty at the trauma center, and Dana found him hanging around the intake desk. A nice break. Evan was always good for a little harmless flirting, and it would send Tom a message. Dana leaned over the desk and gave Evan a peck on the cheek. Tom turned away and walked toward the cafeteria. *Perfect.*

"Nice to see you, too, Dana," Evan said. His dark eyes danced over her, and Dana felt a surge of possibility for young love ripple through her. "How's your dad's hand?"

Dana startled, her stomach flipping over, as if she'd inhaled some shwag. But it had been a while since she'd smoked at all. It came to her in a few seconds that Evan wasn't referring to her missing father but to her injured father of a few days ago.

"Oh, his hand's fine. I guess he doesn't handle kitchen knives often enough, especially in a strange kitchen." She hoped her father's hand, and the rest of him, really was fine, wherever he was.

"He said he'd been cutting down some bushes," Evan said, sweeping the air with a karate chop.

"Nuh-uh, he was making an hors d'oeuvres tray at his fiancée's house, for her East Coast guests. Maybe that didn't sound macho enough."

Evan laughed—a very pleasant sound, unlike Tom's cackle. "Could be. I was just going off shift at five-ish, so maybe I wasn't paying attention."

Dana frowned. "But he hurt himself around ten in the morning. I figured he came here right away."

"Now, that I'm sure of," Evan said. "It had obviously just happened, and I don't forget people who come in bleeding right as I'm leaving."

Dana's look must have been intense, because Evan hurried to explain. "Just kidding, just kidding. I was happy I was around to take care of him. It only took a few minutes, anyway. In fact, I left right after that, so I wasn't here when Tanisha . . . you know." Evan rapped his knuckles on his forehead, ruffling unruly dark waves. "Geesh, Dana, you must think I'm some kind of jerk."

But Dana wasn't judging Evan's professional demeanor; she was thinking hard about last Friday. She'd let herself and Tanisha into Elaine's house around noon, during a lull, to drop off the fresh flowers for the guests while Elaine was at work. Dana had insisted. Elaine was always doing nice things for her. Finding her books to help her study for the MCATs; sending everything from casseroles to furniture while Dana was moving; even paying to take care of Dana's Jeep when she scraped it, so Dana wouldn't have to tell her dad.

Dana remembered seeing the beautiful hors d'oeuvres tray. She'd slapped Tanisha's hand playfully when her partner tried to steal a shrimp wrap.

Dana took a deep breath.

"Evan, are you sure—"

Evan had already opened the large register and turned it

toward her. He'd flipped back to last Friday evening's log-ins. Dana saw her father's name above Evan's finger and read across to the time: 4:54 P.M.

Friday's timeline ran through Dana's head. She and Tanisha had arrived here at the trauma center, where Tanisha was shot, about 6:15. So her father had been here an hour before. She ran the timeline farther back. The call had come to pick up Patel at 5:45. Say it had taken Golden State Hospital about forty-five minutes to bandage him up and make the call. That meant Patel and her father were both wounded around five o'clock.

So what?

Dana shook her head and blew out a loud breath.

"Are you okay, Dana? Why is this so important?"

"Thanks, Evan. I'm fine."

Evan took her hand and squeezed it. He gave her a smile that would have knocked her out in different circumstances. "Let's have coffee sometime, huh?"

"Yeah, sure."

Dana turned toward the door. Cute as Evan was, her flirting mood had passed. She needed some air. She couldn't figure why her dad would lie about when and how he'd slashed his hand. Or why he wouldn't have said something about being at the trauma center right before Tanisha's murder.

And now he was missing. Surely he couldn't be involved in Tanisha's death, or Patel's.

In the next minute, Tom came out to her. "Hey, couldn't find you. They're already finished with Señora Santiago. That's a surprise."

At this point, nothing would surprise Dana.

CHAPTER NINETEEN

According to his secretary, the message that interrupted Phil's presentation sent him to another meeting "in an hour." That would put the urgent meeting at about three o'clock on Monday afternoon. But where was the rendezvous? And with whom?

We bent over the local map spread on Elaine's farmer's-style kitchen table, like treasure hunters looking for a chest of gold, or human genome researchers seeking clues to genetic markers.

What would be a likely spot? we asked. I put the stylus of a compass—neither Elaine nor Matt was surprised that I'd have one with me—on Dorman Industries. I was ready to swing it around in a circle of radius one hour.

"Do you think we can assume it would take an hour for Phil to get there?" Elaine asked. "Or that the other man needed an hour? Or each needed half an hour?" She threw up her hands. "This is too much like the word problems I always hated in freshman algebra. 'If it takes three men four days to chop down six trees . . .'"

"Then those men aren't working very hard," Matt said.

Elaine laughed, but just barely. "It's hopeless," she said, and I saw the same look in her eyes.

We abandoned the map project and put together a list of questions that would have simple answers. If only we had the legal right, or the nerve, to ask them.

"We could just ask Robin what she was doing with one of Lokesh Patel's IDs," Dana said. "And why she changed my incident report to Valley Med before she printed it."

We turned to Matt, the only one with any authority or training to evaluate the situation. I knew he was skittish about investigating in any formal way. He'd want to put together a reasonable presentation for Russell.

Matt's look said it wasn't good news. "Russell's already claimed no interest in Robin," he said. "First, Dana gave the uniforms at the scene a stack of IDs with Patel's photo and different names. One of them might have been accidentally—or deliberately, for all he knows—held back. The card could have fallen from Dana's pocket onto Robin's closet floor. They are roommates, after all."

Strike one.

"Same with number two. We have only Dana's word that Robin changed the report. Dana was clearly stressed and could have marked it incorrectly or, in a fit of honesty, marked it correctly—indicating that drugs *had* been involved in the incident."

Elaine bristled. "Are you saying—"

Matt held up his hand. "I'm only saying what the Berkeley police have said and might well be investigating. Let's say Dana files a formal complaint against Robin, accusing her of fraud with respect to the report. So we have to ask, what will we gain by doing that, or by approaching Robin without real proof that she had something to do with the deaths?"

"What about confronting Julia with the fake invoices?" I asked, bracing for a third strike.

"Same thing, really," Matt said. "There are any number of explanations for those sheets of paper. Besides, they're obviously copies. We have nothing to take to Julia or the Berkeley PD at the moment. They're never going to issue a search warrant on what we have. We'd essentially have to catch her in the act. Whatever that might be." He gave an apologetic shrug, the bearer of bad news.

"So, we have all this evidence, and all these crimes, but not enough of anything, no way to connect them," I said, mostly to myself.

"Then there's my dad," Dana said in a weak voice. I figured it cost her a lot to throw her father into the mix of suspicious characters. "He knew about Patel's briefcase. He *had* the briefcase. And he lied about his hand."

"His hand?" Elaine asked, her voice exasperated, as if this were the last straw. She couldn't even count on her fiancé to have a legitimately slashed hand.

Dana briefed us on a conversation she'd had with an intern at the trauma center.

"Didn't you actually see Phil cut himself while working on the shrimp?" I asked Elaine. "You mentioned all the blood—I assumed you were there and drove him to the ER."

Elaine looked sheepish. "No, no. I was at work when it . . . something . . . happened. I just repeated what Phil told me."

I understood. Elaine seemed to have adopted the same storytelling technique Rose had always used. Even when Rose related an event from the days of the nineteenth century about one of the more famous Revere natives, Horatio Alger, she spoke as if she'd been present at his speeches. I'd always thought she'd have made an excellent history teacher. More recently, her description of the blown-up hearse had all the elements and drama of an eyewitness report.

"So, Phil told you he slashed his hand here, in the morning." I turned from Elaine to Dana. "But the intern told *you* he arrived, bleeding, at the trauma center, just before five o'clock?"

Dana and Elaine nodded. "I believe Evan," Dana said. "He showed me the log." She turned away from us, as if embarrassed for her father's lie.

"Okay," Matt said. "We can certainly ask Phil to explain some of this, if . . ."

If we can find him hung in the air.

I wondered if there was a sport that allowed four strikes.

When the phone call came from Rose, we were at an impasse. That might have been the reason I didn't hesitate to take the call when her number appeared in my cell phone display. It had taken us a moment to determine whose cell phone was ringing, since four of them were on the table, at different angles and positions, like a cross-sectional snapshot of the positions of particles in a plasma.

"Hi, Gloria. Mail call!" Not only was Rose's voice cheery, it was innocent. I'd told her nothing of the crime wave sweeping through our little corner of the Bay Area.

"Anything interesting?" I asked. Maybe Matt and I had miraculously won the Massachusetts lottery. Doubly miraculous, because we never played the games, and also, I doubted the winners were notified by mail.

"An interesting package came," Rose said. "Besides the usual, like a note from your cousin Mary Ann. Doesn't she know you're away?"

"I told her. She forgets."

Mary Ann was old-school in many ways, besides her age. She lived in Worcester, only about forty-five miles from Revere— many Californians commuted that far to work every day—but she still wrote me weekly letters rather than call. When I phoned her, she'd end the call within three minutes.

"Before they cut us off," she'd say. I often wondered if she contacted the operator every time to put the call through for her, as in the old days. *Number, please,* I remembered hearing on our old party line. I couldn't imagine Mary Ann adjusting to my new cell phone, with directions for making a call on page twenty-four of the instruction manual.

"What about the package, Rose?" I asked.

"It has an Oakland postmark. I can't read the date, but I thought you might like to know about it. Maybe someone sent you a present and you should thank them while you're there."

Rose's impeccable logic. I imagined her on her white wicker porch, where her own mail was deposited every day by the same man who'd brought it for decades.

"Is there a return address?"

"None. It's just your name, not Matt's, and it's handwritten. Also, your name is spelled wrong. They have it "Lamerina." An *a* instead of an *o* on the end. It's one of those brown padded envelopes. I thought it might be a videotape, but it's bigger than that. And it's flatter than an audiotape but thicker than a compact disc."

I wished I could put Rose on speakerphone. It didn't seem fair that my companions in Elaine's kitchen were not privy to a comedy routine that could bring smiles to their pensive, straight faces. Or maybe, except for Matt, they wouldn't realize how amusing it was to hear my near-Luddite friend use electronic devices as measuring criteria, rather than her bread box, knitting needles, and garden tools.

"Rose, please open the package."

While Rose undid whatever held the package together, I covered the mike and briefed Matt, Elaine, and Dana on the call, mostly to explain my recess from the work at hand, and noted relatively uninterested nods all around.

"Oh, it's one of those new memo things." Rose sounded disappointed, as if she might have been hoping for a film with mature language and content. "Robert and John have them, and now even William wants one. Have you seen the new cell phone holders, by the way, Gloria? Some of them are obscene. William's friend—a girl, but let's not go there—has one that's a miniature black leather thong, the underwear kind, with rhinestones. William wants one for his birthday. I don't think so!"

"If it weren't for you, Rose, I'd be so out of touch with pop culture. But tell me, is there a tape recorder in the package, after all?"

"No, it's one of those devices that looks like a mini-mini laptop computer and you don't even use a pencil."

"A PDA?" Someone from Oakland sent me a personal digital assistant? Though I was generally on the other end of the scale from Luddism, I'd resisted the technology that squeezed an appointment calendar, address book, e-mail, music, and games into the palm of my hand. I thought my life was not that busy and my eyesight not good enough to read a three-inch-square screen comfortably.

I heard a faint snapping of Rose's fingers. Or maybe I imagined it, from knowing her so well. "A PDA. Right."

"Is there any note of explanation? An invoice or a packing slip?"

I covered the phone and addressed Matt, sitting next to me. "Did you by any chance order a PDA?"

Matt frowned and shook his head, as I expected. I knew it was unlikely.

I was about to tell Rose to set the PDA aside and I'd deal with it when I got home. Then it came to me.

"Rose, can you turn it on for me and see whose it is?"

"You're kidding."

"You're smarter than it is, Rose. I'm sure there's a power button in an obvious place."

I heard her sigh. "A power button? Okay. I'm pushing this red button at the top right. Oops!" I envisioned Rose jumping back as the screen came to life in her hand. "It worked. The screen says "This device is owned by,' then there's a space. Hmmm."

I tapped on the table. "Rose!"

"Gloria, it's not often I have the upper hand, you know."

She was right. Also, I reminded myself that Rose had no idea what we'd been going through since Friday evening. For all she knew, we'd been wining and dining at the tourist sites of San Francisco and overdosing on wedding talk, all of which Rose would enjoy immensely.

"I don't mean to be impatient, Rose. It's an important piece of"—I looked at Elaine and Dana, both with heavy expressions—"a business matter for Elaine's fiancé."

"Oh, okay. The owner's a Lokesh Patel. Must be Indian. I think half our Indian clients are named Patel, and Frank has to be careful to put the red dot . . . sorry, this time I wasn't trying to tease you."

I gasped at the sound of Patel's name, the first time Rose said it. Elaine placed a cup of coffee in front of me. She held out a plate of biscotti and raised her eyebrows. *Want one?*

I shook my head. I was reeling from the information from Rose, and from the idea that Patel's PDA had been mailed to me. By whom and why had yet to be processed.

"Lokesh Patel," I said out loud. Elaine pushed her chair back from the table; Matt and Dana leaned in.

"The address is . . . are you ready?" Rose asked.

I pulled the pad of paper I'd been doodling on closer to me and picked up my pen. "Very ready."

"127 Woodland Road, Berkeley, then there's a telephone number—510-555-9712."

"Anything else?" I asked Rose, as if I hadn't heard enough.

"There's a note on the bottom of the screen. It says, 'If found, please contact me.'"

Too late, I thought.

"Something's going on there, Gloria, isn't it?"

"You might say that."

"You're not just rehearsing your walk down the Rose Garden aisle in pretty shoes."

"No, we're not."

A pause, while Rose plotted, I was sure. "Robert is good with these things. If I get him to dig out whatever's in here, do you promise to tell me why it's so important?"

"I do," I said, as if I were a bride.

"Why would Patel send his PDA to you?" Elaine asked. "You didn't know him, did you?"

I put my hand to my chest. "Not at all." I felt an unwarranted defensiveness, as if Elaine were accusing me of withholding a connection that might help exonerate Phil.

I'd determined from Rose that although Lamerino was spelled incorrectly (what else was new?) my Fernwood Avenue address was correct; there was no mention of Matt; and the envelope had no other distinguishing features, such as scent or unusual markings.

"Someone who knew we were away must have sent it to our address for safekeeping, so to speak, figuring it wouldn't be opened for a couple of weeks." Matt smiled. "They weren't counting on Rose."

No one expressed the obvious out loud: All the West Coast people who knew I'd be in California for two weeks were now in Elaine's bright kitchen. Except Phil Chambers.

I looked at the clock above the sink. About four o'clock in the east. Robert wouldn't be available for PDA hacking for a couple of hours.

Might as well have biscotti.

The next call interrupted me in the nick of time. I'd been about to express the theory I'd held for a while: that Phil, Robin, and Patel were involved in industrial espionage, at least, if not treason. I'd concocted scenes where two of them pass by each other in front of the Indian fabric store on University Avenue, and one slips a computer disk into the pocket of the other.

I envisioned Phil taking Patel's PDA when he killed him—I knew I needed a motive here—and mailing it to me, to get it out of town. It didn't make sense, but I couldn't come up with anything else. I tried to think whether I'd ever heard Phil pronounce my name. Did he say Lamerina? I tried to remember, but I realized that if I condemned everyone who mispronounced or misspelled my name, there wouldn't be enough striped fabric in the world to make their prison uniforms.

I wished Matt and I were alone. I wanted to ask him, among other things, what the chances were that Phil would send damaging evidence—if it was damaging, another *if*—through the mail, where it would ultimately be discovered, rather than toss it into San Francisco Bay, or off the cliffs of Grizzly Peak, or into Tilden Park, very near his Kensington home?

As for Julia's scams, I'd come up with a plausible scenario where Phil framed Julia, generating the false invoices himself, in order to deflect suspicion from his spy ring. *Whew, quite an exercise,* I thought.

Lucky for me, I hadn't yet had time to polish the theory for public scrutiny before the phone rang.

"It's for you, Matt," Elaine said. "Inspector Russell."

Matt took the phone and walked to the small hallway off the kitchen, keeping his back to us. *Not fair.* We all strained to hear at least his side of the conversation.

"Uh-huh."

Pause. A long breath. "Is that right?"

Pause. "Sure, sure. Understood."

Pause. "How soon?"

"Appreciated."

I knew before Matt told us, and looked across the table at Dana and Elaine, both of whom wore heavy expressions.

"They found traces of coke in the briefcase."

"What?" Elaine's voice had reached a pitch higher than I'd

ever heard from her. "We looked. We didn't find any drugs."

"We don't have trained dogs," Dana said. Her voice was a match for Elaine's, high and tight.

"They want us to go down to the station for questioning."

"Us?" Dana asked. "You mean me."

"Look, if it were really bad news, they wouldn't call Matt. They'd come and get you," I said. The last part came off stronger than I meant. I looked to Matt for confirmation and was relieved to see his nod.

"I'm sure they just want to ask some questions." He paused. "Dana, they're going to ask you straight out, do you use? Did Tanisha use? That kind of thing. They're fishing at this point."

Dana put her head on the table, landing on the map a little south of where we were sitting, and folded her arms over her head. I had the feeling she had a secret that was on the brink of discovery.

"Do they want me now?" she asked in a tiny voice.

"Sometime in the next couple of hours," Matt said.

"So, not immediately," Elaine said. "That's a good sign."

"A very good sign," I said. The lawman's partner.

"It was never more than pot," Dana said. "I have no idea where that coke came from. I know they think Tanisha was stealing those medical supplies to feed her habit, but that's crap, too. And now, why do they think I had something to do with it?"

"The briefcase was in your custody," Matt said.

And Phil's, I thought, but not out loud.

I was surprised to hear marijuana still called "pot" and wondered if it was a Berkeley thing. After all, you could still buy hand-dipped tie-dyed T-shirts on Telegraph Avenue. And I'd heard about a new campus hot spot called the Mario Savio Café, after the young man credited with starting the Free Speech Movement in the sixties.

For me, I'd hidden in the basement of the physics building during those turbulent times, playing it safe under a white lab coat.

"How much?" Matt asked. "Daily, weekly, what?"

Dana blew out a breath. She'd finally raised her head and moved her folded arms down to chest level.

"It's probably better to practice here, with us," Elaine said.

Dana nodded and looked at me, though it was Elaine who'd spoken. I was sure she wasn't happy talking about her illegal habits in front of her future stepmother.

"We never got into the hard stuff. No E, no crack, none of that junk. All the EMTs use weed now and then. Well, all the ones I hang with. It's a very stressful job."

"What color is it?" Elaine asked. "Just out of curiosity."

I stifled a laugh, but Dana answered as if she were taking a quiz. "Some is brown, some is green, kind of like *grass* grass, but never as green as *grass* grass."

"Did you smoke alone or in groups?" Matt asked, his questions being more in tune with what the Berkeley PD might ask. I expected they knew what color pot was.

I had a flashback to the days of confession with Father Matussi at St. Anthony's Church in Revere. *Did you sin alone or with others?* he'd ask, in a heavy Italian accent.

"Both," Dana said. "Sometimes when I get home, I just light up a joint, get quiet. A few guys smoke on the job, if you can believe it. Not me. And not Tanisha. Once in a while at a party we might pass around a pipe."

"Does it make you more social? Uninhibited?" I asked. It wasn't every day I had a chance to learn firsthand about the wild side. I'd heard about marijuana-laced brownies, which was the only way I'd ever try a drug, if pushed.

"Not more social, though it depends on the particular strain of weed and on the person." Dana shrugged. "It's like alcohol in a way. It affects different people differently. But mostly with weed you kind of go into your own space, almost like an anesthetic. You get introspective. If you start out depressed, it could make you more so, depending . . ."

"Let me see if I have this right. You go to a party, smoke a joint or pass a pipe around, and then retreat into your own separate relaxed or depressed states?"

Uh-oh, I thought, *I'm sounding like someone's old-school parent. Or my cousin Mary Ann.* I was relieved to see Dana smile at my borderline sermon.

"That's about it," she said.

"Where do you get this stuff?" Elaine asked.

I wasn't sure if this was still the practice quiz or whether Elaine thought she could use some herself. I had the same question about availability, however. This was Berkeley. Was there a weed section on some supermarket aisle that I avoided, like those full of pet foods or baby products?

Medicinal marijuana was legal in Massachusetts, and Matt's oncologist had offered the program to Matt to alleviate the effects of his cancer treatments. I wasn't surprised when he declined.

Matt put his hand on Dana's. "I'm sure Elaine doesn't want you to name your sources. We're just curious, is all." Matt the mediator.

"You just know someone who knows someone. It's not that we go down to the docks and meet a boatload from Colombia or anything. Once you're out of school, it's harder. The network dries up, but you'll always find a friend's friend's friend who brings it around, you know."

"Do you have any with you?" Elaine asked.

"I think it's time to go," Matt said.

Matt and Dana left for the Berkeley PD. Elaine said she needed to return some work-related phone calls and retreated to her office.

Left alone, what was I to do? It was only three-thirty in the afternoon. The heat wave had broken, and a cool, sunny day awaited me.

I tore off the sheet of paper with Patel's address and headed for 127 Woodland Road.

CHAPTER TWENTY 39 88.90585

Patel's neighborhood was the posh district off Claremont Avenue in Berkeley. No ordinary Plexiglas bus stop shelter in this affluent locale; here the shelter looked like a tiny villa, built of stone and wood in an attractive design. Enormous stone pillars with large lanterns on top of them led into an area of winding streets and cul-de-sacs.

Even with Elaine's worn, but correctly folded, Berkeley map on the seat beside me, I had to make a number of U-turns in my search for Woodland Road. Either there were several tennis courts sprinkled through the region or I passed the same one many times.

One of the false streets I started down had a huge eucalyptus in the middle. The trunks of two trees were twisted together like Watson and Crick's double helix, rising from the middle of the road, spitting it into two narrow lanes just big enough for one car in each direction.

I drove down the right-hand lane, dense with tall trees—eucalyptus and willows were the only ones I could identify—on both sides. The branches of the trees seemed to reach across the road to meet those on the other side, high up in the air, forming a lovely but eerie arch that stretched the equivalent of a long city block. In this area of Claremont, you could hardly tell it was a sunny day.

Fine with me.

"My car is your car," Elaine had said when she disappeared for her phone calls, but I doubted she had this trip in mind for her Saab and me.

The houses were magnificent, each a different style, but all architecturally complex and interesting. Long sets of multilevel stairs led up and around the backs of the homes. The landscaping reminded me of the Rose Garden in miniature, with rustic terraced designs and colorful blooms.

I finally arrived at Woodland Road, another densely wooded street. I slowed down to check the addresses, discreetly lettered on homes and mailboxes. I knew better than to expect a linear array of numerals when it came to assigning numbers to residences in Berkeley, where a single street could end at one intersection and then pick up half a block away at another intersection with the same name but a new numbering sequence.

Woodland was a short street ending in a wide cul-de-sac that served as a turnaround. I came to the end and breathed a sigh of relief; there was no house with the number Rose had given me as Patel's address. It dawned on me that I'd been hoping the address was bogus, since I had no plan for the reality of finding (and entering?) Patel's home. In fact, it was stupid coming here alone, I reminded myself. What had I been thinking? If Matt knew, he'd be irritated beyond argument.

I bore left, around the circular part of the road, heading home. An enormous house faced me as I passed the eleven o'clock position in my counterclockwise drive. Flat gray and orange stone, as many of the houses were, this home was set closer to the road than most, but its trees hid most of the facade. The address was spelled out in blue and white tiles, probably imported from Holland, over an elaborate wood-and-glass door.

127 WOODLAND ROAD.

My stomach clutched.

Not that I couldn't simply keep Elaine's car in drive and continue on.

The whole of Woodland Road was quiet, and even more so around the house isolated at the end. I cocked my head to get a closer look at the large stone structure. Like the other houses in this neighborhood, it seemed to belong in another country and time, with its dark, majestic lines and overwhelming greenery. I imagined servants' quarters in the basement. A stark contrast to the bright new developments growing up these days, where the trend was pastel stucco landscapes with only the hint of trees to come.

There was no sign of life inside or outside the home, no open windows, no mothers with strollers or minivans, no gardener's truck on the street. The newspaper reports of Patel's death hadn't mentioned a family, and I felt certain we would have known by now, from the media or from Verna Cefalu, Patel's Dorman Industries secretary, if there had been a widow or children.

The Saab was in park. My palms were sweaty, my fingers alternately slipping and tapping on the shiny wooden knob of the gearshift. I needed to make a decision. Go shopping and surprise Elaine with a little gift from a bath shoppe? Take in a movie at the nearby Elmwood Theater? Get some exercise on a long walk through the winding campus roads? Just because I'd found the address didn't mean I had to do anything about it.

In fact, this might not even be where Patel lived. Rose could have read the address incorrectly. PDA screens were hard to read, and her eyes weren't what they used to be. Or Patel might have entered a false address. He was a spy, wasn't he?

I reasoned carefully. If this was *not* Patel's house, and I went in, it would be a serious B&E perpetrated on some innocent people. If this *was* Patel's house, the police had surely been here, and there would be nothing for me to discover.

Either way, it was a bad idea to enter.

But what's one more bad idea in a career full of them? I asked myself.

I moved the car about twenty yards farther around the circle and partly onto the gravel that served as a sidewalk, until tree branches brushed the windshield. I was grateful I wasn't driving my own car, a Cadillac handed down from the Galigani Mortuary fleet and much too difficult to maneuver on these roads or to hide under a tree.

I turned off the ignition, got out of the virtually hidden car, and walked toward 127 Woodland Road.

Once I realized how absurd it was to try to break into the house, it seemed quite reasonable to just look around outside. *I'm thinking of relocating to this area and I thought I saw a* FOR SALE *sign on this house,* I could tell a suspicious neighbor. Or the police. I put thoughts of my cop fiancé out of my mind.

I wished I'd seen more contemporary movies—I was sure there was a standard way to do this. I began by slipping into the side yard through the unlocked garden gate. The heavy, old wooden door was splintery, reminding me I should have gloves, for more reasons than one.

I stepped onto the loose gravel path that surrounded the house and faced the side wall, glad I'd changed into indestructible black oxfords. I kept my body close to the building, my shoulder brushing the cool stone. I moved along the wall slowly.

The first window I came to was almost as large as a typical patio door, but raised a couple of feet from the ground. I peered in through gauzy curtains at an elaborate living room suite with a maroon velvety look that reminded me of the Galigani Mortuary parlors. The objets d'art seemed perfectly placed. Godlike statues on small tables, vases in all sizes on the floor and mantel, paintings hung in complementary groups of three. Everything said *professional interior decorator*—no ordinary Pottery Barn shoppers had furnished this home.

A breeze ruffled the trees behind me, making a low, whispery sound, almost hissing, as if to warn me. If the noise had been a word, it would have been *tresssspassing.*

I traveled more quickly to the other side of the window, still conscious of the crunching gravel, scanning the room as I moved. There were no photos or personal items that I could see; no books other than a matched set in the built-in bookshelves. Too far away for me to make out the titles. The Harvard Classics, or the works of Shakespeare, I guessed. Or the Indian equivalent.

Maybe Patel had a family still in India. My grad school classes in the sixties had been filled with men whose families had stayed behind in other countries. Wives who'd been given in arranged marriages waited in China, Taiwan, Thailand, India, for their husbands to return. One Korean student I'd gotten to know hadn't seen his children in more than two years. The plan was that Ha-Neul would earn his degree and then go home to make a good life for them. I wondered if that cultural pattern had survived into the new century.

Reminiscing, philosophizing. Sure signs that I'd found nothing of interest in the present moment.

I decided to give the grounds in the back a quick sweep and then leave. The area behind the house stretched to about twenty yards, not large by mansion standards. It was nicely landscaped with bushes and flowers of modest proportions. It was also empty—no toys, bikes, swings, outdoor furniture, barbecue grill. There was no sign that anyone lived here recently.

I turned to make my getaway, calling myself lucky I hadn't gotten arrested, and spotted two medium-sized garbage containers.

No, I told myself.

But I lost the argument.

I stayed close to the walls of the house and approached the small, raised wooden pallet that held the cans. I lifted the top of the first one and peered in.

Empty.

On to the second one.

Not empty; in fact, quite full.

I stepped back and slammed the lid shut, as if the contents might attack me. I thought back. Patel died almost a week ago, on a Friday. There must have been a garbage pickup since then. Both barrels should be empty. The only way this one could be full was if pickup was last Friday, the morning of the day Patel died, and he'd managed to fill it up again in the hours before he was shot.

At the top of the refuse container was a thin white box. The unmistakable shape of a takeout pizza box. Was Patel's last meal a pizza?

I lifted the cover of the trash barrel and tilted the carton so I could read the top. I noticed many more takeout containers underneath. The pizza place was an independent, evidently, named Giulio's, on Ashby. A delivery slip, filled out in neat handwriting and marked with oil stains, was Scotch-taped to the top of the box.

128 WOODLAND RD., it read. Not Patel's address but across the road. Under special instructions: *leave outside by tree, pick up cash in mailbox.*

The handwriting was clear cursive, like Palmer Method, except the is were dotted with small circles. I envisioned the writer as a sixteen-year-old girl with a tiny waist, earning money for her cheerleading outfit. Unfortunately, my imaginary minimum-wage employee wasn't as careful with the date. In that section, she'd written only *Wednesday*. Probably only days of the week mattered at that age, I figured. Work Wednesdays, study Thursdays, party on Fridays and Saturdays. Since there were no mortgage payments or pension checks to keep track of, the month and date weren't relevant.

No matter. Either someone had eaten pizza in Patel's house last night or the folks at number 128 dumped their garbage here. I could look for that address on my way out. But in my single-mindedness, I discounted that possibility and others quickly. That the police had been snacking on the job, for example. Or teenagers partying in the neighborhood. Or that an empty box in a garbage can meant nothing in the first place.

Above the garbage pallet was a small window. The frosted glass said *bathroom*. It was transom-shaped and slightly open. Before I could talk myself out of it, I tipped the empty can over and, with great effort, lifted myself up and stood on it. There was no chance any human other than a toddler could slip through the opening, but I got a good look around the side of the metal frame, through the triangular gap. I felt I'd sunk to a new low, peeping through a man's bathroom window. Fortunately, the shower curtain was open and the tub unoccupied.

I saw a razor, shaving cream, and a small bottle of aftershave on the counter around the sink. The fixtures seemed old, either original equipment or new faucets designed to appear old. I'd come to accept the Restoration Hardware look, though I couldn't understand it. I knew I'd never own a telephone that had a 1940s look on the outside and the latest digital technology on the inside.

The door to the rest of the house was closed. A distinctive citrus smell wafted through the opening.

Nothing unusual—except the toiletry items were spread out on the counter in front of a black carrying case. And the toothbrush lay half inside a long blue holder, probably plastic.

Question: Why would a man groom himself out of a travel kit in his own home?

Answer: It's not his own home.

Click.

The noise startled me. To me, in my edgy state, it rang out in the silence, sounding like an entire lab cabinet of beakers crashing to the floor. Someone was entering the bathroom. I ducked down and lost my balance, falling onto the ground, making another noise that thundered through the quiet Claremont afternoon.

I got up as quickly as I could and limped out of the yard. To minimize the sound of my footsteps, I moved out from the house onto the grass, aware that I could be seen more easily.

A cat. A raccoon. A squirrel. I gave these words emphasis in my thoughts, as if to put them into the mind of the resident of 127 Woodland Road. *Let him think an animal tipped over his garbage can,* I pleaded to no one in particular. My only saving thought was that no adult could fit through the bathroom window opening to pursue me. I wondered how long it might take for a person to run through the house and meet me as I crossed in front of the entryway. My heart pounded in my ears as I slipped through the garden gate and out to the gravel sidewalk.

I dug for the car remote as I ran painfully to the Saab. I got into the car and drove away. I didn't look back except mentally, to berate myself. One more second and I would have seen the current occupant of Patel's house. Also, one more second and the occupant might have seen me. It was a trade-off, and I'd played it safe. For once.

I didn't relax my shoulders until I reached the Claremont-Ashby intersection and saw nothing that looked like a car in pursuit behind me. Then I remembered the odor from the bathroom window. It came to me. It was aftershave. Citrus aftershave. The last time I'd smelled it was in a bagel shop on Monday afternoon.

I'd found Phil Chambers.

I drove to the Berkeley marina, at the end of University Avenue, wanting to put as much distance as possible between me and the open bathroom window on Woodland Road. Though I would have appreciated a walk on the long public fishing pier stretched out before me into San Francisco Bay, I sat in the Saab, in case a quick getaway was in order.

Also, my ankle hurt badly. Not enough that I thought it was broken; just a sprain, I hoped. I removed my shoe, rubbed the sore spots, and took two aspirin. That would have to do for medical attention.

It seemed clear that Phil had been hiding out in Patel's Claremont home. I hadn't allowed myself the leisure of checking to see if there was a number 128 Woodland Road, but I felt sure Phil's fingerprints were on that pizza box. I pictured him at an upper window, watching for the delivery truck, then sneaking across the street, probably at two o'clock in the circle, to pick up his dinner.

Why he was there, I could only guess. At the top of my list was fugitive Phil, guilty of two murders, hiding from the police. That thought made me want to climb into one of the lovely boats berthed in the water to my right and sail away before I had to face Elaine with what I suspected. I tried to declare Phil not guilty, on the basis that a double murderer would flee farther than a few miles from his own home. Still, innocent people didn't go into hiding at all. And the home of a dead man was as good a place as any to lie low, especially since Patel apparently had no family, and the police were not likely to return.

I tapped my steering wheel, deciding on my next step. Matt was unavailable, unless I wanted to call his cell phone and interrupt his meeting with Dana and Russell at the Berkeley PD. Also, I wanted more evidence. More accurately, *some* evidence that Phil was at Patel's. If I'd thought to grab the pizza box, I might have been able to persuade Russell to dust for fingerprints. As a government employee at BUL, Phil's prints would be on file. So would mine, I realized, a match for those on the gate and the garbage cans of 127 Woodland Road.

I had one other idea.

I picked up my phone, hit 411 for information, and then punched in the number I was given.

"Giulio's," said an upbeat, young, female voice.

I smiled; I'd been right about the cheerleader. "Oh, hi. Are you the one who's nice enough to arrange for my husband's pizza to be left outside the door?"

"Um. Yeah, is this Mrs. Boyle?"

Ha. Boyle's Law, a key topic in every freshman chemistry class. I had to give Phil points for keeping his sense of humor in a crisis. He'd taken the name of a seventeenth-century chemist credited with formulating the relationship between the pressure and volume of a gas.

I almost hung up then, having assured myself the Boyle connection was no coincidence, but Courtney, or Ashley, or whoever was on the other end of the line seemed too sweet to leave hanging.

"Yes, this is Mrs. Boyle. Thanks for being so accommodating," I said.

"Hey, no prob. Your husband says he doesn't want the doorbell to wake the kids."

"He's a doll," I said. "And by the way, could you please put anchovies on the next order? He always forgets to ask."

CHAPTER TWENTY-ONE

When my cell phone rang, it woke me from a fantasy world where I tell the police where to find Phil Chambers; they arrest him for the murder of Lokesh Patel (co-spy, who wanted to turn Phil in for revealing secrets of a new nitrogen-based weapon) and Tanisha Hall (wrong place, wrong time); and at last my best West Coast friend, Elaine Cody, thanks me for saving her from marrying a traitor to the country.

"I have some news," Matt said.

"Me, too." I leaned back and enjoyed the sounds of seagulls, carried on a rejuvenating breeze that flowed through the open windows of Elaine's car. Not quite Revere Beach, though. For crashing surf I'd have to drive to San Francisco.

"Let's meet somewhere," Matt said.

"Fine. Where's Dana?"

"They're holding her a little longer."

I gasped and sat up straight. "She's arrested?" *My fault.* I'd failed to account for Phil's daughter in my dream world, where everything works out fine.

"No. I'm pretty confident they won't arrest her." Matt sounded tired, and I felt a pang of concern that he was overstressed. "They're checking out her statement. Anyway, I'm taking her Jeep until they're ready to release her."

"Is that your news?"

"No."

"I'm at the marina, in Elaine's car."

"Is that *your* news?"

"No."

It wasn't clear why Matt and I decided not to share our biggest news cell phone to cell phone, since they were better than land-lines, as far as not being able to trace calls or set bugs. I'd brought my Galileo book and had read only a few pages before I saw Matt pull up in Dana's Jeep. He parked it a few slots away and joined me in Elaine's car.

"Want to walk on the pier?"

I pointed to my ankle. "Not today. I'm a little lame right now."

"How did that happen?"

"I just . . . tripped."

Matt clicked his tongue, willing to move on, but I knew he'd come back to it.

It couldn't have been a more beautiful setting, in spite of our agenda. It was five-thirty, still light out, but the promise of a magnificent sunset was ahead of us, with the Golden Gate Bridge and the San Francisco skyline as backdrop.

I wished we were on vacation.

"I know where Phil is," I said.

"So do I," Matt said. "You first." Our version of cop banter, the kind that Matt claimed was necessary to survive day after day of stressful, life-and-death situations.

"I saw him," I said. Meaning, I saw evidence of him. The way scientists say they see atoms.

Matt raised his eyebrows. "Oh?"

"He's hiding out at Lokesh Patel's home in the Claremont dis-trict. Remember the address was on Patel's PDA? Well, I—" *Oops.* I hadn't meant to be quite so open about my adventure in snooping. I swallowed. "He's there, is what I'm telling you."

"Am I going to be upset about how you know this?"

I gave him a special, distracting smile. *My sweetheart.* "Not too much."

"Is that how you hurt your ankle?"

"Where do you think he is?" I asked. Using Matt's own technique, answering one question with another. Not bad.

"Russell evidently took me more seriously than I thought the other day, and he did some checking on Phil. Pretty impressive, without a formal report. A Dr. Philip Chambers booked and boarded a flight to Hawaii on Monday night."

I stopped in my mental tracks. "That can't be. Are they sure?"

Matt treated it as a rhetorical question.

Elaine's cold-feet theory came to my mind: Phil got wedding jitters, clutched at the last minute, and bailed. My spy theory wasn't shot to pieces yet, however. I wondered if the mainland had extradition reciprocity with the Hawaiian Islands. Probably, since Hawaii was a state, I reminded myself. I'd been to Maui a couple of times, and to Oahu to tour Pearl Harbor, and while there I often forgot that I was still in the United States.

"What if whoever Phil works for—" I started.

"Dorman Industries."

"I mean his . . . handler," I said. "Like the KGB. What if they faked his travel?"

"The KGB is defunct."

"You know what I mean." I took a breath and formulated a plan. "I have an idea," I said.

I dug my cell phone out of my purse and hit Patel's phone number. An answering machine picked up immediately.

"You've reached 510-555-9712. Please leave a message." A nondescript utility-generated voice.

"This is a message for Robert Boyle," I said. "Please call Galileo on his cell phone. You have the number."

Matt threw up his hands. He didn't say anything, but I heard, *Amateurs!*

I knew Elaine would be wondering where I'd taken her car, though she was nice enough not to probe when I called her.

"We're picking up dinner," I told her. "And we're cooking for you."

"Thanks. I guess I haven't been a very good hostess."

"Not true, Elaine. Just have the coffee ready."

I knew Elaine would have told me immediately if she had any news of Phil. Evidently Russell had charged Matt with updating Elaine on the whereabouts of her fiancé. For me, I was getting to be a pro at withholding information from my friend. On the phone with her, I didn't tell her that I was with Matt, that Russell had allegedly tracked Phil to Hawaii, or that I thought I'd found traces of Phil at Patel's house. My evidence should also have an "allegedly" tacked on, I admitted.

I wondered which reality would be more upsetting to Elaine—that her fiancé had fled to Hawaii, or that he was on a fast-food diet in hiding a couple of miles away.

My ankle was throbbing, and the bottle of aspirin I kept in my purse was empty. I needed a painkiller and a bandage. I slipped into the downstairs bathroom, minimizing my limp, hoping to find a first aid kit. Elaine didn't fail me. There was a small white box with a red cross on the cover in the bottom drawer, and aspirin in her updated medicine cabinet. Elaine had had the downstairs bathroom remodeled; the new cabinet featured extrawide glass shelves and lit up when you opened the door, like a minirefrigerator. No rust marks on metal shelves, as in our old Fernwood Avenue cabinet.

It took about ten minutes for my self-medication and self-treatment.

Hooray for pants, I thought, happy that my trouser leg covered the bandage. All I had to do was be careful not to limp and hope Elaine wouldn't notice that her first aid kit was short about two feet of adhesive bandage. If it came to that, I was prepared with a story about walking on the pier and tripping over a bucket of bait.

I'd persuaded Matt to at least wait until we'd served a decent meal before breaking our news. Matt and I both had enough reserve weight to carry us through the summer, but I was concerned about Elaine and Dana, who looked as though they'd lost several pounds right before my eyes in less than a week.

The table was set, the eggplant parmigiana cooked and ready, and Dana was still not back. We kept it warm, hoping Dana would call soon and not be receiving takeout at the Berkeley PD. Matt played down her absence with Elaine.

"It's routine," he said. "They'll want to check out her story."

"Her story about what?" Elaine seemed to be running out of patience. I couldn't blame her.

"Dana, or someone, indicated there were drugs involved in the killing of her partner. That's number one. Second, drug paraphernalia was found on Tanisha's body—"

"Rolling papers," Elaine said, waving her hand. "I might even have some around here."

I doubted it.

"Third," Matt said, continuing as if there'd been no interruption, "stolen goods were found in her partner's residence."

"It seems like busywork to me," Elaine said.

Matt raised his eyebrows and tilted his head in what we might have construed as agreement.

Elaine had put on a CD of classical piano, a little too tinkly for me, but I was not a great fan of classical music except for Italian opera, the more tragic, the better. Either that or Perry Como. Still, the piano notes filled the tense silence as we waited for Dana to call for a pickup. During one soft interlude, Elaine leaned forward from her place on the couch.

"Is there something you're not telling me?" she asked. She lowered her head and seemed to steel herself against an unwelcome answer. She ran her hands through her hair, starting at her ears and ending with both sets of fingers at her temples.

I'd been keeping track of Elaine's emotional temperature this week. I'd watched her go from EXCITEDLY HAPPY (I envisioned such a check box on a questionnaire) over her wedding and our arrival in town to ANGRY with me for trying to vet her fiancé. Since Phil's disappearance, she'd kept a NERVOUS BUT STEADY attitude of waiting. Now I thought I was seeing another milestone, where HYSTERIA might step in at any moment.

"Keeping something from you?" I asked.

RRRing.

How lucky can you be? I thought. I grabbed my cell phone from the charger and punched it on.

"Hey, Auntie Glo." The voice of young William Galigani, Robert's son, representing the newest generation to call me aunt. "I played around with that PDA Mom gave me. Dad was kind of stuck."

"Thanks, William. I really appreciate this. I know it's past your bedtime."

"I don't have a bedtime anymore, remember? This was fun. And it got me out of taking out the trash."

Rose's usual good negotiating skills at work. "I'm glad there was some reward for you."

"I'd have done it anyway, but Grandma doesn't have to know that."

I was sure she already did. "So, did you find anything interesting?" I thought a moment later how William, a sophomore at Revere High, would have a very different "interesting" list than I did.

"I'm just starting playing around, but I can get a few things right away. There's a lot of names in an address book." *There* are *a lot of names,* I wanted to say, but William was doing me a great favor and could be allowed a minor slip in grammar. "It's running Windows, so I can download it into my computer and send that to you."

"Perfect. Let me give you the e-mail address here."

"My grandma has it." Here William laughed. It sounded like *And a lot of good it does her.* "Then there are some things in the Notes section, but they're written by hand and I can't make out most of it." William made handwriting sound like a prehistoric pastime, and in his world, it was probably rare. I pictured a laptop at every desk in his homeroom and USB ports where there used to be inkwells.

"Can you e-mail the notes, too?"

"Done. I'll keep at it, okay, and I'll call if I find anything else. I might have to charge it, but it's okay because me and my friend figured out where to get the right cradle."

"You're terrific, William." *My friend and I,* I said to myself. "Anything I can bring you from California?"

"A Forty-Niners cap."

"What?"

"Just kidding, Aunt Glo. How about a T-shirt from the physics department at Cal?"

"Now you're talking."

I sat at Elaine's computer, which was becoming as familiar to me as my own. I scrolled through subject lines that were clearly junk mail. Shouldn't it be common knowledge in the world of e-marketing that Elaine Cody had lived in this house more than thirty years and no longer had a mortgage? And that she had no interest in discount clothing or hot teen ch*&^ks?

There was nothing yet from William Galigani.

I got up to stretch and paced the small office. Elaine's wedding dress hung on the outside, on a hook attached to the closet. If an outfit could look forlorn, this was it. The lovely cream-colored fabric hung loosely on the hanger, as if its owner had shrunk to a skeleton. The dress was what we used to call tea length, the skirt straight, the bodice sparkling with delicate crystals and pearls stitched into a design that reminded me of graph paper.

I wondered if Elaine had done anything about alerting her wedding staff that the groom was missing. She hadn't mentioned doing so, but I imagined that caterers, photographers, and other wedding vendors needed some notice of change or cancellation. Was there an emergency backup plan, such as all Californians were expected to have for earthquake readiness? I decided not to ask.

I walked to the windows for a glimpse of what was left of the glorious sunset. One window looked down on Elaine's driveway. Garages and driveways were a novelty in the crowded residential areas of Berkeley; Elaine always claimed she had one of only six decent driveways in the whole city, long enough for two cars and wide enough to allow flower beds on both sides. Her garage, on the other hand, was built for a Volkswagen bug and housed only her gardening tools, old files, and items destined for charitable donation.

Something seemed off this evening. Elaine's Saab was as far to the front as possible. I'd driven way in to make room for Matt to pull Dana's Jeep in behind me and clear the sidewalk comfortably. But where *was* Dana's Jeep? Maybe I'd been distracted and didn't notice that he parked on the street instead.

I called down the stairs. "Matt, where did you park the Jeep?"

"It's in the driveway, right behind the Saab."

Not anymore.

CHAPTER TWENTY-TWO

Dana sat in the hot, crappy interview room in one of the Berkeley PD's substations. She took in the peeling paint, the rust spots on the ceiling, and furniture that was a lot worse than in most of the homeless shelters she'd seen.

Did they purposely not have air-conditioning in police stations? Is this what they meant by sweating a confession out of a suspect? At this point she was almost ready to confess to *something,* as long as the jail cell was cool.

Nobody had told her exactly why she was sitting here, waiting. She assumed they were searching her house. *Great.* Another household was being upset. She wondered if Jen or Robin would be home. She imagined Jen, who didn't do well under stress, curled up on the overstuffed floral chair Elaine had given them. Jen would be whimpering about how she had homework to do and was going to flunk her summer class in the Age of Enlightenment if the cops upset her papers and lost her place in her textbooks. Robin, on the other hand, would probably scare the shit out of the cops.

Dana needed a shower. She needed to change her clothes. Mostly, she needed a smoke. The thought of her stash at home unnerved her. Scenes from all her favorite cop shows came to mind. In nearly every episode, suspects waited in shabby rooms while TV detectives Sipowicz and Clark, or Briscoe and Green, or Benson and Stabler, went out and searched their houses. If the Berkeley cops *were* searching her house now, how thorough would they be?

Neither Jen nor Robin knew where Dana kept her little Baggie, but the police might think they did and grill them, too. She didn't have much left of her latest bag. Would they find it, tucked under the top tray of her jewelry box? It wasn't enough to send her to jail, but a citation and a fine would not look good on her med school apps. And what if whoever changed her incident report got into her room and planted drugs, the way they'd planted the stolen supplies in Tanisha's house?

The crime of "possession" didn't seem to apply to her. The term should be reserved for somebody with kilos of coke or a truckload of crack, not for the casual user she considered herself and Tanisha to be. It was practically medicinal, she and Tanisha had decided, except that to be legal they'd have needed the approval of a doctor.

"The job make us sick," Tanisha had said, using her street grammar as she did whenever she was joking. Dana felt a great sense of loss and renewed her resolve to make things right with Tanisha's mother. She'd visit Marne as soon as she got out of this pit.

Dana couldn't believe the questions they'd asked her.

"Who's your dealer?" some guy in a tacky polyester suit had demanded, his face contorted. As if she were connected to some drug lord in East Oakland. *Save the loathing for the hardened criminals,* Dana wanted to tell him. She was totally sure her friend Sergeant Matt Gennaro wouldn't use these tactics.

"Do you have a regular pickup and drop for the drugs?" This from a young female detective, probably trying to make a good impression on her senior partner.

Truthfully, Dana didn't know how the weed got to her hands. She'd told Elaine and Gloria and Matt the truth about that. She assumed it was grown somewhere in South America and was passed through a network in every city that was near a port.

Oakland was in an ideal position for that, being an international hub for cargo transportation and distribution.

Kyle, an EMT at another ambulance company, was her current contact. Dana knew Kyle was far from the big-distributor end of things. She'd met him at a training class just in time to fill in the gap when her own college contacts had gone away. Kyle was apt to bring the weed to Dana as small branches, which she didn't like. She'd have to clean off the branches and get rid of the seeds and stalk before she could roll the grass. She kept meaning to investigate further contacts at parties and raves in the neighborhood. Now it was just as well she hadn't. They might be able to torture the information out of her.

Finally, after what seemed like a month sitting in that gray metal chair, the polyester suit came back.

"You can go," he said. The smell of garlic reeked from his pores. "Just not too far, okay?"

Dana had a lot of questions about what the cops had been doing since they left her, but she had no intention of hanging around to ask them.

She nearly flipped the chair over backward leaving the room.

At the last minute Dana decided not to call Matt to pick her up with her Jeep. She also refused the cops' offer of a ride home. Instead she called a cab.

"Pull over here," she told the cabbie when they got within a block of Elaine's house. She paid him and walked to her Jeep, thankful it was at the back end of the driveway.

She was glad she'd given Matt just her spare car key and still had her own set. She needed to take care of some business, and she didn't want to have to explain herself. First, she wanted to visit Marne and Rachel and do whatever it took to assure Marne she had nothing to do with incriminating Tanisha in anything. Tomorrow she'd confront Julia at Valley Med and find out what the fake invoices were all about and why Dana's and Tanisha's names were on them.

At the back of her brain always was her dad. She flipped between hating him for being so uncommunicative and worrying that he was dead, like Tanisha and Patel.

Dana felt bad about sneaking into Elaine's driveway, but she couldn't see any other way. She'd had enough of being around Elaine and her friends. Elaine was too depressed and, worse, trying to hide it for Dana's sake, she could tell. Gloria was entirely too reasonable about everything, and Matt . . . well, she was becoming way too dependent on Matt, who'd be gone in a week and she'd never hear from him again. Might as well break it off now. Dana had to smile at how much it felt like Matt had been her prom date and would soon be going off to college.

Lights were on in the kitchen and dining room, and she figured they were holding dinner for her. It looked so inviting, but . . . some other time, she thought. She knew if she went inside, they'd all try to talk her into resting, eating, staying overnight again, and she didn't have the energy to resist.

She rolled back into the street without headlights and pulled away as quietly as possible.

Dana had never been so happy to climb the stairs to her own house. Her plan was to go straight to the shower and then out again to Marne's house across town. On the way she'd pick up some blueberry marble ice cream, Rachel's favorite flavor.

She unlocked the door of her house and entered the foyer off the living room. She wouldn't have been surprised to see her things turned every which way, left a mess by cops with a search warrant.

What she hadn't counted on was seeing her boss, Julia Strega, one room away, in her dining room.

Julia and Robin were bent over pages strewn across the dining room table. When Dana walked in, Robin jumped, as if a firecracker had gone off. She came into the living room to greet Dana with a hug—when had that ever happened?—while Julia pushed the papers together.

"Hey," Robin said, all cheery. "How are you doing, Dana?"

"Hey," Julia said, with a guilty grin. She made a mess of the papers while trying to act casual about shoving them into a shiny gray-and-silver duffel bag.

Dana couldn't think of any business Julia and Robin would have together. As far as she knew, Robin hadn't worked at Valley Med for more than a year, certainly not since Dana had started there.

"How's it going, Dana?" Julia asked, as if she hadn't seen her in years, instead of at work that very morning. Then, "I'm just about to leave," she said, without waiting for Dana's answer.

Here was Dana's chance to face both Julia and Robin with her questions: Robin, where did you get those new clothes (okay, not that important), and why was Patel's ID in your closet (very important), and why did you change my incident report (most important)? Julia, what's up with those phony invoices and listing me as a driver on calls to fake facilities?

Matt was a cop; he had to worry about breaking rules of interrogation or whatever, but Dana could just ask anything she wanted.

Julia had already swung the duffel bag over her shoulder and brushed past Dana, heading for the door. Dana needed to act fast. But another image came to her—Tanisha swinging the duffel bag that belonged to Patel. The same bag? Dana shook her head. There must be millions of duffel bags in Oakland, and half of them gray, but what a coincidence that this one, with its distinctive wide white zipper, looked exactly like the bag Tanisha had been carrying when she was shot, the one with Patel's tennis balls.

Dana swallowed hard and pushed away the image of her partner sprawled on the trauma center driveway.

The whole scene in her house was very curious. And starting to get very scary. Julia kept going toward the front door. Dana heard her clump away in her clogs, down the outside steps. Robin faced Dana, her look threatening, as if to say, *Go ahead and say something.*

Dana went to her room and sat on her bed. She wanted to curl up under the chenille throw, but she knew she was too edgy to relax. Maybe it wouldn't be a bad idea to stay close to Matt for a while.

She listened for movement in the rooms outside and heard none.

She wished she had a lock on her door.

Dana showered quickly and left her house, slipping out her bedroom door, around to the foyer, and out. She didn't know whether Robin was still home until she noticed her old blue Ford a half block down on their street. She'd wanted to pack some things and camp out at Elaine's but decided to come back later with reinforcements, like a certain Massachusetts cop. Amazingly, she'd remembered to check her jewelry box for the stash. It was gone.

She pictured some uniform taking a toke at her expense.

Dana pulled the Jeep up in front of Marne's house at about eight-thirty. She knew Marne was a late-night person and hoped she might be more mellow the later it got.

Up a flight of stairs from the street, ringing Marne's doorbell, Dana didn't feel any braver than she had when she'd seen Julia and Robin together. She couldn't figure why the scene had freaked her out so much, except it was one more creepy thing among too many lately. Maybe Robin was applying to return to Valley Med, but she hadn't mentioned it, and Dana hadn't been aware that the two women had even kept in touch.

Dana couldn't believe what a coward she'd been, not only

abandoning her legitimate questions but cutting and running—a gutless wonder. And she was feeling more spineless by the minute on Marne's front porch. She hoped Marne wouldn't yell at her; she didn't think she could handle it again.

No answer on the first ring. Dana thought she heard footsteps on the other side of the door and figured Marne saw her through the peephole. She pictured her friend's mother scowling, hands on her narrow hips, as she was at Hutton's Funeral Home.

She nearly cut and ran again, but instead she gave the bell a firmer push.

"Come on, Marne," Dana said. "I just want to talk to you for a sec." Her plea had been loud enough to penetrate the door, she hoped.

Maybe too loud. On the street below, several kids in baggy pants and sweatshirts stopped under the streetlight and looked up at her. Marne's neighborhood—she used to think of it as *Tanisha's* neighborhood—was an array of small, neat houses and mostly well kept front yards. The kids hooted and whistled. Though their gestures and taunts were obscene, Dana took them as harmless. Maybe this was the most interesting drama going on in their young lives. A white girl begging to be let into their neighbor's house. In any case, they were certainly less scary than Robin had been earlier, in Dana's own living room.

She rang a third time.

"Please, Marne. I have blueberry marble." She glanced down at the kids, who'd already moved on.

The door opened, and Marne's smile lit up the night. "Careful what you say, Miss Dana. People around here get mugged for less than a quart of ice cream."

Dana nearly fell over the doorstep into Marne's arms. Marne patted her back, as if Dana were the one who'd lost her only child.

"You're not . . . mad?" Dana asked when she caught her breath. "I thought you weren't going to open up."

"I was in the back, putting Rachel down, but I'm thinking I'll get her up for the treat." She took the bag from Dana. "And, oh, I *was* angry." Marne led Dana into the house. "Truly angry. But now I believe you'd never do anything like that. I should have known."

"How—"

"That cop came by," Marne said. "The one with the Down East accent."

Dana felt her shoulders relax. At least there were some things she could still count on.

Rachel sat on Dana's lap and ate her blueberry marble ice cream, careful to keep spills away from her soft purple nightshirt.

"Are we friends again?" the little girl asked. Her deep brown eyes seemed to be pleading for more picnics and trips to the planetarium.

Dana kissed the top of Rachel's head. She breathed in a sweet lavender scent. Evidently baby shampoo products had branched out from the smells Dana remembered as a child.

"Of course we're friends," Dana said, relieved Rachel wasn't interested in what had caused the nasty interlude at the funeral parlor.

"Tell me the airport story," Rachel said. She put her bowl and spoon carefully on the table and turned sideways so she could see Dana's face.

Dana swallowed hard and tried to psych herself up for Rachel's favorite ambulance tale.

"It was a spooky, rainy night," Dana began, her voice low and scary.

"And what happened?" Rachel asked.

"And a great big plane slipped on the wet runway and banged into a truck and some people were hurt."

"So they called Mommy."

"That's right. And Mommy got in the ambulance and put on the sirens." Dana made high-pitched noises, and Rachel joined her. "And the lights." Dana fluttered her fingers in a flashing motion, tickling Rachel. "And Mommy drove that ambulance down the runway as if she were flying a plane." Another elaborate flying gesture. "Vroooom!"

Rachel clapped and squealed. "And she saved everybody."

"She did," Dana said, holding back tears. She dared not look at Marne.

"Knock, knock," Rachel said, kicking her feet enthusiastically.

"Who's there?"

"Lemon."

"Lemon who?"

"Lemon me give you a kiss," Rachel said, with a wide smile and a giggle that was too close to her mother's for Dana's comfort.

Marne's house was spotless. The kitchen counters were free of clutter, the bright yellow curtains freshly laundered. Every inch of the swirl-patterned beige linoleum looked washed and waxed, unlike the floor covering Dana and her roommates had inherited. Dana knew Marne used to clean other people's houses until Tanisha had put in enough overtime to afford Marne's staying home full-time with Rachel. She imagined Marne now putting all her housekeeping skills to daily use in her own home, even though it was a rental.

Once Rachel was put to bed for the second time that evening, Marne's tears flowed. Dana didn't know whether to cry with her or to tell more knock-knock jokes.

When Marne got around to talking about the police search, her tone turned harsh.

"Pigs." Marne spat out the word. "Some of them brothers, too. They come in here and upset Rachel and her friend. Scared them half to death." Marne poured blood-red Rooibos tea into thick multicolored mugs. Her deep coral lipstick looked fresh, and Dana wondered if she'd applied it just before opening the door. "Flipping over pillows, lookin' into cereal boxes, liftin' up the cover on the toilet tank. And finally they find this laundry bag in

Tanisha's closet, full of meds, you know, all kinds of pills. I tell you, they was *planted.*"

"What made you think I sent the cops?" Dana kept her voice low, hoping soft sounds plus the tea might calm Marne. In the background she could hear a singsong bedtime tune from the tiny boom box Tanisha had bought for Rachel only a few days ago, when her raise came through.

"One of them dumb white cops . . . I ask him, 'Why you here?' 'A tip,' he says, 'from your sweet girl's partner.'"

"I swear, Marne—"

Marne waved her hand. "I know, I know. Somebody had it in for you, too, I figure. You know, they come looking for one kind of drugs, and they find meds. I watch TV, and I think that's not supposed to count. If it's not on the paper and they find it, it's rotten or something."

"Fruit of the poisonous tree," Dana said.

"That's it. If I could afford a lawyer I'd sue them. But it don't matter now. Tanisha is gone anyway."

Dana nodded, but her mind had wandered, thinking how this was something else she and Tanisha had in common—they'd both been objects of police attention lately, though Dana had no direct evidence that the cops had been to her house; she just assumed they were the ones who took her stash. She'd have to ask Matt if cops could search without informing the person, either before, during, or after executing a warrant.

She thought back to her dates with the rookie, Derek. "Your senses cannot trespass," he'd told her, as if he'd just come from passing a pop quiz with that question on it. "If you can see it, smell it, taste it, you know, the senses, then it's fair game."

So unless the Berkeley PD had smelled the little stash in her jewelry box, they had no right to take it, unless they had a search warrant.

What a lucky break that Tanisha was between stashes, she thought. But as Marne said, she was gone anyway.

Dana slipped into Tanisha's nightshirt, a long-sleeved tee with a decal of Will Smith and Tommy Lee Jones in *Men in Black,* and about three sizes too big for her. She was so grateful to Marne for letting her stay in Tanisha's old bedroom for the night, or for as many nights as Dana wanted, with no explanation. Which was good, because Dana would have had a hard time explaining why she was afraid to return to her own house. Even to herself.

She looked around the small room, one she'd been in a few times during their friendship. Dana had been surprised the first time that the room was so feminine. Not your typical firefighter-in-training décor. She guessed the ballerina music box was pretty old, but the collection of elephants that lined the dresser and shelves was an ongoing "thang," Tanisha called it.

"I have a *thang* for elephants," she'd say, laughing.

Dana recognized a spongy gray elephant she'd given Tanisha for her last birthday, and a small malachite model Tanisha had found in a hospital gift shop.

For Dana, her girlhood obsession had been shells. Real shells from walks along Monterey Bay, fake shells from souvenir shops on San Francisco's Fisherman's Wharf, shell jewelry from who knows where. She wondered what Rachel collected, other than an enormous number of different colored beads to hold her braids and cornrows together.

Dana stretched out on Tanisha's bedroom floor and started leg exercises. Flat on her back on the brown shag rug, she pedaled the air as fast as she could. Why did she bother paying health club dues, she wondered, when she carried out most of her fitness program on her bike or her living room floor? One twenty-dollar floor pad was all she really needed.

Dana remembered Tanisha kept a floor pad under her bed and thought she'd indulge herself in a little comfort. She shuffled sideways, spreading her left arm to feel the floor under the twin bed. Nothing within reach. She twisted halfway to get a better look at the whole area. Maybe Tanisha had shoved the pad under the bed from the other side. She shifted her body farther in. Dust filled her nostrils and she sneezed. The bedsprings were few inches from her face.

So was an envelope, stuck among the coils. Dana's heart skipped. She jerked up and hit her head on the coils and part of the frame. She blinked her eyes and twisted around until she was flat on her back.

Leave it alone.

Not likely.

She took a deep breath. She tugged at the envelope, a regular business-size white envelope, the kind you might a pay a bill with, held closed with a thick rubber band.

As soon as Dana removed the elastic band, the envelope fell open.

She couldn't believe the police wouldn't have found this. It didn't say much for their thoroughness.

So, the cops had come looking for drugs, they'd found stolen medical supplies instead, and they'd missed this envelope full of cash.

CHAPTER TWENTY-ThREE

$\mathbf{S}$omeone stole Dana's Jeep?" Elaine asked. More a sentence than a question, as if nothing could surprise her.

"I don't think it was stolen," Matt said. "My guess is that Dana got a ride back here from the uniforms and drove off in her car."

I tended to agree. In fact, I hoped he was right. Otherwise, I could imagine the buzz at the Berkeley PD. *Gloria Lamerino arrives in town, and the crime rate shoots up. In a week we have two killings, a missing person, and now a stolen car.*

"Don't you have her keys?" Elaine asked.

"Just this." Matt produced a miniature blue-striped beach sandal hanging on a chain, along with a single key. "I'm sure Dana has another."

"Why would she do that? Just sneak off."

I felt Dana had had enough of us, but I didn't express that to Elaine. "She probably needed some space" was how I put it. I thought it sounded holistic enough for a Berkeley native.

We sat in front of dried-out eggplant parmegiana, limp salad greens, and strained conversation, until Elaine called us to order.

"Okay, I've consumed about two thousand calories here. It's time to come clean."

Well, at least the food brought back her sense of humor, I thought.

We laid everything in front of Elaine, including the two Phils:

one in Hawaii and one on Woodland Road. There was a way quantum mechanics could account for colocation, through the eigenstates of a system, but I knew it wasn't the time for a modern physics lesson.

I could tell Elaine was running the possibilities through her mind. "He could have business in Hawaii," she said finally, casting her vote against my first-rate evidence. "Did they tell you which hotel he checked into?" she asked Matt.

I had to admire my friend, keeping it together while asking *my* fiancé what the police had reported on the whereabouts of *her* fiancé.

Matt shook his head. I searched his face for signs of strain. The bags under his eyes were a permanent part of his Italian American look, I knew, so I wasn't worried about them, and I calmed myself by remembering that his doctor had given him a referral to a Berkeley physician in case of emergency. "I think they quit at the airlines stage," he told Elaine.

Elaine put her napkin aside and got up from the dining room table. "Excuse me, please. I need to make some calls."

I followed her as far as the stairway and gave her a hug.

"I'm here," I said.

I was sorry I had so little to offer.

Once again I was on my own.

I'd heard Elaine's office door close, shutting me out of the e-mail and attachments that might be coming from the young PDA genius, William Galigani. I imagined her coursing through every hotel on the five Hawaiian Islands.

Matt had fallen asleep on the couch to a mellow jazz saxophone. He'd found a CD of the Monterey Jazz Festival among the collection Elaine's old boyfriend Bruce had left behind.

It was a good thing my cell phone rang, to keep me from being bored. I picked up on the first ring, not to disturb Matt, and carried the phone to the empty kitchen, which still smelled of cooked tomatoes and oregano.

"Hello?" I said.

"Galileo?" A man's voice.

I nearly knocked over a stack of dishes on the counter. I couldn't be sure it was Phil. But who else? Even if someone else had heard the answering machine message I'd left at Patel's phone number, he wouldn't know who Galileo was. Or was I more transparent than I thought?

"Yes," I said. A soft, quick answer, not wanting to wake Matt, and even less to betray my fear and ignorance of who was on the line.

"Come to the house. Alone."

I held on to the phone with both hands and talked in a whisper. "What house?" As if I didn't know. "Who is this?" As if I couldn't guess.

But the line had gone dead.

I tried to remember my phone message to "Robert Boyle." I'd referred to my cell phone number only, knowing that Phil had it— he'd used it to change the location of our lunch date. There was no question in my mind; the house was Patel's, the caller Phil.

I told myself how *foolish* it would be for me to respond, un-escorted, to such a message. Then I rationalized. How *superb* it would be if I got some valuable information, especially something that cleared Phil in all our minds. And if he meant to hurt me, surely there were easier ways to get to me than to lure me with a nebulous phone call.

I checked Elaine's freezer. No ice cream. *Good.*

I walked upstairs and knocked on Elaine's office door.

"I'm going out for a bit—we're out of ice cream." I talked quickly, hoping to sound desperate for dessert, with no time to chat.

"Oh, sorry, and thanks, Gloria. I'm plugging away here. We'll have some ice cream when you get back." Elaine seemed no more eager to chat than I was. "Was that your phone I heard?"

"Wrong number," I said.

I drove to Woodland Road, my brain split between *This is unwise; you're going to be killed* and *What a lucky break; we can settle this and get back to the plans for the wedding.* I never thought I'd long for chats about who would be seated with whom at the ten-person tables at Elaine and Phil's wedding reception.

The Claremont neighborhood, so beautiful in the daytime with its magnificent, dark, leafy trees, had an eerie cast at night. The cul-de-sac Patel lived on seemed even quieter and farther away from the city streets than it had during the day.

I pulled up to the house I'd cased a few hours earlier. A single dim light showed in a downstairs room, more likely to be an automatic night-light on a timer than a reading lamp for a current occupant. I sat in the Saab, its motor still running in case I decided to leave, and took some breaths. What did I hope to gain? *Information,* I answered. I cursed myself for not being a normal person who spent Thursday nights in front of the television with a favorite sitcom or hospital drama.

I drove up to the spot I'd been in earlier in the day and parked the car, again mostly hidden by the trees. I walked up to the front door this time, poised to ring the bell. A visitor, for tea. I told myself once again that this was not a dangerous scenario. What attacker sits and waits for his victim to ring his doorbell?

I'd told Elaine I was going out for ice cream but had left no note for Matt. I was afraid he'd see through any sentence I'd construct. If he woke up before I returned, maybe he'd believe Elaine.

And maybe they'd be having this conversation at my funeral services. Why did I continue to put myself in danger? I hated to think my motive was to win approval, an attitude that had dominated my childhood and young adult life. Growing up with a mother who would never be pleased can have that effect.

Look, Ma, I'd say, *I got all As.*

So? she'd say. *You don't do anything around here but study. Who couldn't get As with your life?*

But that was a long time ago. What was my excuse now? Was I so insecure in Matt's love that I felt I needed to be heroic to win his approval?

Crrrash! A loud noise coming from the bushes by the side of the house where I'd been snooping this afternoon.

I froze. A *raccoon,* I told myself, *going after the pizza boxes.* A rational explanation from my brain, but my body took over, and I turned and ran down the path, back to the car. My heart pounded, and at once I saw the ridiculousness of being there alone. I made my usual bargain with the universe: If I would be spared, I'd never do this again.

I'd put the keys in my pants pocket. I pulled at them, but they were caught on some loose threads that I'd meant to cut. *A little careful homemaking would come in handy at times like this,* I thought. I managed to get the keys free and clicked the remote.

I didn't hear a beep—and remembered that I hadn't locked the car.

I dove for the driver's side, jumped in, and pushed the lock button, at the same time wrestling with the key to fit it into the ignition. After an interminable amount of time, the key clicked in. I drove away without looking back.

At the first traffic light, I caught my breath and steadied my hands. I looked in the rearview mirror, but I knew I'd never be able to tell if someone was following me. All I saw was head-lights, one set indistinguishable from another.

At the next light, I was stopped directly under a streetlight. An unfamiliar reflection from the passenger seat caught my eye.

I looked over to see a small white padded envelope.

Someone had entered the Saab on Woodland Road and made a deposit.

I stepped into Elaine's living room with a quart of chocolate showers—Loard's delicious version of chocolate chip ice cream—in one hand and an audiotape in the other. I found her and Matt across from each other. Elaine's eyes were red; the nearby wastebasket overflowed with tissues. I suspected there was no Dr. Philip Chambers registered in a hotel anywhere in the Hawaiian Islands.

It might have been the first time in my life that I postponed ice cream in favor of an audio recording.

"You got this tape where?" Matt asked.

I put my finger to my lips and pointed to Elaine, who had pushed the PLAY button on her old portable tape recorder. I remembered the little black machine from the days when she'd record meetings to be sure she got work assignments and due dates right. I had fond memories of the time she'd been the lead editor for a program I worked for, making it legitimate for us to have long lunch meetings.

"Okay, Howard, it's just you and me here, and we need to get some things straight. It's almost the middle of June, and I need to find out what you want me to do, how far we're willing to go, and so on."

Elaine pushed the STOP button. "That's Phil's voice," she said. She took a breath and held it.

"He wants to establish a record," Matt said. "He's giving us who's there, the date, and the agenda. I'm guessing Howard didn't know this was being recorded. Very smart."

"Phil *is* very smart," Elaine said, as if she'd been trying to tell us this for a long time and we were getting it at last. I wondered if she felt a bit of relief, just hearing her fiancé's voice. " 'Howard' must be Howard Christopher, Phil's boss."

Matt nodded. "Gloria and I met him at Dorman the other day."

I was itchy to push PLAY, which Elaine finally did.

"What do you have so far?" Howard Christopher's voice.

"I have more than enough to take this to the next level. First, as I told you, I've been tracking missing nitrogen in Washington's database of special substances. You can see from this table"—(rustling)—"that Patel has been at the site in all these highlighted cases."

"Phil's giving us a review," Matt said, nodding approvingly.

"We've been over this. So Patel was in the vicinity of reported material losses. That could be coincidence. The man travels a lot."

"You sound like you don't want him to be guilty."

"Not at all. I'm just trying to keep you honest, Chambers. (laugh) I want to get to the bottom of this more than you do. When you came to me with this, what did I do? I gave you a full go-ahead, relieved you of other duties. You know that."

"Okay, you're right. I'm just telling you now what I've found out. I told you I saw Patel download from the classified system in the VTR. I walked in on him and he tried to cover it up, but I'm positive that's what he was doing. Our work is paid for by the U.S. government, and that's all who's meant to see it. Patel is stealing."

"Let's say he is stealing. What's he going to do with the information?"

"He could have been transferring everything we've been working on. Those files contain all the equations for nitrogen-enhanced molecules and all the device designs."

"And what's he doing with them, in your view?"

"Making money, I presume. India is, what, third place in the world economy? We've been hearing for years that it wants to become a member of the nuclear club."

"This isn't nuclear."

"No, but it would go a long way toward getting them into the big weapons club."

"And isn't this a little racist, Chambers? Just because the guy's Indian?"

"Okay, some other country. He could be sending the stuff anywhere."

"You know, Patel could also have been uploading, not downloading.

Maybe his only violation was to use a classified computer to upload his PDA calendar with his kids' birthdays, for God's sake."

"He doesn't have kids."

"Geez, Chambers, maybe it was his tee times. You can't be sure he was downloading classified information."

(Exasperated grunt) *"You're right, Howard. So, you want me to back off?"*

(Sigh) *"Yeah, you get back to work, Chambers. We need you back on the bench. I'll take it from here."*

The machine went silent, except for the whiny noise of the clutch. The meeting, obviously held before Patel's murder, appeared to be over.

"Phil might have taped this for his own protection," Matt said. "Maybe he'd begun to suspect his boss of being in on it."

"*It* being some kind of industrial espionage or even national security violations," I said. *Aren't you sorry you didn't pay more attention to my nitrogen lesson?* I thought, but considered it too flip to say at the moment. "And that's why he mailed the PDA to me instead of turning it over to his boss."

"Why not the police?" Elaine asked.

"No context," Matt said. "If I were the cop who got this, I'd need a long explanation. On its face, there's nothing but two guys disagreeing about a third."

"But the third one is dead," Elaine said.

No one mentioned the "missing" status of the second one.

Matt yawned. As much as I felt we were making progress, I wanted us all to retire for the night.

"I'm not saying Phil made the right choice. But he knew Gloria was investigating." Matt ticked off the evidence. "She asked him pointed questions at lunch—"

I felt my face flush. "You weren't there."

"Did you?"

"Lucky guess," I said.

"Let's say it is Phil at the house. He probably saw her the first time. He'd have to wonder how she got the address and realize she'd accessed the PDA."

"She could have gotten the address from the police," Elaine said.

"Not likely," Matt said, apparently thinking, as I was, that the police were not bending over backward to include us in their investigation, nor to share information. "Then, if he had any doubt, she left the Robert Boyle message."

"And he might have gotten anchovies the next night," I said.

Elaine looked bewildered at that, but I didn't take the time to explain.

"Hmmm, it almost looks as though you've been doing the work of a cop," Matt said.

"I prefer to call it research, acting as a consultant, as usual."

"You know what this means," Elaine said, ignoring our banter. Her voice had all the confidence of a moment of enlightenment.

Matt and I gave her similar looks. I, for one, hadn't begun to see the clear picture Elaine had apparently worked out.

"What *does* it mean, Elaine?" I asked, since she seemed to be waiting to deliver a punch line.

"Phil's one of the good guys."

I should have realized how much it would mean to Elaine for Phil to be the guy who was ferreting out a spy, and not be a criminal himself.

I gave her a hug. I heard the faint sound of wedding bells.

All we had to do now was straighten out a few loose ends. It was looking good for Christopher as the murderer, and I looked forward to working out the logic more carefully in a session with Matt.

And to luring Phil out of hiding and down the aisle.

Elaine went upstairs shortly after we heard the tape-recorded meeting between Phil and his boss. I heard a soft "Thanks, Gloria" as she left the room. She looked weary beyond words. I sensed that hearing Phil's voice had brought her about a microliter more hope than she had the day before.

Matt and I called Patel's phone number a few more times, to no avail, then agreed that we needed a fresh start before outlining murder scenarios and listing all the questions that still remained to be answered.

William Galigani called long before we'd had enough sleep, however.

"Hey," William said. "I'm surprised you're up this early. But I have some stuff to send you."

I guessed this was a teenager's version of *you had to wake up anyway to answer the phone.*

"What did you find, William?" Words spoken through a wide yawn.

"There's no games on it," he said, through boyish chuckles. William's voice was in the transition stage; I expected any day to mistake his voice for his father's, as had happened with Rose's two sons. "And only a few hot chicks."

"Nice, William."

"Sorry, don't tell Grandma, okay?"

"I wouldn't dream of it."

And I wouldn't, though I thought it curious that William was more concerned about Rose's reaction to his little jokes than his parents'. But William had probably been up half the night working on my project, and he deserved a little fun. At least school was out for the summer and I didn't have to worry about keeping him from his homework.

"Okay, well, there's a calculator, and an expense sheet, and then some book downloader, but no books," William said. "Then there's some charts, with columns, like the first heading says 'storage places,' and there's amounts, and it says 'missing materials.' I think it's, like, a list of missing chemicals and stuff, plus dates." The facilities Phil mentioned on the tape, with evidence that Patel was in the neighborhood during the time period of recorded thefts. "There's a lotta equations, too, and formulas and reactions. They don't look that complicated, though."

"Do you recognize the equations from your chemistry class?"

"Yeah, they're sort of like TNT and nitroglycerin and ammonium nitrate. Stuff like, you know, we studied this year, except there's one term that might be off from that. Well, it's hard to explain, but I'm just sending it all now and you'll see what I mean."

"Thanks, William. You're the man. Is that the right expression?"

"Wow, Aunt Glo, you talk the talk. Call me back if you need anything else, okay? And, oh, I think Grandma is going to be calling you in a few minutes."

"William, do me one more favor and tell her I'll call her later. I'm just walking out the door."

"I get it."

When we hung up, I had the awful realization of what a bad role model I was to children everywhere.

CHAPTER TWENTY-FOUR

Matt and I sat in front of coffee and sourdough toast, both of us a little bedraggled. I'd put a load in the washing machine so that at least our clothes would be fresh and unwrinkled. My brow, on the other hand, had felt more furrowed with each day in California. Looking back over the week, I realized our only crisis-free moments with Elaine had been our time in the rush hour traffic from the San Francisco airport to Berkeley.

There was still no sign of Elaine from the upstairs quarters, and I hesitated to rattle around in the office, lest I disturb her.

I'd done enough of that.

From William's assessment, I thought we wouldn't get much more from Patel's PDA anyway. Probably the most useful information had been the owner's address and phone number, which had allowed me to find Phil in the first place.

Also, for my purposes now, the equations themselves weren't as important as the fact that Patel had downloaded them. I was sure William's observation about "sort of like ammonium nitrate" but with an unfamiliar term or two had to do with reworking a standard high-explosives equation to accommodate a new, more energetic nitrogen molecule.

For those reasons, I didn't mind delaying my access to Elaine's computer.

About one hour and two pots of coffee later, Matt and I were well into the construction of scenarios that would account for two murders. To make it easier to follow our trains of thought, we wrote on a large piece of newsprint I'd tacked onto the bulletin board in the kitchen.

I'd found the pad in the guest room closet, left over from when Elaine had taken drawing classes through local adult education programs. I thought again how alike Elaine and Rose were, always exploring new subjects, trying different crafts— Rose's current project was making glass beads. *When I retire,* I'd told them, and myself, but I'd come to realize that people hardly ever take up new interests in retirement.

Except for police work.

My current craft was sketching plausible threads as Matt and I talked about the events of the week. One thread seemed very neat.

Howard Christopher

▼

Shoots Patel
(to cover up security breaches)

▼

Follows ambulance
(to finish job and confiscate materials in briefcase and duffel bag)
(disks? printouts? extra PDAs to hold all the equations?)

▼

Shoots Tanisha Hall
(wrong place, wrong time)
(thinking duffel bag had information, not tennis stuff)

We also managed to account for Phil's wounded hand. Not from creating our shrimp-wrap hors d'oeuvres, we knew from Dana's intern friend.

"What if Phil was there at the scene when Patel was shot and got wounded himself?" I asked.

"The timing's right," Matt said.

"And it would explain how Phil knew about the briefcase and the duffel bag." It seemed ages since our word games over the briefcase/duffel-bag mix-up, and I felt vindicated that I hadn't made a fuss over nothing.

Matt scribbled out a timeline for our first Friday evening, working backward from the pickup call to Dana and Tanisha at about five-forty-five. "By then, the wounded Patel had made it back to his car, driven himself to the wrong hospital, got bandaged up—"

"But Phil probably went straight to the trauma center." I drew a thick black line that went nowhere but helped me think it out.

"A little tip he'd picked up from his EMT daughter."

"So Phil was already at the trauma center when Dana and Tanisha pulled up in the ambulance with Patel in the back, though he couldn't have predicted they'd meet. He must have ducked into a closet when he saw them."

"Or gone out the side and shot Tanisha."

I sighed, or rather, whined. "That puts us back to 'Phil shot Patel.' I thought we agreed on Christopher."

"Okay, we'll save the 'Phil is a double murderer' thread for later. For now, we'll go with 'hand slashed by Christopher at the crime scene.'" Matt ticked off that question from our list of loose ends. "If only our checkmarks made it so, huh?" he said, always the reality checker.

I'd been asking Matt all week, in one way or another, how he felt about working during his supposed vacation. I asked again, "Are you still all right with this . . . project?"

He took my hand. "I'll warn you when I'm going to faint again, okay?"

"Don't even joke about it."

I was satisfied with the thread that linked Christopher to Patel's and Tanisha's murders. But Matt was not, his tick marks notwithstanding.

"We have a tape," he said. "We have no authentication so far, from either party."

"But it must have been Phil who put that envelope in my car. It's his voice. Elaine recognized it. And it was a live meeting."

"So you say."

Of course, Matt was right. I thought about how deeply technology influenced the rules of evidence. On the one hand, digital cameras had time and date stamps so you could always tell when a photo was taken, to the minute, or even the second with some systems. On the other hand, anyone bright enough could alter that information. The audiotape we listened to could have been made up; the PDA material could have been tampered with. *Even by young William Galigani,* I imagined a defense attorney saying.

"And think about it," Matt continued. "There's nothing really incriminating on that tape. Just upper management who didn't want to acknowledge a problem area so he wouldn't have to deal with it. How common is that?"

Temporarily defeated, I moved on to the second thread. "Julia Strega," I said, indicating the name at the top of our second column.

Julia Strega

▼

*Steals supplies and meds
(through her EMTs? which ones?
Tanisha??)*

▼

Sells to ??

▼

Launders $$ through phony pickups and deliveries

It bothered me to list Tanisha's name as a potentially corrupt EMT, but until we had some reason to believe the evidence was planted, we felt she belonged there.

"This thread's not so neat," I said.

Matt tapped his pencil on our list of questions. "We do have one or two leaps and bounds and a few fringe items."

I had to agree. "The Robin connection, for one—the fact that she had one of Patel's IDs and that she apparently altered Dana's incident report."

Slap. Something hit the kitchen table while we had our backs to it.

We turned to see Dana as she pointed to an envelope she'd slammed on the table.

"And the fact that Robin and Julia had their heads together over something fishy yesterday, at my house, and the other *enormous* fact that Tanisha had this wad of cash stuck under her mattress."

Dana looked as bad as we did, only a younger version. Sleep-deprived, on edge, frustrated. Her shorts and top looked as though she'd worn them while she slept—or tossed in her bed.

"I'm so angry," she said, adding to the emotional inventory I'd concocted for her. "Tanisha. She *did* steal those meds and supplies. She *was* a thief."

Matt put water on for tea. By now we all knew where Elaine kept the special African teas Dana liked.

Dana sat down and gave us a dramatic rendition of how she'd found Robin and Julia at her house, and how Robin all but threatened her life, sending her into Marne Hall's arms. All this was a lead-up to how she happened to roll under Tanisha's bed, which I understood. But she didn't have a good explanation of why she took the money.

"I'm not going to *use* it," Dana said, sending a scowl my way when I asked.

"We know that," Matt said.

"I just wanted to get it out of the house, I guess. In case the cops went back."

Dana buried her head in her arms on the table. I could hardly imagine how difficult it would be to find out your good friend was a criminal.

"Could there be another explanation for the cash?" I asked.

"No." No hesitation. "I remember now, certain things. Like, she'd never want to gossip about the stolen meds, the way me and everybody else did. She'd always change the subject, and God knows she'd gossip about everything else. And she'd be hanging around the pharmacies here and there, and she had a lot of private meetings with Julia that she never talked about. Things like that. Plus, lately she's had all this extra money so Marne could stay home and take care of Rachel. She said it came from overtime, but she didn't seem to be putting in much more time than I did. She said she got a raise, too, and now I'll bet she didn't." She pushed the envelope away from her. It slid to the edge of the table and stopped, as if it had some internal sensor that kept it from falling. "Unless you count this as a raise."

I wasn't used to sharing my investigative activities with another layperson. I had to struggle even to think of myself as "lay," especially since George Berger, Matt's partner at the RPD, had come to accept me as a de facto member of the police team. Still, I welcomed Dana's input.

I changed my thinking—from Tanisha as victim to Tanisha as scam artist—and edited our newsprint diagram accordingly. I struck out a few question marks in Julia Strega's column.

▼

(through her EMTs? ~~which ones??~~
Tanisha~~??~~)

We were getting close but still had kilometers to go.

"Thanks for speaking up for me, Matt," Dana said. "I can't believe you actually went over there, to Tanisha's house. I suppose cops know all the addresses in the universe." She smiled, a worshipful look. "It means so much to me to at least have Marne and Rachel back in my life."

It was the first I knew about his side trip to the Hall residence. I figured he must have stopped off there one of the times when he had Dana's Jeep to himself. I decided to leave Dana and Matt alone, hoping that her near adoration of him might calm her enough to help even further with our posted schematics.

I headed up the stairs to retrieve the equations William had sent. I walked past Elaine's still-closed bedroom door quietly, though I was beginning to think I should wake her, or at least check on her.

In the office, I booted up Elaine's computer and watched the software icons take their place on Elaine's tapestry desktop.

"That's a very famous tapestry," she'd told me a while ago. "See that lovely unicorn in the middle of the fenced-in area?"

I would have been more impressed if the fantasy animal could have speeded up the start process.

I walked to the window over the driveway and gazed out at a sunny day. Perfect for a BART trip to the newly renovated Ferry Building in San Francisco, for example. Though I'd never get on my knees in the dirt, I loved looking at flower gardens. Elaine had planted a strip about two feet wide of low-lying deep purple flowers along the fence between her yard and her neighbor's. I gazed at the colorful blossoms on both sides of the driveway. And then I noticed . . .

Not again.

A missing car.

This time it was Elaine's.

I knocked on Elaine's bedroom door, but I knew there'd be no answer. I shoved it open. Empty. I had a good idea where she was.

I pushed the buttons for William's cell phone, shifting from one foot to the other while I waited for the connection.

"Hey, Aunt Glo. I have caller ID, so I could tell this call was from California. Cool, huh? Did you get the equations?"

I hadn't checked. "Yes, thanks a lot, William." Lying to a minor, again. "I have another question, though, a quick one. When you called this morning you said something like you were surprised to know I'd be awake?"

"Right."

"How did you know I'd be up in the first place?"

"Oh, your friend Elaine called around seven o'clock California time. So I figured you'd be up, too. She called Grandma first, and then she called me and she asked me for that address from the PDA."

I was right, but not happy about it.

Matt, Dana, and I piled into her Jeep, and she drove us across town to Patel's Woodland Road home. By now I knew the windy route by heart and could direct her easily.

It wasn't clear why we decided, with almost no discussion, that we needed to go to the house in Claremont immediately. I realized in retrospect that it was the first Dana had heard that her father might be alive and living at Patel's, and she naturally would want to see him. For me, I wanted to support Elaine in what must have been an overwhelming need to see and confront her fiancé.

I suspected we all also felt an undercurrent of fear.

Because it might not be Phil, but a murderer waiting for Elaine? Because it *was* Phil, and he was a murderer? No one offered a conjecture.

I pushed the numbers for Patel's phone. "We're on our way," I said to his answering machine—again, without a clear reason for what seemed like a warning to Elaine. I felt like the leader of a posse. The effect of being out west, I figured.

I navigated as Dana took a left from Claremont Avenue and eventually a right onto Woodland.

And into an emergency situation.

A sliver of sunlight made it through the morning fog and bounced off a bright red fire truck, a stark white ambulance, and the spinning blue lights of a police car, giving the scene a patriotic look. The emergency fleet took up most of the cul-de-sac in front of Patel's house.

Dana gasped and slammed on her brakes, throwing us all forward, as if our bodies were mimicking our minds: stunned, doing double takes, straining to look more closely and understand what was happening.

I didn't breathe again until I saw Elaine, in her familiar Burberry windbreaker, standing by a police car.

I stayed to the side, a few yards away, in the small, albeit slowly accumulating, crowd in the cul-de-sac. Mostly women in jeans and T-shirts, I noticed. I wondered if I was in the land of stay-at-home wives and mothers, though I didn't see any children.

We'd arrived in time to see two paramedics push a gurney into the ambulance and lock it down. Matt joined the Berkeley police officers who were questioning Elaine, and so far they were letting him hang around. Dana talked to a uniformed young man she seemed to know. I didn't see Inspector Russell in the contingent of two uniforms and two suits, and I couldn't hear anything of the conversations. I was determined to keep out of the way and satisfied myself with the thought that I'd be briefed shortly.

After a few minutes, Dana climbed into the back of the ambulance, whether as the victim's nearest relative—I assumed it was Phil's feet I'd seen on their way into the bus—or as visiting EMT, I didn't know. I caught Elaine's pained expression as the imposing vehicle pulled away, sirens blaring.

I wanted to wave to Elaine, to make sure she knew her closest supporter was handy, but I held still, feeling helpless.

———

We convinced Elaine to leave her car in the cul-de-sac and ride with Matt and me in Dana's Jeep. We seemed to have spent a lot of time figuring out car logistics on this trip.

"It was just routine out there, Gloria," Matt said from the driver's seat. Meaning, *You didn't miss anything.* "They want us all down at the station in the next day or two."

"The paramedics wouldn't tell me a thing," Elaine said, "except that it seemed to be a gunshot wound and that Phil's alive." She took a long breath. "I told the police about Howard Christopher. And I heard Dana talking to her cop friend about Julia and her scam. Phil had those invoices, and maybe Julia knew he was on to her. I'll bet the police are sorry they didn't listen to us before."

We were all sorry for one thing or another, I thought. My biggest regret was that I might have led the shooter to Phil.

At some point I'd have to face that.

CHAPTER TWENTY-FIVE

We sat in the stark waiting room of the trauma center where Lokesh Patel and Tanisha Hall had died. *And countless others,* I thought. I had an urge to ask the young Asian nurse at the desk if anyone left here alive. My heart went out to Elaine. An image came to me of Al Gravese, my own fiancé who died, and I tried to brush away the connection. Phil was still alive, I reminded myself. There could still be a wedding.

"I *had* to go over to that house, you know," Elaine told us. "I couldn't stand it another minute. I needed to know, was he in danger? Was he just having a crisis of faith in our marriage? Was he . . . ?"

"It's okay, Elaine," we all said in different ways, from our multicolored plastic chairs. Dana was slumped in an orange one, her arms across her chest.

Elaine stared at the wall, at a landscape that even I knew was not fine art. "I got there and the front door was open. And I heard moaning from the living room or library, whatever it was. Phil was on the floor."

I pictured the area I'd peeked in on from the side yard, with the bookcase full of matched sets. I tried to imagine what I would have done if I'd seen someone sprawled on the carpet of the elegantly furnished room.

Elaine choked back tears. "He was bleeding from his side," she said, patting her own. She was in a dark green sweatsuit I'd never seen, with rubber-soled shoes that also looked strange to me. Apparently Elaine had a whole separate wardrobe for slipping out of her house undetected.

Matt handed her a second bottle of water from the six-pack he'd picked up somewhere. I thought he might remember this vacation as one where his main function was driving strange cars and providing water and comfort to frazzled females.

Elaine took a long swallow and continued. "I panicked. I tried to talk to him, to find out who did that to him, but he didn't answer. I guess he was unconscious. I didn't know what to do to help him, so I just ran to the phone on a little table and called 911. Maybe I should have done something else. I had no idea how to stop the bleeding. I was so afraid if I touched him I'd make it worse, so I just threw a throw on him—" Here she was able to giggle at the idiosyncrasies of our language and help us all relax a bit.

"You did just the right thing, Elaine. You probably saved his life," Dana said. Coming from an EMT and a doctor-to-be, the assurance had to make Elaine feel better. *The tables have turned,* I thought, with Dana comforting Elaine instead of vice versa.

I resolved to take a first aid course at the earliest possible opportunity.

We nearly force-fed Elaine cheese and crackers from the cafeteria. She'd taken aspirin, too, and declared that she was fine. I had the feeling this situation, with Phil in an intensive care unit, was only marginally better for her than not knowing where Phil was.

Dr. Brandon, the physician in charge of Phil at the moment, approached us. He was gray-haired and soft-spoken, and older than anyone I'd seen in a medical capacity lately. I had a flashback to the bouncing blond ponytail of Trish, Matt's oncologist in Boston. Youthful energy aside, I preferred at least the appearance of wisdom and experience.

"He's sedated," Dr. Brandon said, taking Elaine's hand. "He lost a lot of blood, but he's stable now. I can't tell you when you'll be able to talk to him. Your best bet is to go home and stay by the phone. But I'm sure you won't want to do that." He gave her a kindly smile. "So I'll simply tell you the cafeteria is at the end of that hall, and there are more comfortable chairs in a lounge downstairs."

"He's so nice," Elaine said. "He's in good hands." A little slip of pronouns, but Elaine's grammar was not in the best shape this week, and we all knew what she meant.

Would I forget Newton's Laws under similar stress? I hoped I'd never have to find out.

Matt and I left Dana and Elaine at the trauma center, with a plan for staggering the waiting room watch. We hoped to convince Elaine to go home for a nap, but we knew it wouldn't happen too soon.

Once buckled into Dana's Jeep, I let loose with the tears I'd been holding back. Matt knew immediately what was wrong.

"It wasn't your fault," he said.

"I led the killer to that house. Someone followed me to Patel's, knowing it was a good bet that I was also looking for Phil." I shivered at the realization that I'd put more people than myself in danger. I was over blaming my mother, Josephine Lamerino, for all my faults, tempting as it was. I let Josephine off the hook. "I'm responsible, Matt. And don't give me that line about how it was the shooter who hurt Phil, not me."

Matt was silent. Suddenly I wanted that comforting line. "Well?" I asked.

"Okay, you might have led the shooter to Phil. Or he may have found Phil himself. Or Phil may have called him, not knowing he was a shooter. Or a hundred other scenarios. But you're right, one of them might be that you were followed."

"Twice," I said. "I went there twice. Just in case once wasn't enough."

By two o'clock in the afternoon Matt and I were back at our newsprint pad and charts. We had another event, Phil's shooting, to account for in our scheme, but not any additional data.

"How does it feel to be working without access to police files or reports?" I asked him.

"You mean, do I like being reduced to a kitchen bulletin board?" He put his arms around me. "It's useful to see how the other half lives," he said.

Too bad we didn't have the luxury of taking the rest of the day off.

I had many questions and directed them at Matt, my closest law enforcement officer. How soon would the police check the bullet from Phil's side to see if it matched the one taken from either Patel or Tanisha? (Ballistics was on it, he was sure.) Was it time now to tell the Berkeley PD all the loose ends we'd been working with? (Yes, we were on our way, with full cooperation on both sides, he thought, once we talked to Phil.) What if the PD had the complementary evidence and could pull the whole solution together? (They probably did, and all this would be resolved in time for a glorious wedding.)

A phone call from Rose took me away from more theorizing, but I knew I'd put her off long enough.

"Your grandson's a genius, Rose," I said. My way of making up for my recent neglect of her.

"You can skip the schmoozing," she said.

I laughed. "As long as you know I tried."

"I'm waiting." I pictured Rose, my diminutive lifelong friend, hands on her hips if she didn't have to hold a phone, pouting slightly, frustrated that she was out of the loop on what had gone on since I left her neighborhood.

I summarized our week, with all the background stories. It drained me to talk about the events that took the lives of two people, and to have to tell Rose that we still didn't know what the prognosis was for Phil.

"Poor Elaine," Rose said. "I can't imagine. You weren't kidding when you listed those disasters the other day."

"No." *In fact, I played them all down,* I thought.

I heard a long whistlelike sound, then maybe the longest silence in Rose's telephone history.

"What's new with you?" I asked.

Her laugh seemed to let out a breath she'd been holding in. "Well, nothing like you're going through. But there was a break-in here. I didn't want to tell you, once I realized *something* was going on with you, though you took your sweet time telling me. Not that I guessed it would be *that* big." Another long whistle.

"There was an intrusion at the mortuary? Was MC at home?" I felt protective of my old apartment, and even more of Rose's only daughter, my godchild.

"MC was there; it was the middle of the night. But they never got upstairs. And the best news is we caught them. Well, the RPD caught them. Even without Matt." A teasing laugh. "So it's over for now."

I felt completely out of touch with Revere. I didn't remember ever feeling so disconnected from Rose's daily life, even in the thirty years we lived a whole country apart. "I'm not getting it, Rose," I confessed. "What's over?"

"The mortuary chain, Bodner and Polk. You do remember that part? That they were trying to put all us independents out of business?"

"I remember." *Barely.*

"I faxed you the police report about the exploding hearse at O'Neal's. Do you remember that?"

"I remember." *Barely.* I was flunking my Galigani quiz.

"Well, you don't have to worry anymore. Ever since all this started—the switched clothes and all?—we beefed up security at our place. George Berger—you do remember Matt's partner?" A laugh here, as sarcastic as Rose ever got. "He recommended this excellent service. I think they're ex-wrestlers or boxers. Big, big guys. So when the goons broke in through the basement window, our guys were waiting. It was beautiful. It took about five minutes for the gorillas to give up their bosses. You guessed it. Bodner and Polk." A pause, and then, *"Done."*

I pictured Rose brushing her palms against each other, as if she herself had taken on and cleaned up a messy situation, though I doubted either Frank or Robert would have let her anywhere near the "gorillas."

"Rose, I'm sorry I didn't get to—"

"Don't give it another thought, Gloria. Now that I see what you've had to go through, I'm sorry I bothered you in the first place. I'll bet you'll be glad to get home."

"Indeed I will."

"I mean, you have just as much excitement here, right? And Matt probably misses being near his sister. And then there are those earthquakes you have to worry about."

Matt's sister, Jean, lived on Cape Cod, not exactly "near" her brother, by East Coast standards. Finally I realized what Rose was thinking. Each time I went to California for a visit, she worried that I'd stay there. Not paranoid on her part, since I did have a history of impulsive cross-country moves.

As for earthquakes, that was another matter. The worst one I'd been in had sent me under the conference table with my boss at the time, while books from the shelves on the wall tumbled over us. No harm to people that day, but the quake, a 5.3, left the physical plant a mess, and we all went home early.

I couldn't keep my friend on the hook any longer.

"Rose, I'll be *home* soon."

"I know, I know. Just checking."

It seemed a long time before I'd be packing, however. The

week ahead loomed in front of me, shadowy and unpredictable. I tried to imagine a wedding at the end of it.

The picture was very fuzzy.

Matt and I pulled up in front of Patel's house for the sole purpose of reclaiming Elaine's car, partly buried under the same trees I'd used for cover the day before.

I got out of Dana's Jeep and started toward the Saab, which I was to drive home. I paused at the front driveway and glanced at the door, a few yards away. The graceful branches of large old trees couldn't minimize the effect of stark black-and-yellow crime scene tape.

I stood there and looked back at Matt. He got out of the Jeep and walked up to me. He put his arm around my shoulder and led me toward the Saab.

"Don't even think about it," he said.

Obedient as an electron in a magnetic field, following a predetermined path, I got into the Saab and buckled up.

I had no intention of breaking through police tape.

It was much too bright out.

CHA[Pt]ER TWENTY-SIX

There was good news on Friday evening. Matt took the call as we sat in Elaine's living room. Phil was not only alive but awake and talking. Not that he'd said much. Phil had told Elaine and Dana, and the police, that he didn't get a look at who had shot him.

We also learned that the bullet had grazed past all Phil's important organs without penetrating them. He would have bled out (Dana's words, we were told), however, if Elaine hadn't found him.

"So it was a TNT," Matt said to me when he'd hung up.

"Trinitrotoluene? Why are you back on nitrogen compounds?" I asked him. "Not that I wouldn't be happy to go into the fascinating history of nitrogen, like the fact that it was first called 'burnt air,' as in, air that has no oxygen."

Matt put up a halt sign with his hand. "'Through and through.' That's what we call it when a bullet goes straight through a body, leaving both an entrance and an exit wound. TNT, for short."

I was sure my idea of what TNT stood for was much more common than Matt's.

Elaine met us in the hallway of the hospital, animated and seeming relieved that the worst was over. "The bullets came from outside the house, through the patio door," Elaine said. "The first one just shattered the glass. The second—" She swallowed. "The alarm went off and made a lot of noise, but Patel apparently hadn't paid his monitoring service bill, so no one came, and the neighbors didn't pay attention. They never do. But at least it scared the man with the gun, because he didn't stay around to try again."

That was Elaine in her I-might-as-well-have-been-there story-telling mode.

An older African American nurse ushered us into Phil's room, where Dana sat beside him. The nurse, whose name tag said BUNTING, was pleasant, except for reminding us sternly that she planned to return shortly to usher us all back out.

"Too much traffic for this man," she said, shaking her head of tight black curls. "Police, fiancée, daughter, friends . . ."

Phil was sitting up, forced into an erect posture by stiff wrappings that were partly visible over his blanket. "I'm so sorry to have put you all through this," he said. "I suppose you think I'm a coward."

We shook our heads vigorously. I caught a whiff of food from a tray table that had been pushed to the side. I wondered if the gray and brown lumps on the plate made Phil long for a pizza from Giulio's, with or without anchovies.

"I had to hide," Phil said. "I had no idea who to trust in my own company. I'd been working with a friend outside the company, Rob Driscoll—"

"That computer geek?" Elaine asked. She turned to us. "He's a very nice guy," she explained, "but too brainy, if you know what I mean."

I did.

"Right," Phil said. "Rob called me Friday and said he'd hacked into Patel's files and seen some action that shouldn't have been there. Patel was what we called an ATM. Not your local cash withdrawal machine but an authorized transfer manager. He was the go-to guy if you needed to send something out of the company, say, to another consultant or to a lab."

Phil's attention seemed to drift. I wondered if he was in pain. When he started up again, it sounded more like stream of consciousness.

"It's so much more complicated now. We all sit in a window-less room and work on portable hard drives that have to be locked up at night, and we have these metal inserts that we put into computer drive slots to keep anyone from inserting and downloading, and on and on." Phil eventually found his way back to his recounting of events leading up to this moment. "Ev-idence was mounting against him. So I faced Patel, to give him one last chance to give himself up."

"And that's when whoever shot Patel found both of you on that Friday evening," Elaine said.

Phil nodded and held up his hand, still bandaged, as evidence. But the strips of gauze paled in contrast to the massive wrapping around his torso. I thought I saw streaks of blood on the pad and worked hard at not staring at them. I wondered what kind of matter the bullet had gone TNT, as Matt had put it. I was certain there'd been great trauma to Phil's body, no matter what the doc-tor had said about the bullet's not hitting anything "important."

Besides first aid, I needed a course in biology, sadly lacking in my science education. When I was in school, biology was the stepchild science, without a solid theory behind its catalog of data and random bits of information. Rutherford once called it stamp collecting. Now—and during the days of discovering the extent of Matt's cancer—I wished I'd paid more attention to my one high school freshman class in anatomy.

"I eventually managed to unlock Patel's briefcase and get his PDA out of it." He gave Dana a smile. Evidently they'd already discussed how he took it from her house.

"What about the duffel bag?" I asked him. "Why would Christopher, or whoever was the shooter, want the duffel bag?"

Phil shrugged the shoulder on his good side. "I knew there was nothing of value in the duffel bag."

"No value as in misinformation, or no value as in gym clothes?" I asked.

"Gym stuff. Patel was a tennis nut," Phil said, his voice sad. "Either the shooter didn't know that or he was really after Tanisha."

"Are you getting tired?" Elaine asked. "We don't have to do this now."

"I'm fine for a while," Phil said. He gave his fiancée a loving look, then said softly, "I missed you."

If we hadn't all been so curious, I'm sure we would have left the two lovebirds alone at that point, but nobody budged. For me, I was willing to let Nurse Bunting decide when Phil had had enough.

"You got an urgent call on Monday afternoon," I reminded him.

"Right. Rob called me on Monday and said he'd broken another password barrier."

"And you rushed out to meet him," I said.

Rob Driscoll, computer geek, was the strange, urgent voice Ms. Cefalu had been hearing on the phone lately. Somehow, I'd pictured a darker, more shadowy spooklike figure.

"I got the PDA back from Rob, and you know the rest. Originally I'd just meant to have it in a safe place while I thought about what to do."

"And the flight to Hawaii?" Elaine asked.

"You'd be surprised how easy it is to fake a departure."

Surprised and dismayed, I thought.

"I still don't get why you had to play spy in the first place," Dana said. "Isn't that why we have the FBI and the CIA and the DOE and all those other alphabet orgs?"

I understood Dana's question—an amateur had been sent to do the work of a professional. *Sort of like me,* I thought.

"Funding sponsors," I said.

Phil nodded, his disheveled hair and dark-ringed eyes taking little away from his good looks. "When there's a problem like this in your company, you don't necessarily want to alert your funding sponsors. You try to solve it in-house first. You're competing with a lot of people, and something like this could tip the balance against you."

"If you can't handle your own staff and security, why should we give you big bucks for research?" Elaine added. "Happens all the time in my department."

"What's worse is that, in this case, we're dealing with national security, not just company secrets. The NNSA has shown interest in our project, for example. The National Nuclear Security Administration. In the wrong hands, this nitrogen molecule could do us a lot of harm, military-wise."

"Is that a word? 'Military-wise'?" Elaine asked. I was glad to see the editor was back in form.

"We were this close," Phil said, illustrating the small gap with his thumb and index finger, "to being able to sell our nitrogen design to a national lab for development. We'd had a couple of briefings with them already. Then I started to see some signs that Patel was not quite straight up."

Phil's voice was fading, his eyelids drooping, and I worried that he was going to drift off to sleep before we had any new information or confirmation of our newsprint theories. "It seems Christopher didn't take your investigation seriously. Was he in on it?" I asked. *Could he be the man with the gun?* I meant, but couldn't bring myself to articulate the thought.

"I think so. But it's hard to imagine him a killer. Hell, it's hard to imagine anyone you know as a killer."

I shivered a bit as I thought how easy it had been for me to think of *Phil* as a killer.

"I took my concerns to Christopher right away," Phil continued, "and he told me to look into it, but when I did . . . well, you heard what he thought about it."

"Why didn't you go to the cops?" Dana asked, clearly still shaken from nearly losing her father.

"What could I have done? Given them Patel's PDA? They

wouldn't have understood the context," Phil said. He glanced quickly at Matt. "No offense."

"None taken," Matt said. He stood back from the bed. I loved his serene expression and took it to mean he wasn't hurting. I was glad he'd been in the almost constant company of an EMT on this trip, however.

I looked at my watch. I wondered how long we had before the curfew nurse returned and cut us off. I needed more from Phil, and I didn't have much time.

"What about the invoices in your house, Phil?" I asked. "From Valley Med."

Phil looked surprised. I realized he'd been missing in more ways than one. He had no idea of the extent of our investigation. How could he have guessed we'd been rooting around behind his kitchen bulletin board?

He glanced at Matt. "You're a good detective," he said.

I supposed it was natural that Phil would think it was the cop among us who'd been pursuing the case. This, in spite of our Robert Boyle/Galileo messages. Old stereotypes died hard.

Matt smiled, wisely letting me decide whether to call Phil on his false assumption. I let it go—he was recovering from a TNT gunshot wound, after all—and Phil continued.

"Well, I was looking for missing special materials, not just nitrogen but other controlled material, to try to trace it to Patel. I searched everywhere, both classified and unclassified Web sites, and I hit on a lot of lists with details of incidents and reports of missing substances, nuclear and nonnuclear. These would be either illegal or hazardous in the wrong hands."

"And the missing hospital meds came up?"

"You'd be amazed. There's nitrogen in Viagra, for example. And nitroglycerin. And of course morphine, $C_{17}H_{19}NO_3$, which, coincidentally, I was offered a shot of this afternoon."

I was impressed that Phil could rattle off the chemical composition of a complicated molecule like morphine. And I'd had no idea it contained nitrogen. He shifted a bit and his lips tightened. He had to be hurting, I thought.

Elaine put her hand on his forehead and made another offer to let him be. "Phil, are you all right? Do you want us to leave?"

A breeze blew in from the slightly opened window, past a shabby credenza, carrying light perfume from a large basket of flowers from Elaine. I wondered if she'd used her wedding florist. I assumed she and Phil had had a wedding talk during the day. I figured I'd learn the parameters—on/off, postponed/canceled, full throttle/scaled down—when I needed to. Phil looked like he was only one good nap/shower combination and a tux away from walking down the aisle, but I knew there was more to it than that, and not just physically.

"I'm fine," Phil said. "I'm trying to do this without morphine, and it's a little rough right now."

"Miss Emma," Dana said, getting a smile from her dad.

I was learning a lot—not only the composition of the drug, but one of its street names as well.

"So, with the N atom in there, nitrogen will show up on the missing morphine list. Check your friendly DEA controlled substance list and you'll see what I mean."

Dana smoothed her long hair back from her face, making a temporary ponytail, then a bun at the top of her head. It fell back into the original arrangement as soon as she let go. "I've been thinking about this, Dad. I know the procedures. These facilities do a daily inventory of controlled substances. It requires a strict accounting, including the signatures of people going off duty and the people coming on duty."

"I know, sweetheart, but then how do supplies ever go missing in the first place? We know how it's supposed to work, but—" Phil shrugged the wrong shoulder and winced again.

I felt certain Dana was thinking of how her own friend and partner had managed to find a way to skirt inventory rules.

"They're supposed to write incident reports," she said. "I guess eventually someone did, and that's how you got to see it on those lists."

Phil nodded, but weakly. He was fading, and I wasn't finished. I switched topics again.

"The interview with Howard Christopher? Was that the only one you taped?" I asked.

"Yeah, unfortunately. By the time I caught on that he might be involved, it was too late. And even with the interview I gave you, I'm aware I didn't quite get him to give himself away. I can't prove he knew about Patel's downloading to his PDA."

The dull white walls of Phil's room seemed to light up as I had a flash of memory.

"Maybe you got more than you thought, Phil. I'll have to check the tape when I get home, to be sure."

I was finished for the time being, and it's a good thing, because the door opened and Nurse Bunting gave us a you're-out gesture that we would have been foolish to disobey.

CHAPTER TWENTY-SEVEN

Dana had to keep herself from resenting Gloria just because she'd be taking Matt home with her. After all, it was Gloria who'd located her father at Patel's house in the first place, and then her bravery had allowed him to pass on the PDA while Dana was hiding at Marne's. Her own discovery of Tanisha's money counted only as serendipity, not courage or investigative ability.

Dana watched as Gloria pushed REWIND then PLAY on Elaine's tape recorder. They all listened to the whole interview between her father and Howard Christopher once through, and then Gloria rewound to the passage she wanted.

The voice of Howard Christopher:

"Maybe his only violation was to use a classified computer to upload his PDA calendar with his kids' birthdays, for God's sake."

"I don't recall Phil's saying anything about a PDA before this point in the meeting, do you?" Gloria asked. "I think this is what we need." She glanced around the room, her expression too smug for Dana's liking. Matt gave a thumbs-up; Elaine clapped lightly, a wide smile on her face; Dana was quietly thrilled that her Dad might have successfully stopped a threat to national security, however remote.

She shuddered at how close her father had come to dying this week—twice. She had a new respect for Robin, losing her father at nine years old, and in a way that couldn't help but mar her for life. Maybe Dana should cut her roommate some slack.

Dana was glad she finally knew how and when her father had hurt his hand—tussling with Patel and his killer. Probably Howard Christopher, from the sound of that tape. It was awful enough that Tanisha Hall had turned out to be on the wrong side of the law; she wouldn't have been able to take her father's being a bad guy, too.

"Can I call Dad and tell him?" Dana asked. She wanted to be the one to give her father the good news—that they finally had something to take to the Berkeley PD. She was pleased at how quickly everyone agreed, Gloria first.

"Of course," Gloria had said. "That's the best idea."

Dana certainly couldn't claim that Gloria was selfish or hard to get along with, and she was attractive enough for an old lady. It wasn't Gloria's fault that Dana hadn't found anyone her own age who was worth her time.

Now that things were getting cleared up, her life looked doable again. She might dig out those medical school applications and play up her EMT experience. Popular opinion was that it would go a long way to counteract her less than stellar academic performance.

As for dating possibilities, she'd exhausted the pool of guys at Valley Med; every eligible male was either an ex-boyfriend, like Scott Gorman, or a never-to-be, like Tom Stewart. And she'd already dated too many premed students. They all wanted to practice their phlebotomy procedure on her.

"It's no fun pretending to draw blood from a straw," Scott had told her as he stuck her arm.

She remembered how conscientious he was, getting down at eye level with the needle, so he could be sure to keep it between fifteen and thirty degrees. Too bad he wasn't that meticulous about being faithful to her.

She might have to start doing the singles thing. *Nah.*

———

Dana's phone call to her father was short, since her father was still being monitored by Nurse Bunting, but he was clearly happy and relieved that his ordeal might be over.

"You know, at the time that nagged at me, that Christopher mentioned the PDA, but I couldn't put my finger on what was off kilter. Good for you, sweetheart."

"It was Gloria, really," Dana told him.

"But you were always on my side, I know, and that means a lot."

Not always.

Dana remembered the Robin/Patel connection, still unresolved in her mind. But her recuperating father didn't have to know that.

Dana sat in front of the TV in Elaine's living room. She noticed Elaine had a new piece of furniture for her television set—an "entertainment center" that looked like a huge dresser, but with doors. She wondered if she'd ever have a home like this, where everything matched and all the prints were framed, or if she was doomed to stapled posters and dormitory décor forever.

"Make yourself at home," Elaine had said when she went upstairs. Matt and Gloria went up, too, and Dana decided to hang around Elaine's a little longer.

She'd put together a late-night snack of milk and crackers and peanut butter, too lazy to make popcorn with Elaine's non-microwavable raw kernels. She got comfortable with an old Doris Day and Clark Gable movie. Good enough to stare at while she decided what to do next.

Dana hated to admit she was afraid to return to her own house. She hadn't shown up there since she'd walked in on Robin and Julia shuffling papers, looking guilty (Julia) and angry (Robin). Jen, who seemed oblivious to the drama-filled days Dana had been having, had called to check on her, but she'd heard nothing from Robin, of course.

"Are you there alone?" Dana had asked Jen. She imagined

Robin somehow taking her anger out on their petite roommate.

"Wes is with me. Why? I came back to get some things, and I thought as long as you're not depressed or anything, I'd stay at his house."

Sweet thought, Jen. "Do it," Dana had said.

Dana tried to get her head around Tanisha's being involved in the medical supply scam. Tanisha had had enough talent and personality for four; she could have made it without getting sucked into Julia's scheme. Dana smiled, remembering the time Tanisha had talked down a crazy old guy. He'd been throwing furniture out the window of the convalescent home, yelling, "Satan is making me do it," when they arrived. Everyone was afraid to approach him, except Tanisha. She'd put on a scary face and said, "I'm from Satan, and I have a message for you."

That had stopped the guy just long enough for the paramedics to come in with straitjackets.

She tried again to come up with another reason for the wad of money under the mattress—ten thousand dollars in twenties—but she couldn't. The irony was that Tanisha apparently hadn't been shot over stealing the meds but because she happened to be carrying Patel's duffel bag with some sweaty T-shirts and socks. At least that's how it seemed.

Dana hoped that in time the old *knock-knock* Tanisha would prevail in her mind, and not the image of her friend tiptoeing around nursing-home medicine cabinets and making deals with the guys who monitored the hospital pharmacies. She also hoped everyone who participated in the scam would pay. She knew that a couple of Julia's EMTs had already been suspended by the county office. Even so, it wouldn't cost any of them as much as it had cost the Hall family.

Robin Kirsch's behavior was still a little hard to understand. It was obvious now that she was still working for Valley Med, not as an EMT but as part of Julia's scam, and that was probably what had set her off when Dana appeared to be—make that *was*—snooping in her closet. But how was she involved? As far as Dana knew, Robin didn't have access to meds, unless one of the companies she did home consulting for was a pharmacy. Robin had never told them specifically what she was consulting about.

Another thing that didn't make sense was that Patel ID in Robin's closet. The cops had suggested that Dana herself dropped it there; maybe they were right. She did have a bunch of them in her pockets, and she'd been tense while she was rummaging through Robin's new clothes, that much was for sure.

Dana wondered if Tom Stewart was also involved. Part of her wished he was, but she knew that was only because she wanted to make a trade—let him be guilty and not Tanisha.

Dana was due at the PD in the morning, along with Elaine and Matt and Gloria. So, by this time tomorrow, the police could have everything they needed to arrest all the perps. Everyone who wasn't dead. She heard herself sound like Jerry Orbach/Lenny Briscoe on the original (still her favorite) *Law & Order*. She pictured Julia Strega and Howard Christopher in dull gray jumpsuits sitting at Rikers (so what if this was California, not New York City) with Sam Waterston/Jack McCoy and a model-thin lawyer from his office, offering them a deal.

Dana brushed cracker crumbs from her shorts. She'd been in them more than twenty-four hours, except for a brief stint in Tanisha's T-shirt. She remembered her father saying he'd acted cowardly, but Dana felt *she* was the wimp in the family, hiding out wherever they'd take her in. Matt would be anything but proud of her. Look at what Gloria had accomplished by her courage and willingness to take risks. If Dana had been braver, she might have been able to help.

Wouldn't it be cool if she had more to bring to the table at the PD tomorrow?

Something concrete.

Maybe it wasn't too late.

But the first thing she needed to do was get a good night's sleep in her own bed. How brave did she have to be to do that?

Dana unlocked the front door, ready to jump back if anything or anyone lashed out at her. *It's pretty sad when you're scared to enter your own house,* she thought, but there'd been too many creepy scenes lately, too many creepy places. Her Dad's empty house in Kensington; Patel's huge house in the Claremont district. She hadn't entered Patel's home, but her cop friend, J. J., had described the scene as bizarre, with the blood soaking into an Oriental carpet, making a surreal pattern. That was before he realized he was talking to the victim's daughter.

Dana pushed open the front door and took a deep breath.

No sounds, no lights, except the little Washington Monument night-light in the hallway. Jen had brought it back from a trip she took to D.C., *to gain an appreciation for our national treasures,* she'd said in her totally white-bread way.

She knew Jen was with Wes. Robin was either asleep or out. On Friday night, most likely the latter.

Dana put her ear to Robin's bedroom door. Not a sound.

Jen's door was open a crack and Dana pushed it a little more, until she got a look at Jen's empty bed, neatly made up with a quilt from her mom. No surprise that it was a bright, cheerful flower pattern. Dana wondered what it would be like to have a mom who quilted. Her mom had spent most of her time at tennis and fitness, and ended up marrying her personal trainer.

Dana walked around the empty house, flipping light switches, her arms outstretched, doing twists from the waist. It was good to be home. She felt her body relax, warming to the idea that home was safe again.

The dining room table was messy as usual with mail, newspapers, and a pile of books for Jen's summer class project on a French artist. Dana studied a painting in a huge, propped-open art history book. It was of a young girl reading, holding a book up, her elbow resting on the arm of a chair. *Who holds a book that way to read?* Dana wondered. *And who could write a whole paper on one painting?*

Dana leaned over to pick up some papers that had fallen to the floor. Junk mail, mostly. She shook her head and pictured Jen and Robin deliberately tossing their catalogs and local ads on the floor around the wastebasket.

One loose piece of paper didn't fit the profile of a credit card offer or a special rate for a magazine subscription. The red-and-white Valley Medical Ambulance Company letterhead stood out—an original this time, not a copy like Gloria had found behind her dad's kitchen bulletin board.

Dana scanned the page, a spreadsheet. It looked like part of a tax form or a memo about finances. The totals and itemizations were of no interest to Dana—she already knew Julia's books were fraudulent. But the signature at the bottom *was* news. The document was PREPARED BY ROBIN KIRSCH.

Robin was doing Julia's books. More accurately, cooking them.

Chapter Twenty-Eight

I gave up on trying to sleep. I closed the door on Matt's light snoring and went down the hall to Elaine's office. As I passed the stairway, I saw the flickering light of the television set, telling me that Dana was still in the house. Dinner smells had dissipated, replaced by the fragrance of a large jasmine-scented candle, one of many in the house, its flame newly snuffed out.

I wanted to make the most of my interview at the Berkeley PD in the morning, and a review of our information would be handy. I was a self-designated consultant, it seemed. A part of me that I wasn't proud of hoped that Russell would be on sick leave, but only because he didn't seem the type to take a vacation.

The case for theft and fraud in People v. Julia Strega, dba Valley Medical Ambulance Company (I wasn't sure what the charges would be, technically, but it was amusing to pretend I was) seemed unbreakable. If there were EMTs other than Tanisha Hall involved in her side business, the Berkeley PD could ferret them out.

I was also sure we had a vacuum-sealed case against Howard Christopher. He'd given himself away with his comment about Patel's method of getting classified information out of a VTR. I pictured the Indian scientist, a trusted transfer manager, skulking around the vault-type room, taking the steps to remove data, copy equations, even record a note to himself—all the while appearing to be just doing his job, preparing media for the transfer of material to unclassified sites.

It was easy to think of possible scenarios for intercepting secret information. I knew that some PDAs could beam data to each other at a distance of a couple of yards, no cable or computer required. I wondered if Patel had a partner, another operative receiving his information across the room. So high-tech—I gave some thought to getting myself a PDA after all.

I had a harder time imagining the end user of the information Patel had been stealing, but that was because I was embarrassingly out of touch with international politics. Give me a quiz on the status of the world's major accelerators, from BESSY in Germany to KEK in Japan, and I could get an A. I was current on which countries were participating in the research program called ITER, the international collaboration for the advancement of fusion science and technology (Korea was still in; Canada had pulled out). But if you asked me to name the current leaders or political leanings of any non-English-speaking country, I'd be lost. Even for my native land, I was more apt to follow the press releases and decisions of the president's science adviser than of his attorney general.

I'd always thought I'd do more nonscience reading when I retired, but I'd simply switched technical fields, from spectroscopy to forensics.

In Elaine's office late Friday night, I had my ear to the sounds from outside the house. I'd opened the office window a crack and heard only light traffic. This was a quieter neighborhood than the streets closer to the campus, where weekend nights especially were alive with party noise from the many fraternity and sorority houses.

I was downloading and printing William Galigani's attachments—the equations he'd mentioned, drawings of molecular configurations, notes, e-mails—when I heard Dana's Jeep start up in Elaine's driveway.

Finally.

I looked out the window, hidden, I hoped, by Elaine's draperies. Dana backed out and onto the street. I assumed she was heading home, having mustered the courage to face her roommate. My heart went out to her; it couldn't have been easy for Dana this week. Elaine, at least, had a few life experiences under her belt. Dana was only twenty-four, a little older than I was when my fiancé died. All in all, Dana had acted in a more mature way than I had. For one, she didn't flee the scene and avoid dealing with the problem.

There was another reason I was happy to see the Jeep pull away. Dana had been parked behind Elaine's Saab, and I had an errand to do.

In a few hours everything would be out in the open. Julia Strega and Howard Christopher would be in custody, and the rest of us could get back to wedding plans.

So why was I driving to Patel's house late Friday night when sensible people were either partying or sleeping? The only difference between the first two times I snooped around and now would be a bloody spot on the library carpet.

At least no one will be following me this time, I thought. It was late at night, and besides, the Patel case was over. I asked myself again what I hoped to gain with this excursion.

The only thing I could come up with was that lately I'd been generating the same curiosity for crime scenes that I used to reserve for the results of the latest NASA mission. I had to admit also that I was searching for a link between the two cases. Patel's ID card in Robin's closet was tantalizing, and we still had no ballistics information about whether the bullets that entered Patel, Tanisha, and Phil were from one, two, or three guns.

For now, here I was, the poor man's answer to Einstein, who spent much of his life trying to tie gravity and electromagnetic forces together, in one grand unified theory.

Winding through the narrow streets in the Claremont district, needing a U-turn in spite of my having been here before, I wondered how anyone could have followed me that first time without my spotting him. But assuming it was Howard Christopher, Patel's boss, all he had probably needed was to realize the direction I was heading. Then he could have figured out that the Woodland Road home must be Phil's hideout.

I pulled into the cul-de-sac, drove around under my own private hide-a-car willow tree, and stepped out of the Saab. No sounds other than whispering branches; no rooms lit up in the neighboring houses. No rowdy frat parties here. But there was a dim light in an upstairs room of Patel's house, not the night-light I'd seen on the bottom floor on my last nighttime trip. Inadvertently left on by the crime scene team, I figured.

Light from the streetlights at two and at ten o'clock in the cul-de-sac circle bounced off various shiny surfaces—the chrome bumper of a car in a driveway (the least worthy vehicle in the family, I guessed), the handle or hand brake of a bicycle, and then the shiny yellow plastic of the crime scene tape. The strip of tape fluttered in the slight breeze, and as I approached the front door, I saw why.

The tape had been cut.

I froze.

Someone must be in the house. Someone also addicted to crime scenes? A curious neighbor who'd witnessed the drama earlier in the day? Not the police—the only cars in the cul-de-sac besides mine were tucked into driveways, and whoever had a right to be here wouldn't need to hide his vehicle or nose around inside in dim light.

I'd gone halfway up the walk; my feet seemed attached to the flat stones. I strained to see if the door was open; it appeared to be slightly ajar. My body swayed involuntarily, following my mind. To go forward or to run back to the car?

I took a short step toward the door, mesmerized by the

shadows, the breezes, the dim light, the yellow tape that seemed to glow.

In the next second, the upstairs light went out, and a shot rang out over my head.

I unstuck my shoes from the walkway in record time and ran.

I arrived at the car gasping for breath, my already injured ankle and my knees hurting badly. As I ran, I'd kept my head and shoulders low—no mean feat for someone without a well-defined waist, and now my limbs were protesting. My heart pounded somewhere up in my throat. I fumbled to put the key in the ignition, dropped it to the floor, picked it up, and tried again. When I finally roared out of the cul-de-sac, I checked the rearview mirror. I noticed no cars or people following me or even looking after me.

The shot had sounded like an early firecracker.

I wanted desperately to think that was what it was.

This time there was no interesting package on the front seat, no amusing prank I could play with a pizza delivery person.

Possibilities ran through my mind. My best guess was that Howard Christopher had broken into Patel's house, suspecting his time was running out, trying to destroy any additional incriminating evidence at the last minute.

Halfway across town I caught my breath. I realized I would have been dead if the shooter had been seriously trying to kill me. I'd been the world's best target, standing under a streetlight, my hips wide enough for any sighting mechanism, especially if this had not been the shooter's first experience with a gun.

I was sure the person was only trying to scare me off.

It worked.

I pulled into Elaine's driveway. Unlike the Patel house, in Elaine's all the lights were on. I'd been found out. Comforting as the lights were, I knew it would be a specious welcome.

"You could have been killed," Elaine said. Not one to talk after her stunt this morning. Except she could claim that her instincts saved Phil's life; all I'd done was endanger mine.

My aborted visit to Patel's house had been so upsetting that I'd blurted out the truth before I could stop myself.

Matt's silence unnerved me. I wished he would yell, though yelling wasn't his style. It had been a long while since he'd chided me for putting myself in a dangerous situation. I hated the thought of his being angry with me.

"I was curious." It sounded lame, even to me. "And I guess someone wanted me to mind my own business, so they . . . scared me off."

"Shot at you," Matt said. "Someone shot at you. Is that right?" His tone was gentle; his voice would sound cool to anyone but me. I heard the undercurrent of distress and frustration.

"Yes, a shot went *way* over my head," I said, making it sound as if I'd been able to calculate the harmless trajectory of the bullet. I looked at the kitchen clock. One o'clock; my fiancé and my hostess, each holding—almost leaning on—a mug of coffee, looked exhausted and tense. "I'm so sorry. I caused all this."

Matt, not usually given to public displays of affection, finally came over and embraced me.

Elaine let us have our private words, then gave me a hug and went upstairs.

Matt wrapped an afghan around me on a living room chair. I was glad he didn't lecture me. I convinced him to go up, too, and let me stay downstairs for a while, to get my bearings.

He left the room, taking Elaine's keys with him.

Inspector Dennis Russell sat across the table from Dana—a very narrow table, Dana noted, so that he was in her face. His big ears and pointy chin gave him a comical look that put Dana more at ease than she normally would have been in a police station interview room.

She'd wanted to talk about Robin Kirsch, accountant for Julia Strega, scam artist, and fraud. But Russell made it known that he was in charge, and this interview was about Tanisha Hall.

"Did Ms. Hall seem upset about anything in the days before her death?" he asked her.

"No," Dana answered, determined not to reveal anything negative about Tanisha. If the police were going to make a case against Tanisha, they'd do it without her help. It wasn't as if her partner's illegal activities had anything to do with Patel's shooting, or her father's. There was Rachel to think about, and Marne, both of whom deserved a dignified memory of Tanisha. Dana had been trying to think of a way to get the money to them; she couldn't care less what the disposition should be legally.

Dana wished she knew Russell's thinking. Who did he suspect killed Tanisha? Russell wouldn't even reveal how much he believed about Julia's scam.

Behind Dana's firm no to Russell, that Tanisha had not seemed upset lately, was the awareness that there *had* been signs of trouble. And Dana might have been able to help, if only she'd been paying closer attention to her partner.

"What if you were stuck in something?" Tanisha had asked her, during what would be one of the last EMT shifts of her life. "You know, before you knew it, you'd got yourself on a track . . . maybe for the right reason, but it's wrong anyway. And you can't see a way to turn back."

Dana had figured Tanisha was referring to the nasty custody battle with Rachel's father, that Tanisha might be having second thoughts about keeping him as far from their daughter as possible.

"This is about Darryl, isn't it?" Dana had asked.

Dana remembered the long silence. Then, "Yeah," Tanisha had said. "Yeah, it's about Darryl."

But now Dana suspected it wasn't about Darryl's weekend visits with Rachel. What if Tanisha had been trying to get out of the fraud business, and she was looking to Dana for support? Strangely, that thought cheered Dana—that her friend was about to give up on the scam and blow the whistle. She was ready to be a heroine.

The nerve of Robin, Dana thought, going to great lengths, like tampering with her incident report, sending the cops to Tanisha's house to look for drugs, knowing it was highly likely they'd find a bag of supplies. For all Robin knew, Tanisha had already given her up to the cops, and Robin had to protect herself.

It was depressing to think she'd known so little about her supposed friends. She'd have to sit down with Jen one of these days and ask some pointed questions so she wouldn't be caught off guard again.

Dana managed one-word answers to the rest of Russell's questions. Did Ms. Hall seem to spend more money than she was earning? (No.) Had she missed a significant number of workdays? (No.) Had she acquired any new or different associates recently?

"Associates? Do you mean people?"

"Yes."

"No."

A few more nos and Russell was ready to move on.

"Okay, Ms. Chambers, now let's talk about your roommate Ms. Kirsch. You indicated you have something you wanted to report?"

She rolled her eyes, but not so much that he would notice; she wasn't looking for trouble *that* much hard. Dana handed Russell the spreadsheet.

Cops, she thought, and wondered where Matt was.

"How soon am I going to get over this whole thing?" Dana asked Matt. She'd found him in the lobby of the PD, waiting his turn with Russell, and had taken a seat next to him.

"It depends, Dana. There are so many variables, most of which have nothing to do with you, like whether other people let you get over it, for one thing."

"What if something like this happens again?"

"I'm not going to lie to you. It might. You have to admit that. You like to think you're in control. You wear a respected uniform. You have all the equipment you need. Communication tools hanging from your belt. Then something like this happens, a loss, the potential for physical harm to yourself—and you lose confidence. But what you're going to do is, you're going to strengthen your coping skills."

"My dad is already making noises like I should find another profession. He thinks I can just switch my head around and teach third grade or something."

Matt had his arm along the back of the uncomfortable wooden bench. He was paying attention to her. *Why couldn't more people just pay attention?* Dana wondered.

"Can you tell me how you're responding so far? Some people would be very angry and lash out at those around them. Others might withdraw."

"Both, I guess. I'm angry inside, but I withdraw. That shrink I saw asked if I wanted medication, but I don't. It wouldn't look very good on a med school app, for one thing. But how am I going to be a doctor if I'm going to get emotionally involved?"

"How can you do it if you don't?"

She wanted to bury her head in Matt's shoulders. Not sexual, she knew that. Fatherly, or brotherly.

Maybe she just needed to give her own father another chance.

It was getting a little better all the time, Dana admitted. One week, and she was able to call up happy memories of Tanisha. And she'd taken some action for Marne and Rachel. She'd opened an account with the money she'd found, and told Marne that since Tanisha died in the line of duty, Valley Medical Ambulance Company had offered compensation.

"Well, I'll be, if that isn't nice," Marne had said. "My girl took good care of us right to the end."

Dana inhaled some good weed, a miraculous present from Kyle that came with a note: *Heard about your troubles. This is on me.* Sweet guy. "Dope shit," Tanisha would have called this batch. Dana smiled as another memory came to her.

They have a repeat patient, an old black man named Antwon. They know he's okay, but they still have to ask the four A&O questions— alert and oriented. What's your birthday? Tanisha asks. Who's the president of the United States? What month is this? And then, when she knows Antwon is fine, What was Puff Daddy's greatest hit?

Dana took a toke, maybe her last, she thought. She didn't need this anymore. She was going to be the cleanest MD there was.

"Here's to you, Tanisha," she said into the cool night.

CHAPTER THIrTY

I'd been involved in so many interrogations, formal and informal, with Matt, and at times with his partner, that it seemed unusual for two regular Berkeley PD detectives to be on tap to interview me.

To my relief, Inspector Dennis Russell didn't bring up the nature of our interaction on my last trip to California. You might think we'd just met, starting from scratch, with mutual respect. Unless you were paying close attention.

"I've been looking forward to this," I said to Russell and a female detective, introduced as Inspector Ariana Gilmore.

"I'll bet you have," Russell said.

Russell allowed me to go through the two separate threads it had taken a whole team of us to work out. He'd already talked to Phil, Elaine, and Dana and apparently was saving Matt for last.

I thought about how differently I'd worked this week, as part of a group. More reminiscent of my research days than my recent police consulting. Usually Matt and I worked together to put the pieces of a puzzle together, whenever a science-related homicide came to the attention of the Revere PD. At most, we'd be joined by his partner, but more and more in special cases, Berger left Matt and me alone when I had a contract.

This time it had taken several of us, combining information and abilities. Phil had found a way to expose Patel, in spite of the odds against him; Dana had shared all her discoveries, no matter how difficult; Elaine had stood firm, and in the end saved Phil's life; William, from three thousand miles away, had extracted the PDA data; Matt had provided support for Dana and a link to the Berkeley PD that surely helped us all. Ironically, the one "fact" Matt had learned from Russell—that Phil had boarded a plane to Hawaii—turned out to be incorrect. But Matt's ego withstood that, and he continued to work effectively behind the scenes, even going out of his way to help Dana and Marne reconcile.

I looked at Russell and pictured his grade-school report card the antithesis of Matt's: *Little Dennis does not work well with others.*

Our whole time together on Saturday morning, Russell used me as a character witness.

Did I have any reason to think Phil would betray his company or his country? Did I think Dana was really innocent of any drug-related charges? What was my impression of Howard Christopher? Of Julia? Of Robin? Was there anything else I wanted to say?

I laid out my understanding of Howard Christopher's role, from the tape. Russell listened but didn't comment. When I was finished, he asked again, "Is there anything else?"

Yes, but I'd better not say. "Nothing at the moment, thank you," I said, and left the room.

"Robin flipped on Julia," Matt said, pouring us ordinary coffee in Elaine's kitchen. The one without an espresso maker. "Julia's being charged with a number of counts of theft, drug-dealing, fraud."

"So Robin is free and clear?" Not exactly a whine, but close.

"Free and clear. In the other matter, Howard Christopher is being charged with two counts of murder, one attempted."

"That 'attempted' is for Phil, right?" I asked, meaning, *You didn't tell Russell about the shot fired at me, did you?*

"For Phil, yes," Matt said, frowning. Neither of us wanted to talk out loud about the bullet that passed way over my head.

"I'll bet Christopher gets a better deal than Julia gets," I said. "They'll want all the details of the information that got leaked."

"Same reason cops make deals every day," Matt said. "Damage control. You want to know the big picture. In this case, what did they sell to whom, and for how long?"

"And that's the message we're sending. You can beat a murder charge if you've also been involved in selling government secrets."

Matt gave me a that's-life shrug. Sometimes I was happy that I hadn't spent my career as a cop.

"In any case, Russell seemed to like Christopher for Patel and Tanisha. He thought it seemed likely Christopher assumed the duffel bag might have something that incriminated him."

"Why wouldn't Russell tell me all this?" I asked.

"It's a cop thing."

Oh, well, I thought, *a person didn't have to like all cop things to marry one.*

CHAP T̲e̲R THIRTY-ONE

M att and I spent a good part of the next week shopping for our wedding present of choice for Elaine and Phil—the most up-to-date espresso/cappuccino maker in Berkeley.

"Almost as pleasant as searching scientific supplies catalogs," I told Matt.

We decided against a bronze model with a mythical bird on top. Matt liked a tall, old-fashioned tower arrangement topped off by an Italian glass dome, but we settled on a squat black version that would blend in with the modern Cody/Chambers kitchen. It was labeled "semiautomatic," and Matt enjoyed pointing out that espresso makers, like weapons, came in automatic, semiautomatic, and manual models.

"It has a three-way solenoid valve," I said.

"That should do it," Matt said.

I didn't tell him it also reminded me of a fast servo tool I'd seen in a precision engineering magazine.

We bought the package that included a pound of special beans each month for a year. Expensive, but we meant it as combination hostess, shower, and wedding present, with maybe an apology thrown in.

"We can deliver it at the shower on Thursday evening," I said.

"We?"

"Wedding showers are not just for girls anymore."

"That's a shame."

Dana seemed excited about hosting the shower for Elaine and Phil, whose doctors declared him ready for anything he thought he could handle. She'd enlisted the help of some friends: her noncriminal roommate, Jen Bradley, who wore a tiny white apron ("I'm here to serve," she announced); Jen's boyfriend, Wes, who plied his short-order-cook trade for our benefit (no on cucumber sandwiches, but yes on man-sized pesto-stuffed mushrooms); and a young, petite EMT, Melissa (who seemed thrilled to be included and allowed to fill coffee cups and collect dirty plates).

It was obvious Dana had cleaned and rearranged things for the occasion. The moving boxes were gone or hidden, the floor vacuumed, and fresh flowers placed on every available surface. The wall that usually supported two bikes was now covered by a stack of presents; the bikes had been moved out of the way into the hallway off the kitchen.

Besides Matt, Phil, and Wes, there were a number of other men present, evening out the population to ten and ten. I was happy to reconnect with some BUL acquaintances I hadn't seen in a long time, most of them part of a group of editors and graphic artists Elaine worked with.

"How's retirement, Gloria? Any new hobbies?" a woman I recognized as an editor asked. She didn't know me well enough to realize I had no old hobbies.

I smiled, calling up the expression I use on small-talk occasions. "I'm keeping busy," I said.

I caught Matt's grin.

I had a flashback to the wedding showers of my college days. All girls, silly games, pink- or (the more creative ones) yellow-and-white crepe paper, doll-sized food, and too much giggling over filmy sleepwear and sexy (we wouldn't have said that word) lingerie. I remembered once having to make as many words as possible from the letters in HERE COME THE BRIDE AND GROOM. The first on my list had been BORING.

I knew I would have felt the same even about a shower for me, but I hadn't been engaged long enough to have one. I made a note to talk to Rose Galigani, in case she had plans for me this time around.

Much of the talk was about the dramatic events of the week, some of which had made the local papers. I listened without comment to opinions about the spy ring in our neighborhood (not the first); about whether the ambulance company owner, Julia Strega, would stand trial or take a deal; about Howard Christopher, whom a couple of BUL editors had worked with, and how he still denied shooting anyone.

Out of deference to the hostess, I guessed, no one brought up Robin Kirsch, who had a deal in the works for a suspended sentence in exchange for her testimony against Julia Strega. Robin was on an employee retreat with her San Francisco bank group, Dana told us, and was sorry she couldn't make the shower.

Everyone doubted it.

As soon as we'd eaten, Matt offered to leave separately, and early, to take the presents to Elaine's house.

"Generous man," I said, leaning into his ear.

"I'm practicing for ours," he said, leaning back.

"Let's serve these delicious mushrooms," I said.

Hearing my nonchalant tone, you might have thought I was looking forward to a shower of my own.

At the end of the evening, I abandoned my privileged position as guest and took my turn with the cleanup crew. By now, all the men had left; most of the women stayed to help. Maybe times hadn't changed all that much.

Elaine was practically giddy. After the meal, Dana had set up three card tables, with different games: mah-jongg, Scrabble, and a board game I didn't recognize. I'd opted for mah-jongg since that table had its own Chinese American tutor, a computer scientist I'd worked with a few years back. Much better than wedding games.

"I can't remember a nicer evening, Dana. Thank you so much," Elaine said. I was sure she meant it, even if the past week would not have been hard to top. She quickly dropped her bride privilege and pitched in at the sink.

The mood was so light and happy, I expected us all to break out into a song like "Whistle While You Work," or the modern-day equivalent.

As my last chore, I wrapped the trash and dragged it into the hallway by the back door. I bent over to settle the plastic bag between two bicycles and an already stuffed waste can.

Something not very heavy hit my head as I straightened up after depositing my load. I'd bumped into a crystal hanging from the handle of one of the bikes.

I remembered it from the first time I met Robin, when she carried her bike into the living room. And from another time . . .

My mind went back to Patel's cul-de-sac, to the third time I was there, after Elaine had found Phil on the floor of the library. I'd gotten out of the Saab and spun around to check the reflections from the streetlight. One was off the bumper of a car in a neighboring driveway, a new Volvo. *And that was the car that didn't deserve the garage,* I thought irrelevantly. Another reflection came from the crime scene tape, and the third from the handle of a bike.

But it wasn't from a handle; it was from a crystal.

I saw it now. Robin's bike had been near Patel's home the evening I was shot at.

"We have what we wanted," I told Matt. "The second link between Robin and Patel. The ID card could be explained away, but not this."

I'd waited until Elaine went upstairs to tell Matt the latest in what was supposed to have been a closed case. Two closed cases. Dana had dropped Elaine and me off; I'd spared her also. Both women deserved an evening and a night's sleep uncluttered with confusing pieces of information.

"This means Robin could have been part of what you lovingly call the spy ring," Matt said.

"It does. It makes Robin part of both threads. But how did she even know Patel? If it were anything obvious, like meeting through Phil or Dana, one of them would have told us."

What I hoped was that this new revelation didn't bring us back to Robin and Phil being *involved* involved.

We tried to devise a way to query Dana about the link without alarming her. Matt was in favor of leaving her out of it. "She must have been thinking about this for a long time already," he said. "Ever since she found that ID card."

I deferred to his judgment.

"Okay, we don't ask Dana. Let's focus on why. Why would Robin involve herself in giving secret data to India—or wherever Patel was sending his downloads? Just for the money?"

"Why does anyone do it?" Matt asked.

"Still," I said, "there should be a reason."

"It's not physics," Matt said.

"Well, it should be."

On Friday morning, the day before the wedding, I had a voice message from Rose, who'd sent a lovely set of linens as a shower present. I knew she'd want a complete description of the party. I tried to remember the menu (mushrooms plus an outstanding seven-layer cake were all I could recall), what everyone wore (California casual), what the other gifts were (general household merchandise, boring as it sounded). I wished I'd taken notes.

Catholic guilt took over my mind, and I decided to dig out and look over the police report Rose had sent me on the exploding hearse, so I could sound as though I cared. *After all,* I thought,

Rose is the person I'll be living near whenever I'm not on vacation in California.

I scanned the report, stopping at a mention of nitrogen, my current favorite element. Apparently the uniform who wrote up the incident decided to include a tutorial on the workings of explosives. I read his description.

Most bombs are like fireworks. They contain nitrogen, oxygen, and carbon, I read. *When the molecules containing these atoms decompose, carbon dioxide and nitrogen gases are released quickly and with great energy, making the explosion.*

Not bad, I decided, and figured that passage was probably the reason Rose wanted me to see the report.

"That was one thing," Rose said, when I reached her. "And I also wanted you to see that list down at the bottom, where the police catalogued the other incidents that they felt were from the same perps. See, I just didn't want you to think I was crazy."

I looked at the sheet of paper with the familiar letterhead. At the very bottom was a list of what the RPD had called "similar pranks," some of which I'd already heard from Rose. Like the switched clothing. My eyes settled on a new one to me.

Deceased had tennis ball stuffed in mouth.

"A tennis ball?" I asked, fishing around my mind for a connection I knew was there.

"Yes," Rose said. "Didn't I tell you that one? That was at O'Neal's, too. Someone came in the middle of the night and evidently went into the parlor and stuffed a tennis ball in the deceased's mouth. Imagine when his family came in for the viewing—"

"Thanks, Rose," I said. "You've just become part of the Berkeley homicide team."

"It was there all along," I said.

"The tennis connection," Matt said. He'd already made the trip to the Berkeley PD, as the official liaison for the team. "Robin hanging out with the rich guys at the tennis club; Patel right there, recruiting for his cause."

It hadn't taken a long discussion for Matt and me to decide to inform Elaine, Phil, and Dana of this new development, for safety reasons first. Robin was still Dana's roommate, after all.

Robin had been in charge all along, we realized. Working with Julia for money, as Dana figured out, and with Christopher and Patel for political reasons. She'd used her skills in finance to help Julia launder money, and her knowledge of international business procedures to help Patel manage his crimes against the country.

"Well, Russell was impressed," Matt said. "That's something, huh? He said they were on it. They've already hit the bank where Robin works with a warrant. Since Robin thinks she's clear, there shouldn't be any problem finding her."

"I knew something was going on in her mind, some real resentment about the way her father ended up," Dana said. "It was like she blamed the government for what happened to the Vietnam vets."

"Many people did," I said.

"But why would she think India was any better?" Dana asked, apparently still trying to make sense of things.

"Not everyone thinks things through," Matt said.

I had a few things to add, but I could see that Dana was satisfied with that.

CHAPTER THIRTY-TWO

Friday night, the wedding eve, at last. We gathered at the viewing patio at the top level of the Rose Garden. The sunset vista was perfect in all directions, from the hills of Marin County straight ahead of us to Richmond on one side and Oakland on the other.

Time for the rehearsal, the official start of the wedding celebration. We were so close to having this wedding come off with no more disasters, I thought I should be breathing easily, but instead I was tense as we walked down the stone steps. The tennis courts off to the side of the garden reminded me of Robin, and I half expected her to jump from behind a lovely bush and attack us all.

I scanned the sparse crowd of people in the garden, some paying attention to us, others wandering among the rows of shrubs, lost in their own conversations or meditations. No one was threatening the bridal party. *Relax,* I told myself, but I kept my shoulders stiff and my gaze alert.

Elaine provided corsages for Dana and me.

"Just for the rehearsal?" I asked.

"Absolutely," Elaine said, nearly stabbing me with a weapon-length straight pin. "It's only a little one. Tomorrow's will be bigger."

Of course. I figured this two-corsage protocol was in a bride book authored by a florist, but I knew such thoughts were anathema at a time like this.

The minister was a friend of Phil's from Dorman Industries. A nice enough man, but I suspected he'd been ordained online.

On the second run-through, my corsage came undone. I unpinned it before it fell off completely and laid it on top of a small bush next to the gazebolike area at the bottom of the garden, where we stood for the pretend vows. We made one more run-through, this one with music from a boom box Elaine had brought.

Though I couldn't name the piece, I knew I'd heard it at about three out of every four weddings I'd attended in my life. It was designed to be meditative and tear-jerking and seemed to be working already, even before the final take. Both Elaine and Dana were dabbing at the corners of their eyes.

I was holding out for a full-fledged cry tomorrow.

Ten minutes later, back at the top of the garden, ready to carpool to dinner at Berkeley's world-famous Chez Panisse, I realized I'd left my corsage behind.

"Elaine is bound to notice," I told Matt.

"I'll get it," he said.

I pointed, trying to aim my finger at a spot six levels down, to where three peach tea roses nestled among dozens of adult roses in full bloom. "I think I'd better go. You'll never find it, and I know exactly where I put it."

I made my way down the steep pathway, using the same aisle I'd used as a rehearsing maid of honor. I found the corsage and started up the steps.

It had turned dark suddenly, as it always seemed to do when the sun made its way down those last few degrees above the horizon. The garden's visitors had left also, as if the sunset had signaled the park's closing, though I was sure a posted sign indicated that it was open until ten o'clock at night. I saw shadows where I hadn't seen them on the way down. They moved in strange ways.

I strained my neck to see the wedding party above, at street level, but it was a long way up, and there were many twists and turns and lattice overhangs between the garden levels and the opening at the street. The tennis players had left, and I felt an enormous distance between me and anyone else in the universe.

On the third level, a shadow materialized and a strong hand grasped my arm.

"I'm here to say good-bye."

My throat went dry. I felt a shiver through my body.

I barely recognized Robin's voice, hollow and menacing. With each word, she squeezed my arm more tightly. Her jacket was torn in several places; she looked and smelled like she hadn't had a shower in days.

I thought I cried out, but I couldn't be sure. I grabbed a branch and earned a few punctures from the thorns. My movie fantasy come true, but with the wrong leading actress.

Robin pulled me down, below the bushes. Even if my team missed me and looked down, they'd never see us. I tried to improve my odds—I screamed. But I'd never had a particularly loud voice, and I doubted anyone heard me.

Robin shoved me down next to her, still holding my left arm. I could hear her breathing, raspy and loud. It wasn't the first time my retirement contracts had put me in the clutches of a killer.

This time seemed different.

Less frightening, as strange as that feeling was, even as Robin took a gun from the pocket of her windbreaker.

"My plan was to come tomorrow and ruin Phil's wedding," Robin said. She sounded drunk, but I smelled no alcohol on her breath. "Now I think this is even better, since you were the one who put all the pieces together."

"Don't do this, Robin," I said. A weak command. "We can work things out. That's your father's gun, isn't it?"

"I want a witness," she said, her eyes glazed over. I knew she hadn't heard a word I said. "My father had no witness when he did it, no one to share his burden."

I knew what Robin meant by *it*—her father's ignominious suicide. And I knew her plans for his gun.

I had one hand free. As it turned out, it was my right hand, the hand holding the corsage. And the long straight pin. I worked my fingers around and extricated the pin from the petals and leaves. I let the flowers fall to the ground and held on to the pin.

Robin raised the gun and trained it on her own head.

I closed my eyes as I always do when giving or receiving pain. I twisted my body and thrust the pin into Robin's side, holding it close to the tip for leverage. The pin bent, too dull to penetrate the nylon jacket, but the movement rattled Robin enough for her to lose her grip on me, and on the gun.

By the time the wedding party reached us, Robin was in tears and the gun was in my hands. I had no clear memory of exactly how the weapon changed hands. Or whether the sound I'd heard had been a firecracker or a gunshot.

"I must be getting used to this," I said to Matt. "I'm hardly shaking."

Then I collapsed into the nearest bush.

CHAPTER THIRTY-Th REE

O n Saturday, July third, Elaine Rita Cody and Philip Lawrence Chambers, both in cream-colored outfits, promised to share their lives and dreams, and one or two other parameters, in a nontraditional recitation of vows. I was happy not to hear anything about obedience on either side. Nor did I hear "forever," but "for all my days." I wondered if there was a difference.

I looked at my strong, beautiful friend and thought, *If Elaine can pull this off, no bride should ever complain about the stressful two weeks before a wedding.*

Firecrackers popped all over the neighborhood. Elaine had given me a flyer advertising a mammoth, all-day celebration at San Francisco's Crissy Field in case Matt and I wanted to attend while she and Phil were honeymooning at an undisclosed vacation spot.

Looking at the events promised by the red-white-and-blue bulletin, I was ready to reevaluate my harsh criticism of the Bay Area's patriotic spirit.

The Rose Garden was in full bloom; a poet might have said the roses were happy. No one seemed to notice a certain bush that was bent out of shape from an altercation the evening before. Even my fancy navy dress was reasonably comfortable.

Elaine's shower guests were at the wedding, plus other BUL employees I recognized but couldn't name. I estimated at least as many passersby attended as invited guests.

Dana and her EMT friends had decorated an ambulance and

parked it in front of the entrance to the garden. "In case you and Elaine need a little hideaway, Dad," Dana had said. For the first time in my acquaintance with her, Dana behaved like a normal twenty-four-year-old having a good time. She'd shed her lost, spaced-out look. Whether for this occasion only, I didn't know, but I hoped not.

The buzz at the reception went from those in the know about the events of the week to those listening in rapt attention.

"I don't blame that ambulance company owner," said a young woman. "It must be hard for a woman to make it in a male-dominated industry."

"Aren't they all?" her female companion said.

I wondered where they got their data.

"So the Dorman Industries guy did it." I heard this from someone in line behind me as I chose an éclair from a platter of pre-cake desserts.

"No! He was completely innocent," said a man next to him.

Not completely, I thought. Though he hadn't committed murder, Howard Christopher had known of and profited from Patel's un-American activities and had been handed over to federal authorities. I didn't respond, however, since I'd promised myself to engage only in happy wedding talk for the day.

"Did you catch the news this morning? It was all spearheaded by one of Dana's roommates," another éclair person said to her partner in line.

"Yeah, she had this grudge against America because her father couldn't hack Vietnam." (Not a Berkeley native, I decided.)

"She had a right to be ticked off. Her father never should have had to fight that war."

"America, love it or leave it."

I moved to a nonpolitical group.

"And she nearly attacked the maid of honor."

Nearly, indeed.

"This was definitely the most beautiful of Elaine's weddings," I said to Matt. He was looking handsome in the one suit he reserved for nonprofessional occasions, a deep brown, almost black, to match his eyes. He'd loosened his collar, letting his gold-and-beige-striped tie slip to the side.

"How about the fall?" he asked.

"Whose fall?"

"For us. We could get married in the fall. Say, on Fermi's birthday?"

September 29. I'd become so used to my fiancé, I was hardly surprised that Matt remembered the birthday of Enrico Fermi, one of my favorite scientists, the first to demonstrate a nuclear chain reaction.

"That would be perfect," I said, feeling a flush of contentment. Just like that, we'd set a wedding date.

In the next few seconds, the country club ballroom went from a comfortable temperature to seriously overheated. I fanned my face with the wedding program. Fermi's birthday was less than three months away.

"Need some air?" Matt asked.

At that moment the bridegroom and his EMT daughter danced close to our table and smiled at us. I thought I heard an ambulance siren pass by outside.

I smiled at Matt. "Air? I could use a tank of oxygen."